Praise For
ABE & ANN

"I love this book about the young, poverty-stricken, backwoods Abraham Lincoln courting his first love Ann Rutledge with nothing but grammar, the poetry of Byron, and hope. To me, *ABE & ANN* is quintessential historical fiction because it beautifully and eloquently upends our revered assumptions about a beloved historical figure. Too often, reputation preserves the famous in a fossilized amber that makes us forget the simple truth that people have to grow into those beloved reputations. But here, in *ABE & ANN*, in glorious, lilting prose, is Lincoln before he became the famous president we revere and thought we knew, in all his uncertain, love-struck, ambitious, underprivileged youth, wrapped in desire and struggling to find his way in the world."

Robin Oliveira, New York Times bestselling author of *Winter Sisters* and *My Name is Mary Sutter* and winner of the Michael Shaara Prize in Civil War Fiction in 2010.

"Gary Moore's *ABE & ANN* is lively, artful, and engaging, but it is also notable in managing to offer an imaginative depiction of this famous romance without altering the basic historical parameters. Perhaps his most impressive achievement is having created a really scintillating Ann Rutledge."

Douglas L. Wilson, Co-Director of the Lincoln Studies Center and author of *Honor's Voice* and *Lincoln's Sword*, both winners of The Lincoln Prize.

"This lyrical novel of the young Lincoln in love not only kept me turning the pages until the wee hours of the night, it also grabbed me as all the best stories do, less a tapestry of a particular time than a universal story of what it means to love and to lose. Gary Moore has written a moving tribute to how the most intimate of experiences can forever change us, and sometimes change the world."

Thomas Christopher Greene, author of
The Perfect Liar

"I have been deeply moved by this book in a way that I rarely am. It is indeed the tale of the star-crossed love between Abraham Lincoln and Ann Rutledge and though many will have heard of their intense relations, none of us have read it rendered so tenderly as if we were in their midst. The telling by Gary Moore, the poet, is what any one would call exquisite. He will stop you in your tracks with the dialogue. And for Lincoln aficionados, avowed and otherwise, the story will deepen the sense of who the man is in a way that the House Divided Speech or Gettysburg Address simply cannot. In these speeches, we see Mr. Lincoln in the grip of politics and war. In *ABE & ANN*, we see the young Mr. Lincoln in the grip of love. This book is worthy of a Pulitzer Prize."

Jim Freedman, author most recently of *A Conviction in Question: The First Trial at the International Criminal Court.*

"Abe & Ann is a splendidly realized fiction in the great tradition of biographical fiction. I was caught its narrative vortex and whirled. Gary Moore is a gifted writer ."

Jay Parini, author of *The Last Station* and
Benjamin's Crossing.

"This heartbreaking novel masterfully blends fact and fiction, giving readers a vivid picture of the young, meandering Abraham Lincoln, while also convincingly imagining what could have transpired in his relationship with Ann Rutledge, the woman who brought so much poetry and love into Abe's young life. Informative, moving, insightful--Moore shows us the kind of magic that well-done biofiction can bring to our past and into our present."

Michael Lackey, Distinguished Professor of English and author of *The American Biographical Novel*.

"Gary Moore's novel *ABE & ANN* tells the story of star-crossed lovers and what might have been. Moore gives voice to a woman largely ignored by history, the first love of a man before he became a legend. Written in gorgeous prose, evocative of the time, this novel had me wishing for a revision of history, rooting for a couple that could not be."

Ann Davila Cardinal, author of *Five Midnights*

"Here is Lincoln as you've never seen him. In the circumscribed world of an Illinois frontier village, the future statesman meets and woos the arresting Ann, a worthy match as she tests the constraints and obligations of her time and place. The young lovers are brought memorably to life in Gary Moore's poignant *ABE & ANN* as only a gifted poet, dramatist, performer, and scholar could portray: richly imagined, beautifully expressed, and authentically informed. In Moore's hands, Ann and Abe are flesh and blood, their joy and anguish genuine and affecting. The reader wonders just how much of Lincoln's iconic character was shaped through his smitten devotion to the complex, dazzling Ann and her shattering loss."

Denise Brown, author of *The Unspeakable*

"Gary Moore's Abe & Ann presents the engrossing story of a young, rustic Lincoln's resolute campaign for the heart of the lovely, brilliant Ann Rutledge. More than a vivid and tender romance both timeless and keenly evocative of its time, Abe & Ann is a passionate novel rendered in lyrical prose seldom found in historical fiction, one that will haunt you long after you have come to its exquisite, bittersweet conclusion."

Don Bredes, author of *Polly and the One and Only World*

ABE & ANN

A Novel

Gary Moore

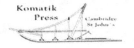

Komatik Press — Cambridge St John's

ABE & ANN, A Novel
Copyright 2019 by Gary Moore
Published in the United States by Komatik Press
Komatik Press
95 Jackson Street
Cambridge, MA 02140
www.komatikpress.com
Library of Congress Cataloging-in-Publication Data in process
Moore, Gary
ABE & ANN: a Novel / Gary Moore
ISBN (Hard Cover) 978-0-9987113-6-2
ISBN (Paperback) 978-0-9987113-7-9
ISBN (eBook) 978-0-9987113-8-6
Cover and Book design by Rex Passion

Cover: The first known photograph of Abraham Lincoln taken in 1846 by
Nicholas H. Sheperd after Lincoln was elected to the House of Representatives.
No photograph of Ann Rutledge is available. The stand-in is American stage
actress Minnie Ashley, 1897.

The author photo is by
Sonia Sanz.

To the Memory of
Ann Rutledge

We know that he started out at the bottom and had to struggle upward, but it is easy to minimize or overlook his anxieties,
for we also know how it all turned out. What is harder to grasp
is the way things were or must have seemed to him at the time.

Douglas L. Wilson
Honor's Voice – The Transformation of Abraham Lincoln

1

Will she remember me?

He's walking through a moonlit night to a woman who doesn't know he's coming. The black shape of an owl coasts silently above his road through deep woods and his eyes go up to it and back down to the rutted dirt in the full moon's dream-like glow. But he's not dreaming and here's the owl again with its still wings gliding the skyway over the road to a clearing ahead. A graveyard. He shivers but shakes it off and shifts his bag to the hand away from the graves and picks up his pace.

He slows when the owl settles on a gravestone leaning close by the road. The owl rises noiselessly as he comes near, then beats its wings a few times into the trees leaving a single spirit-like call over the luminous cemetery. Come even with the marker the bird's just left, he stops and puts his satchel down to look at the worn gray stone. In the gothic moonlit setting and the melancholy feel of the world as he's known it, he half expects the inscription to spell his name: *Lincoln.*

That's what would happen, he thinks, if this were a story.

He's walking into a story that will be told for hundreds of years but doesn't know it. The gravestone is part of it, but not the worn-down run of flowing heading, probably a first name and a last, that time has taken like their owner. Below the unknowable name, in smaller but deeper block letters, are legible words:

> Life is not forever
> And neither is death

A decorative image at the bottom has the last wordless word, projecting rays upward from a setting sun.

Or, he thinks as he picks up his things, *is that sun rising?*

Finished with his momentary optimism, he veers back to habit. *She probably has someone.* As he goes back to hiking the ankle-turning grooves and clumps of the road, he sees pictures. Him the gangling poor boy with only a canvas satchel to his name, speechless before her, dumbstruck. Him bent and stumbling into the woods when she has someone.

What will I do if she has someone?

Give up.

Sometimes he thinks things he doesn't like. It started after his mother died. That windowless cabin in the woods got darker then, and more than from the want of his mother to keep the fire. He was nine and got stubborn and silent like his father, and though his sister Sarah and then his new step-mother gradually brought him back to life, a voice got in him in that dark year and didn't leave. *Take what you want or someone else will*, he thinks and dislikes himself for it. *Cheat a little, everyone does...*, grasping and blaming like the dad he

2

butted heads with every day. Finding something wrong with everything, the voice spews contempt on Abe's father for being illiterate and on Abe for reading. It can't be satisfied. One day it says: *If you stay here with this fool of a father, you'll end up the nothing he says you are.* And the next: *If you go off on your own, you know you'll fail.*

A few months ago, afraid to stay and afraid to leave, Lincoln let go into a long-chained urge to bust free of his daddy's farm. Was it working on him since he saw the slaves? Three years ago his father hired him out as a hand on a flat boat taking farm goods down the Mississippi and he saw the dark men chained in a line being loaded on a steamer. He'd seen a few Negroes walking behind owners when he was young in Kentucky, but never a shackled bunch of Africans put in a boat like cargo. *Woebegone,* he said to himself when he saw their wet bloodshot eyes. *Like ghosts,* he thought and shivered when he heard their chains clank as the white man forced them down below where there was no light.

Nineteen at the time, Abe turned over his earnings for that trip to his father and went back to plowing and planting on the scrubby family farm until he reached twenty-one and freed himself. Now here he is in this year of 1831 just back from a second trip to New Orleans with corn and hogs in a log boat he pegged together himself and piloted for pay that's all his own. His employer Denton Offut wants to use his profits to start a store back up here in the frontier north. It's growing, Lincoln, he keeps saying. You put your money where it grows. Lincoln talked Offut into putting his investment in New Salem, a town they'd stopped in for a day on their way downriver. For all the young Lincoln knows he'll like storekeeping and do it all his life. But why in New Salem?

It's only got a hundred souls but it's the up and coming town of the region and you'll be in before the big money knows. That's what his scheming inner voice said to tell Offut instead of the other truth that New Salem's where Abe saw the woman he wants so much he's walking through the night to get to her. It worked.

3

If she's got a man, the voice says, there are ways to change that. If you're a man.

When he gets to New Salem the sun is still down behind high virgin oaks but the sky is so bright it must be eight. He doesn't come into town from the east where he got his boat stuck on the dam. Better not see that dam first thing, that dam where he was the town fool back in April.

He comes in as far as you can from the dam and still be in New Salem, down at the west end of the town's one house-lined road that runs east a few hundred yards to the tavern by the dam and mill on the river. At first he feels important as the only man striding toward the sunrise-backed tavern like a temple on a sacred day. But then he sees how the shadows come toward him and how he's on display to anyone in the houses fronting the narrow dirt road. Are eyes watching him from hiding? Birds call from trees behind the houses. Why?

One, two houses… he stills his fear by calculating, a habit that helps when he feels uncertain. He counts the houses, or the buildings rather, because he sees… long after he first heard the clanging anvil… the blacksmith's place, and across the road from it the half-bound barrels and leaning staves of a cooper's shop. Left and right, north and south he counts them, all log buildings, not one of frame, and reckons their different shapes the way eyes inside them might be reckoning him.

Not much to reckon, he thinks, but he stiffens as he walks the last of the gauntlet to his goal. He passes a store on the north side of the road and opposite it on the south the office and shingle of "Dr. John Allen." Seven buildings on the north side of the village road, he makes it, ten on the south. And there it is. Where she is.

The Rutledge Tavern. It's a double log building that stops him with the shock that now he has to knock on the door. He overpowers an urge to turn and rush away, and instead puts his bag down and crouches as if to find something in it. There's no way he can know that he'll remember this moment when he enters the White House thirty years from now, and remember what he was looking for.

4

Courage. He stands angrily and yanks the handles of his canvas bag and marches the last steps wiping the defiance off his face and knocks three times on the big plank door.

Will she remember me?

The tavern door swings open, sparks leap from blue eyes in a woman's bright face framed by long auburn hair and she exclaims, "I remember you!"

2

Ann's hair is not pinned for work yet this morning but falling loose around her freckled face and he who's famous as a talker to those who know him feels caught and carried off in its red streams down the front of her brown prairie dress and she says something about the river taking him away before and he doesn't know what to answer.

A nothing has nothing to say, he taunts himself before he thinks in a kinder voice but still paralyzed: *I've got one pair of pants, one year of school, and two jug ears on a face an old lady told me made her want to cry. And a woman is talking to me.*

Women were scarce in backwoods Kentucky and Indiana where he grew up with more bears than people. There was a cabin here, a cabin a few miles over there through the mosquito-swarmed forest, and here and there a clump of buildings where people bought gun powder and beans and went to church if the Sunday weather let them get there on the muddy roads. At church you saw a few skinny farm girls and a few hefty farm girls and some mothers and grannies in shapeless long gray and brown cotton dresses. But church was church and you didn't play much or know anybody much and you'd go back to your cabin where you might have a sister and step-sisters like he did that you could fight with like boys.

A real woman.

In New Orleans the women swished into carriages in hoop skirts and hard-looking make up. Women called from doorways like in dangerous stories. The fear he felt down there jumps on him here: *You gonna get in there or be a boy the rest of your life?* His law partner many years later will say that women liked Mr. Lincoln, and Mr. Lincoln liked them, but that had to start somewhere and as Lincoln now looks dumbly at a real woman… the bright welcoming face, the rounded breasts and hips and the narrow waist between… gesturing him into the Rutledge Tavern in New Salem village on a July morning, he has never before in his life stood face-to-face talking with an attractive woman about his age. And sure of herself.

"Do you remember? Do you 'member, Mr. Lincoln?" She's so… *lively.* The corners of her mouth go up easily and often and her eyes flash and light the zest of brown spots high on her cheeks and across her nose. "We met in April 'cause of daddy's dam. I was sweeping the mill floor when you tried to come over the mill dam below me with your flatboat of hogs. Can I take your things?"

He's never forgotten the way she looked down at him from the mill deck above the river and he looked up like she was Juliet, but he doesn't say it. She says she was sweeping but he thought she looked up from a book. He looks somber remembering and she remembers his face more lively back on the day he got stuck on the dam, but he was the center of a mess back then and his face was full of stir.

"I saw you…" he says as she reaches hospitably for his satchel, but then he pauses and panics and looks grave to mask it as he gives her his bag and loses the thread and doesn't know what to say. He blurts as if talking about some blend of past and present, "I didn't know what to do…," and the voice inside him groans.

7

She goes on eagerly, "Because of the river?" He walks after her unconsciously as she, who at eighteen has known for years what to do when you run a tavern, takes his bag across to where the kitchen and dining room give over to a kind of shed built on as a room for guests. With her back to him she wonders if he's watching her. She wants to prove herself. Not at running the tavern. At... *something.*

He doesn't say, "No, because of you. I saw you watching and I was so afraid of failing...." He remembers seeing sheep grazing on the river banks when he was stuck on the dam and thinking: *Shorn. I won't let that woman see me shorn.* But he doesn't tell her.

He says, "No, Miss Rutledge, but I had to work so hard when the boat lodged on the dam."

"But apart from the boat," she says while she chooses a pillow case she likes and holds a pillow for him under her chin and shimmies her pillow case up and on it in that way women have that means everything and nothing. "I mean, do you remember... that we seen... we saw each other?"

He stares at her red hair and doesn't say, "I've never remembered anything more. All the way down the Mississippi, and all the way back which I came by boat and foot and all night last night by the light of the moon to get to you." But at last he smiles, remembering, and says politely, "Of course I do... Miss Rutledge. Can I help you spread that sheet?"

She won't let him help, so while she gets his bed ready he watches her white forearms splashed with rosy dots appear and disappear as the sleeves on her cotton dress go up and down. Her dress tightens in some places when she stretches and bends and then relaxes and loses shape. She asks questions. He doesn't know how long he'll stay, he says. He's looking for a place to settle, he tells her, or a place that will settle for him. His face lights up when he says that, but briefly. He's afraid to tell her he feels like they've met before. Long before. He doesn't say that when she watched him that fresh April day with her eyes so blue you could see their blue from a distance, he felt like he'd been in that scene before.

8

She remembers thinking he was going down. She saw everything after the shouting started, saw it all from the mill up over the falls where she was reading when she was supposed to be sweeping. His boat was nose-up on the dam and taking on water in the back. There he was, a gangly boatman in his brown jeans pants and blue and white striped shirt and big straw hat, as if on display for her between the woods on the New Salem side of the river and the fields over on the Athens side, about to lose his whole boat full of produce and hogs in the Sangamon River.

But then he started yelling things and he moved the barrels and hogs... he and the two men on his little crew... they carried the casks and pigs from the stern of the boat to the shore so the back of the boat got light and came up on the water and the boat leveled out on the dam. Then he borrowed an augur... she remembers Mentor Graham was there on the bank with a bag of something on his shoulder to get milled and he yelled to gloomy Henry Onstot who owns every known tool to stop gawking and run get one for the stranger.

With the augur this Lincoln... that's what his men said when they yelled to him... drilled a hole where the bow was out over air in the front, drained the water out, banged a round piece of tapered stick in to plug the hole, eased the lightened boat off the dam and into the water below, and saved the day.

After everyone helped him reload his boat, the village men poured into the Tavern on the bluff above the mill to whoop about how handy the lanky young feller was. Ann carried pitchers of cider around the room, but hung back from fussing over the stranger that day, though she didn't know why. It's not that she was shy. But she felt from the first like there was something... what? And she feels that way again, though there's nothing she can call it.

Unsettled by this thought while she tucks his coarse linen sheet in, Ann hums wordlessly as she does when she makes the beds alone.

He knows the tune, *Barbry Allen*, and the words form in his mind:

9

In Scarlet Town where I was born
There was a fair maid dwelling

She's glancing over to read his looks now and then. His skin is worn though he's still a young man, and this goes with the stubborn look of his mouth. His coarse dark hair is a mess over the tops of his wide-set ears and the crown of it flies like hard prairie wind.

"You like the old ballads," he says and runs his hand through his hair as if he saw her looking. He's standing, moving foot to foot nervously, and she can see how his pants, no doubt made by his mama and shrinking every year while he grows taller, come only to the tops of his home-made deerskin boots, but she sees plenty of "high-water" pants around New Salem.

"Do you?" she asks back. "… the old songs?"

Abe hesitates and his face falls back into a sadness that seems natural to it, and she can see how his lower lip projects below the mole on his right cheek, jutting out as if he'd pouted too long and got it stuck that way. His deep grey-blue eyes above high cheekbones stare off into air before he speaks.

"My mother used to sing them," he says. "Was that *Barbry Allan?*"

"Oh, yes, I love that one. "*Barbry Allen* and *Matty Groves* and… well, they're all nonsense of course… all them ones where the people love each other, but something… you know… *girl songs*, Daddy calls them."

He doesn't say, "I wondered if you thought of *Barbry Allen* because it's a love song…." *Say it. Get under her skin,* something in him urges, but he doesn't do it. Her face shines when it comes up from bending to tuck in his sheet, and she goes back to humming but something gay now, and her eyes are dancing, because she finds herself glad even if she's nervous, and she wants him to be happy too.

"Do you sleep cold and need piles of covers even in July?" Ann asks in a way that suggests maybe she's like that. He sees beside her a stack of gray woolen blankets on a chair at the side of the chinked-log room they're in, the shed-like bunk house with beds for six overnight guests. There's a dry sink out there too with a basin and a mirror for cleaning up and shaving, and a few little tables hold lamps to undress by. Instinctively wanting to know how far his bed in this annex will be from the fire in the main room when the weather plunges cold at night, Abe looks to the fireplace out past the trestle table where the boarders take their meals and sees it's far but doesn't care.

He doesn't say, "I'll never be cold with you near."

Seeing him glance at the fire sparks a way she can find out more about him. "You'll be welcome to read by the firelight in the evenings, Mr. Lincoln."

"I'd like that," he says

He does read! Eager to please him she puts her three best-looking blankets on the foot of his narrow bed, meaning, but not saying: *Here, take all I can give.*

Now she wants to know everything. "What will you do for work in New Salem, Mr. Lincoln?"

"Do you think I'll stay, Miss Rutledge?" He surprises himself with his daring and wishes he could take the question back.

"For ever and ever, Mr. Lincoln," she says with a teasing smile.

His face lifts and brightens, and even that pouting side of his lip rises for a moment when he can't keep from showing how pleased he feels, a sight she enjoys as she starts back to the next room to wake the fire. Brushing close as she passes she bends her neck to look up and smile, and his own smile turns nervous and he backs up to let her by.

Alone in the bunk room, Abe lifts his satchel onto his bed and takes things out while Ann absent-mindedly sings *Barbry Allen* in the other room. With his pair of spare socks in his hand he recalls the painted women in New Orleans and marvels at seeing Ann in the next room, so… what?… home-like?… through the doorway with no make-up, and no imposing hoops in her gown, singing to herself in a long brown housedress as she slices with a swift touch a weighty loaf of bread she took from warming by the fire.

11

"Are you coming?" she shouts, then goes thoughtlessly back to her song.

> *In Scarlet Town where I was born*
> *There was a fair maid dwelling*
> *And every youth cried well away*
> *For her name was Barbry Allen*

"You don't happen to be from Scarlet Town, Mr. Lincoln?" She shouts this too without looking but then sees she needn't as he's come into the room and is just across the table.

Being from pretty much nowhere in the woods of Kentucky and Indiana, Abe gets nervous at a question about home from a woman in a civilized house. The table he's just sat at is a trestle table, it's true, but that's what you get when there's no woodworker in town but you can cut a long maple slab down at the mill and sand it and set it on two chunky saw-horses and throw benches together to go down the sides. And when Abe looks across the table to the big fireplace that's the furnace and cook-stove and glowing heart of the Rutledge household, he sees pretty much what his step-mother made his daddy provide, along with a real wooden floor, when she moved into their woeful Indiana cabin. Every house in New Salem has a fireplace like this, he bets, and whether its firebox is log or stone, it has swinging iron fixtures made at that anvil he passed on the way in and hears ringing down the way. And they all have pots and kettles and such on adjustable chains like his first mama probably never saw back in the Kentucky woods when he was too young to know.

But he bets not many New Salem houses have what he sees above the fireplace. A polished walnut mantel clock sits centered between a pewter pitcher and a candle mold. The clock might be English for all he knows, but without language it says *sturdy*. And reliable. Its low tick seems like time itself. A Rutledge heirloom?

The portrait must be. Above the clock, in a gilded frame presiding high on the wall of squared-off logs is the kind of man he's seen before in newspaper engravings of founding fathers. He wears a stiff tie in a stiff collar beneath a stiff face with eyes rising in aspiration. Lincoln has no reason to think he'll ever be in such a portrait, but he wants to be. *It's America*, the out-of-work young farmer thinks. *Everyone has a chance.*

Ann sees Abe gaping and thinks she understands. "Daddy's grandfather's cousin Edward Rutledge signed the Declaration of Independence," she explains, and Abe half-recognizes the name. *South Carolina*, he thinks.

"Or so Daddy says," Ann goes on in what he now hears more like a southern accent, "though Mama disputes his taking on about aristocratic ancestors when he comes from Carolina farmers just like she does. Especially if'n his family made their money from slaves, she says. Her farmers," Ann says with a glance at the clock on the mantel, "didn't own slaves, but they did own — as you see — a grandfather clock. Anyhow," she adds as she puts the bread away, "that might or might not be the signer hisself... himself... up there, but don't you ever cast doubt in front of Daddy."

"I'd be far from taking on about anybody's ancestors," he says, "particularly when I don't know that I even *have* any." It's true that what he knows doesn't go far back, but he knows his father left his own daddy's wilderness farm in Virginia to try his luck in Kentucky, then moved his young family from Kentucky to Indiana to get away from slavery. Not for moral reasons but because a poor man on his own can't compete against bigger owners working bigger farms with teams of slaves. But Lincoln won't go talking slavery to a Southern woman he's only just meeting.

"Maybe," he says, stretching to make a joke, "...maybe my ancestors are from Scarlet Town. Wherever that is."

"Well, it's probably best," she says, "that you got out of there. Because I think them folks in *Barbry Allen* didn't do so well." She remembers a line: "Young man I think you're dyin...." She pushes it away.

13

Abe appears to be transfixed by the wonder of the thick slice of buttered bread he holds up before him, and Ann turns quickly to stoke the fire with her back to him. While he sees how lightly she turns and touches here and there, he doesn't see yet how she uses motion to hide worry. She'll need hot water for the dishes, but right now hot water is something she wants to avoid. What's the way out? "There's a lot in them songs... I mean *those* songs," she says, "... things we never know."

Glad for the chance, Abe reaches for a closing: "I guess they should have been more careful." And he bites into the dark brown bread and savors its wide deep sweet flavor with a surprising edge he doesn't expect down inside it and wonders if Ann made it and if its taste is somehow *her* taste, sweet and unpredictable.

"But if everyone was careful... *were* careful?...," Ann says with a smile at his satisfaction with her bread, "we wouldn't have any songs. Do you think we should be careful, Mr. Lincoln?" She's careful not to look at him when she asks.

"Absolutely," he says between chews. "Never forsake your house and home to run off with the Gypsy Davy, and never be hardhearted to Sweet William so the two of you grow into roses and briars...." She's turned to him now with a pot-holder dangling in her left hand and a ladle in her right and her big eyes shining at him like he's a fairytale. A giant who's come to her village in a shady grove to speak in tongues. No one in New Salem talks like this.

It's her turn. "And never ask the laboring Matty Groves after church to come to my castle while my lord's away."

Abe's heart leaps and he doesn't know why but he has to *unleap* it. He gets up to take his plate to the wash-pot and she says, "Here," but he can't look at her face and he hands his plate into her white fingers and says, "Do you take care of the tavern by yourself?"

She knows what he means. "Father and mother went early to Wednesday market and took the little ones for shoes." Whether to make herself... or him... feel better, she adds: "They'll be back any time now. So what *will* you do in New Salem, Mr. Lincoln?"

"I'm supposed to run a store." Abe settles in his chair while Ann cleans up.

"It has so been decreed?"

Lincoln smiles. No one he grew up with talks like this. "Indeed. By one Denton Offut, entrepreneur. It was his flatboat of produce I lodged on your daddy's dam then took to New Orleans to turn to cash. Offut took a read on this place when we passed through and said it was up and coming and I was up and coming and did I want a job. He should arrive any day with a wagon of sugar and axe handles and gingham he hopes I can turn into cash for him right here."

"Are you an entrepreneur too, then?"

He doesn't know what to say. "It sounds better than shucking corn on the stalk."

"And are we supposed to like what we do?" She doesn't seem to like washing dishes, if he can tell by her indifferent rinsing of the pewter plates.

"My daddy taught me to work," he says, "but he didn't teach me to like it."

"It sounds like you blame your father, but didn't he do what all fathers do?"

"Maybe so, but in a worse mood."

"Then he won't be visiting?"

Lincoln smiles again. "Not for a spell."

"It sounds like you've escaped his spell, Mr. Lincoln. At least you seem to enjoy yourself."

He marvels again at the way she thinks. Her back is to him again as she ladles more water to heat and he stares at her and the shape of her and dwells on her boldly while she can't see what he's doing.

She turns and nearly catches him. Undeterred by his rapt gaze she leans forward on the chair across the table and talks directly to him as if she's decided something. "Well, if I ever get you in a spell, Mr. Lincoln, it will be very different from your father's. I believe in what Mr. Wordsworth writ... wrote. Why do I want so to speak properly with you, Mr. Lincoln? Have you read Mr. Wordsworth?

15

My daddy has the book of Mr. Wordsworth. My daddy has twenty-five books."

Ann nods to the side of the room where Abe sees worn leather spines on a shelf pegged to the wall beside the china cabinet. Abe feels how like him these people are, though better at it. They don't have a lot, but they *appreciate*. Touches. The basil he smells in that tin bowl with the cracked edge on the window sill. And Mrs. Rutledge's white china teapot there she must have brought hundreds of miles safely over rocky roads to display surrounded by gray pewter in the family china cabinet that had to be brought here too, no matter how much space it took in the wagon from Carolina. And Ann's wanting to get the words right. And her daddy's books.

"Daddy used to point to that shelf to get me to read," Ann says. "He'd say that little unfinished pine board holds up worlds," and Lincoln understands when he reads the titles: the Bible and Shakespeare and Sir Walter Scott and Robert Burns and *Pilgrim's Progress* and *Aesop's Fables* and *Poor Richard's Almanac* and *The Rights of Man*.

"Do you believe a woman should read, Mr. Lincoln?" She thinks of her uncle John proclaiming that a sitting woman should sew and involuntarily holds her breath for Lincoln's answer.

Abe remembers his illiterate father slashing him down from a fence for reading when he should have been plowing and says, "I think everyone should read."

Ann breathes her relief and as her lungs fill with air her heart fills with pride and she says, "My daddy has more books than Dr. Allen who came here from Dartmouth College."

"I love books, Miss Rutledge," he says earnestly. "Do you think he'd let me read them?"

"A lot depends," Ann says, "on whether you leave me tell you what Mr. Wordsworth wrote. Allow me, I mean. I mean let me."

He can't keep from smiling at her pluck. "My father sometimes kept me from reading," he says. "I'd never stop you from telling me what's in a book."

Ann recites upward as if proclaiming heaven back to itself:

16

The world is too much with us; late and soon,
Getting and spending, we lay waste our powers:
Little we see in Nature that is ours....

She pauses to see what he thinks and Abe says, "So work can cut us off from nature?"

"Exactly."

"I knew there was something wrong with it! But what *should* we be doing?"

Now she's at the part she glories in and she's taking off her apron as she announces, grinning: "We should be feeling...," she flings her apron away over her shoulder like work itself, "intimations of immortality!"

Lincoln shakes his head in astonishment. "Immortality seems a lot, don't you think?"

"I'm afraid you don't have a choice, Mr. Lincoln."

He demurs, looking down at the floor because he both believes and doesn't believe what he's going to say. "I'm a common sort, Miss Rutledge, lucky potatoes aren't growing from my ears."

"But we're born to immortality," Ann protests, "'Trailing clouds of glory from God who is our home.'"

"Clouds of glory," he repeats, staring entranced at this red-haired marvel.

Whether dutifully or from habit, Ann picks up her apron from the floor and attends to folding it as she goes on. "Tell me we'll always talk this way, Mr. Lincoln. I've only met you and I feel like we've known each other forever." As if to celebrate, she changes her mind about her apron and starts twirling it above her head like a streamer, then turns beneath it, exclaiming: "Since pennants flew from castle walls! You must stay in New Salem and talk with me. Forever and ever!"

"Well then," he says, "you must stop calling me Mr. Lincoln, and I you Miss Rutledge. Agreed?"

"Verily," she says and puts out her hand to shake and when his large hand encloses her small one they're stunned and look for one heart-trembling moment in each other's faces like children before she pulls away. Gesturing with her head to the door as if she heard something, Ann swoops up her apron from the table between them and puts it on quickly as 13-year-old Robert and 11-year-old Nancy and the three tots Margaret and William and Sally bang the front door open and race in jabbering and squealing ahead of Ann's tired-looking mother and father.

Lincoln immediately feels he's in the wrong as he often does when meeting people, and this makes him realize he didn't feel that way with Ann as he works his long frame up to stand and introduce himself. His air of grave reticence descends on him, and he says little more than that he's the new guest if they'll have him. After pleasantries including handshakes with the children, he excuses himself to go look at the town and at the front door turns back and says, "And thank you, Miss Rutledge."

Ann looks up abruptly from putting the bread away and he sees the threat in her eyes as she waves the knife covertly with a little smile, and he knows what she means. But he's less impulsive than she is, and their private ways can't be public for him. At least not yet. Hoping he's caught her eyes alone he raises his eye-brows in comic apology and she curtsies with no explanation and goes back to humming one of her "girl songs" as if she likes a secret. Mrs. Rutledge shouts to him when supper will be, and Lincoln goes out looking for work to hold him until Offut the entrepreneur gets to town with his wagon-load of goods to start his promised store.

After a cordial but stiff supper with the Rutledge family at the Tavern that night Lincoln's alone getting ready for bed with the door closed on his room of bunks off the kitchen.

Why did you lie to her about immortality? he thinks.

I didn't lie.

Maybe not, but you got all humble and you think about immortality all the time.

18

You don't tell people that.

He looks back on the day after his meeting with Ann. The rest of the village wasn't so welcoming. New Salem farmers have plenty of work but nothing to pay with. Their wives offered bread and molasses like they would for any traveler but he felt like a beggar. The businessmen saw him as another store coming when they already have too many. And nobody gave a speech for the hero who got his boat off the dam one day back in April.

It got dangerous when the rough bucks seeing him new in the village sized him up for taking down. They cornered him by the Out House behind the cock-fighting pit... he could see the feathers... and started edging closer as they joked about him being new and needing introduced to the local privy. Luckily he had the wits to laugh as if they were joking and said they must know about Ethan Allen and the privy in England.

They didn't? "Well it seems that Ethan Allen went to England," he said, "on some business or the other, after peace was made in the war. Some fellows there liked to tease him and were always making fun of the backwoods Americans and so on and General Washington in particular, and one day they got a picture of General Washington and hung it in the privy. They asked Allen did he see the picture of his friend in the Out House to spark some fun. Well he gave them some fun. He said he saw it there and it was the perfect place for an Englishman to keep it. Why's that, they said, and he said There's nothing that will make an Englishman shit so quick as the sight of General Washington."

The boys laughed and forgot him and he moved off thankful for stories. He had no way of knowing he'd tell that story another time inspired more by the shit than the outhouse. Years later it would be, in the middle of playing horse-shoes with political friends while he waited to learn if he was nominated for President. And guess who felt like shitting that day?

Escaped from the guffawing New Salem rowdies without fighting his way out of a privy, Lincoln was weary when he got back to

19

the Tavern. He'd walked through the night last night and was on the spot one way or the other all day. Now he looks out the wobbly window glass and across the dark prairie at the blurred night. He faults himself for wanting so much. Not just clean shirts and gingerbread.

Her. I want her.

She's too good for you.

"Mr. Lincoln?" he hears her bright voice, and a tapping at the door. Then a lower, more private tone. "Abe?"

"Come in," he calls, excited and afraid, and Ann pushes in carrying a basin and a pitcher of water.

"Let me, let me, Miss…" he mutters and rushes to help but she pulls the heavy basin back from his hands.

"Miss?" she draws up, offended.

Abe nods humbly and says gently reaching out again for her offering: "Ann?" She softens and their fingers touch as she hands him the clumsy weight and he wonders if she's touching him on purpose and remembers their hands warm together before, and the pitcher of shifting water tips and splashes on their feet.

They laugh. It's perfect.

"It's too full," she says as she turns to go, and they both ask themselves what that means as they say goodnight.

When she's gone a rattling breeze calls his eyes again out his window where the spray of stars reminds him of the freckles splashing across her face.

He wonders: *Is it always going to be like this?*

Ann wonders too. On her way to bed. Wonders at him. She was sure she'd never see him again and now here he is and they talked like she's never talked to anyone before. She's eighteen and the oldest child left in the house. She cleans and bakes and sews and takes care of the tavern and five smaller children and she's never had a man friend and hasn't thought about marriage since she was little and her Grandma back in South Carolina put her to sleep with the tale of a princess who slept a hundred years on a bed made of silver and gold to win a husband. So uncomfortable! How could it be? Oh, yes, and she must know a dozen old songs about people who should get married and don't, and a dozen more about people who get married and shouldn't, and now's not the time to think about that.

Luckily, her bed is better than gold, it's a mattress of good fresh straw in the sleeping loft with the young ones, and she climbs up the ladder thinking of tomorrow making coffee and gathering eggs and baking bread. Abe liked her bread so much he ate four slices. Can he linger and talk while she cleans up after breakfast? That's how far she can see. That's what she can want. That's what makes her feel light and spring up the ladder to the loft as if she were dancing.

3

There's not much time two people can be alone in a busy frontier home, and less when the home is the town's tavern selling meals at the big family table and overnight beds to strangers who come and go all day. Lincoln endears himself to Mrs. Rutledge by begging for chores to do and befriends the children by helping them learn their letters up on his lap while he talks with Ann about his hero Henry Clay as she moves around the kitchen.

"Speaker of the House, Secretary of State, Senator...." He says Clay's titles like honors to long for. "But when he gives speeches he talks," Abe says and Ann sees his eyes shine, "like real people, not scholars quoting Latin. The Senator and chimney sweep both understand him!"

"Then you must like Robert Burns," Ann says.

"Yes!" Lincoln literally leaps from his chair for the Scottish poet's book he's seen in Mr. Rutledge's little library.

Long and long they argue the lines:

> The Honest man, though e'er sae poor,
> Is king o' men for a' that.

Does the idealistic Scot mean you have to be poor to be honest? Is there something wrong with money? With ambition?

Another day Ann spreads her father's Burns book in front of Lincoln at this stanza:

> Had we never lov'd sae kindly,
> Had we never lov'd sae blindly!
> Never met—or never parted,
> We had ne'er been broken-hearted.

And love? Is there something wrong with love? She wants to know and she knows there are some things people don't say in the open but *It's Daddy's book,* she thinks, *so it must be all right to talk about.*

"What does it mean to love blindly?" Ann says casually over her shoulder while she scrapes out a porridge pot and Abe gathers pewter oatmeal bowls after breakfast, and Mr. and Mrs. Rutledge on the other side of the room hear danger like a fire bell and stop what they're doing and look at each other. Mrs. Rutledge goes to Lincoln to ask if he'd kindly bring some wood in for her baking, and Mr. Rutledge is relieved but now he's wondering if it was good to encourage her reading when it can give her… well… *ideas.*

Luckily from Mr. Rutledge's point of view, a week's worth is all the tavern money Lincoln has left from the profits of his flatboat trip to New Orleans, and he moves out of paid quarters to stay with village farmers he works for by the week while he waits for Offut to bring the goods for the promised store. Lincoln is stunned one day when a farmer he's clearing brush with pauses the pole he's using to lever a stump and snickers that he hears Sam Hill's closing in on a deal for the Rutledge girl. Even when you're new and only know a few people, you don't miss gossip this big in a prairie village of two dozen houses.

Of course a gentleman like Sam would court Ann. She's eighteen and marriageable and Sam's got the means. Did Sam hear that Ann takes a shine to the tall new cuss and figure he'd better get in while he's got a chance? Some say it's a wonder it took this long before big-eyed guys started lining up for her freckled hand.

Or did Ann's parents get Sam started? Lincoln's so busy felling trees for a plate of pork jowl and hominy on a farm outside of town that he hardly even knows it's happening, but all through August if Ann's parents aren't showing the village princess off in a new straw bonnet at the Baptist church when they know Sam's coming, they're inviting Sam to dinner and making sure Ann cooks so he sees what he stands to get. Known for the gruff but fair bargaining that's made him the richest man in New Salem, with more real estate than John McNeil and the town's biggest store where the government saw fit to put the post office, Sam is so kind around Ann that many a woman would think nothing of his bald spot or his pot belly coming out through his suspenders, but only see how well he'd take care of her and make her the grandest lady around.

What's Ann holding out for? they wonder when they see her reserve. She's not cold, she's too gracious for that. But careful. Even when she deals with her family about Sam. Her daddy knows her by now and when he sees her holding back he knows she's done set her stubborn red-haired mind and he looks at her sadly one day when she finds an excuse not to bake an extra pie to put aside for Mr. Hill and just shakes his head slowly as he walks away.

One day Abe strides resolutely to the Tavern, urgent to get some kind of claim in front of Ann. He's tired and sweaty from clearing timber at Ike Greene's, but he's got fresh strength for asserting himself after yesterday. Yesterday he clerked most all day for the local election, writing down men's names when they voted, and in the process met everybody and told funny stories to the poll workers and cider-swilling hangers-on. Late in the day one of his new friends raised his spilling mason jar and proclaimed and they all agreed, jolly with democratic spirits, that since this youngster could write and read and tell a good story he should be on the ballot the next time instead of collecting and counting them. Talk and laughter, talk and laughter, but in a year Lincoln's name will be on the ballot, and in two he'll be elected to the legislature and from then on he'll never lose a vote of the people... for legislature, Congress, President... for the rest of his life.

But today his new lift doesn't count for much when Mrs. Rutledge greets him in low spirits at the Tavern. Something's wrong and he can see it in her face. Is there anything he can help with, he asks timidly, while Mr. Rutledge is busy at the mill? Ann is up in the loft now, worried to distraction that her pushy married sister Jane is coming to see her, and her mother, sensitive as ever to Annie's moods, gets Abe organized with some chores while Ann collects herself upstairs.

Abe takes out the fireplace ashes and splits some straight-grained maple to fine sticks for cook wood. He lumbers a heavy iron pot outside and fetches two bucketsful of water from the well to scrub and rinse it in the yard. When he's done and returns inside he sees Ann arguing with Jane in a low voice. He excuses himself to say goodbye hoping Ann will ask him to stay because Jane's just leaving, but no such luck. The best he can get is Ann's surreptitious put-upon look from across the room before he goes.

Outside he feels how little he matters. Like he's not there.

There ain't enough of you to be anywhere, the voice inside him says.

Would he feel better or worse if he could be a fly on the wall hearing Jane give her little sister an earful? If only she'd had the chance Annie has, Jane says, instead of marrying her lazy farmer husband, and so on. And can't she see what this could mean to the family? To her mother and father who gave her everything? All anyone wants is to know is that she'll be taken care of. She hopes God will forgive her if she doesn't marry Mr. Hill. And the silks! Oh, Annie!

25

Because Ann can't stand to be blamed but can't break down in a house full of family and tavern guests, as soon as Jane leaves Ann drops her defiant composure and runs to the barn to throw herself on a heap of straw and cry with her chest heaving like a storm.

A few days later she's behind the Tavern picking blackberries at the edge of the woods in the August swelter.

Alone out there she imagines Abe's patient voice: *Some sweets come with thorns.*

Well then, she answers the invisible Abe while she looks for the next fat black berry. *Why is that?*

I don't know, he says.

I thought you were all-wise.

No, that's you.

Ann smiles but tears rise. *O Abe,* she says, *you are so wrong, and I am so lost!*

Her mother calls from across the yard.

She sees her mother coming up the yard from the house and prickles at seeing her so unlike herself and she knows this won't go well. Any other time she would yell from the kitchen door and expect Ann to come. And she'd not have her best embroidered white apron on and all smoothed out to talk with her daughter. Her mother is Ann's best friend and keeps her heart like no other. But they have a problem.

"Annie," her mother comes up and says, and pauses and twists her white apron string while Ann glances up at her and then back down to picking black berries into her little tin pail.

"Annie...," her mother starts hesitantly, then bursts out, "I never asked you for nothing like this but there's things you don't understand and Mr. Hill has talked with your father and he is serious...." Ann sees only the berries in her pail while she hears but doesn't really listen to her mother's guarded phrases about means and standing and holding your head up and what her father has worked for all his life. Her mother sounds dire and Ann's chest fills with pain but all she

26

can do is keep picking berries and swatting flies and wondering
life has turned so hard.

"Just tell me please, my pretty girl," her mother says in a
bling voice before she gives up, "just tell me you'll listen to wh;
Hill has to say."

Ann nods slowly as she keeps picking. She looks down bet
the bright red fruits on the edges of the bushes to the dark
deeper-in that she wants but can't reach and replies to her motl
will, I will."

Ann means to try, or to try to try, but she knows even ther
she can't do it. And her mother floats away across the yard l
ghost in a long gray dress with a drooping white apron becaus
knows once Ann's set her way she'll never change.

With her mother gone, Ann looks down where her sleeves
pushed up and her forearms sting with thin red scratches an(
remembers Abe saying folks should be more careful. *But how*
thinks. *Hide? Run away? Is there a place where a woman doesn't ｣
one only to hurt another. Please one, hurt another. Please one....*

She puts her pail on the ground and rubs her forearms to so
them but smears them instead with stinging crimson juice. ¯
seep between her closed eye-lids, her heart heaves and she cover
mouth so she doesn't wail. She imagines Sam and how she'll
him, not because she doesn't love him, although she doesn't, not
way, but that's not why she can't marry him. There's another re;
one she can't say. She covers her face with her hands to hide her t
and realizes too late to stop that she's stained her cheeks violent ｜

Look at me! she drops her hands and imagines shouting to
world: *Is this what you want?*

4

L incoln can't know Ann's misery when he sees her so little. And what can he do but feel cheerful on a mosquito-tormented morning when he's cutting rails out front at Ike Burner's place where everybody passes and more than one stops with the news: *Ann Rutledge has Sam Hill fuming 'cause she won't marry him!*

With a new surge upon him Abe finishes the forty rails he owes Ike Burner and moves over to the town forest and starts trimming out trees for the logs to build Offut's store. Yes, Offut's come to town at last with the goods for the store Abe's to run, a wagon load of gunpowder and wool and sugar and nails and O yes that great frontier seller whiskey. In a week the two men throw up a little log building with a window and a porch. They stock it and open for business and Lincoln moves in and sleeps on the counter. True, his fifteen by fifteen domain on the bluff above the mill is narrow for a customer coming down the middle between the shelves on the right and the

counter on the left. But there are kegs and stumps to sit on back by the fire, and on the whole it's not bad for a man with no other prospects, even if the store "lives dim inside" because Offut saved money by putting in only one window.

Inspired one day by opening and tasting a keg of molasses, Offut teases his clerk when he turns down a spoonful of sweetness. "I know what you want, Lincoln. You've got a taste for that rust-haired Rutledge girl, don't you?"

Lincoln blushes and denies it but Offut reads his man right.

"Well, one thing you've got going for you, thanks to me," the entrepreneur goes on, "She seems to like storekeepers. No sooner was she done with old Hill than his young partner McNeil started easing in her door. Maybe she'll want to look at your goods next, laddie!"

Lincoln goes off brooding over a fluttering heart. McNeil wants her now? *What can I do?*

The next time the boys drinking cider on the porch ask for a story he tells them about old Jake, a cuss back in Indiana. Jake was the kind of guy who didn't do much right. Didn't do much at all. But he ate good because he had a knack for hunting prairie chickens. All the other fellows would go out with their fancy new rifles and fancy dogs and come home with their fancy new rifles and fancy dogs. It was rare when they got game. But Jake went out with his rusty old gun nobody else would even handle and came back with four or five wild chickens every time. How did he do it? Again and again the other fellows asked him, but he just laughed. Until one day a hungry hunter must have had sad enough eyes and Jake said, OK, OK, I'll tell you how to do it. Jake took the hunter aside so no one could hear and swore him to secrecy. That done, he revealed it. You go out in the woods, he said, you hide, and you make a sound like turnip.

Abe laughs at old Jake with the others, but when that's done he's still helpless. What can he do? In time he'll know he needs stories the way others need medicine, liquor, prayer. In the unseen years ahead, when a beset Congressman Ashley objects to the President's telling silly tales on a hell night of the Civil War, he'll say: "Ashley, if I couldn't tell these stories, I would die!"

But what's the lesson, he asks himself? That doing nothing is ridiculous? But what can he do? He thinks if he were not so straight-off-the-farm he'd know how to court her. *But that's what you are, ain't it? Rough goods. Paltry.*

Families make it work, he's heard it. Or friends get people together. He's too new in town to have the kind of friends who can get him next to her. And he can't go following her around like a hungry dog. Or walk in like a rich suitor come to call. Sam and John get invitations. They're somebody. With something to wear. He has his one pair of boots he does his muddy work in and his rough linen shirt with the collar coming off. What can he do? He runs a store. *A little store. And look what happened to Sam Hill who runs the biggest store in town!*

Ann does what she must. She doesn't want to hurt her family again, so when John McNeil comes calling she offers him a chair, then some coffee and pie, and when her mother invites him for dinner she tells herself that an invitation to dinner is not an invitation to anything more. Absorbed in helping her father run the Tavern, Ann somehow assumes, especially after eluding Sam Hill's suit, that the family life she has will last forever. Even Sam's courtship didn't make her think about marriage. Not seriously. She scorns the fashionable British novels of propertied ladies scheming to win men of means. She's a country girl and feels more kinship with the women in the old ballads whose loves are fated by something powerful. *But how many live happily ever after? Not in "Matty Groves." Not in "The Demon Lover." Not….*

What do you marry? she asks herself. It's getting cold and there's something about a suitor, especially one with resources, that says warm family home and red rugs and a fire in the fireplace. John can't make her laugh. He isn't handsome, but who is in these woods and that isn't what you marry. He's read some books, yes, though they're

30

church books not Wordsworth. *Will he let me read?* But he's substantial. He's not a rough-neck and idler. He's substantial and there's not a secret reason she can't accept him like there was for Sam. She tries to feel the best she can about him, and finds things to be happy about when he's around.

Her mother smiles and turns the gingerbread out knowing Ann will ice it while John watches so there'll be no doubt she can make things end up sweet. Her mother and father exchange a look while Ann beats the sugar and cream and the blockish John beams proudly in his suit, never one to obtrude with too much to say. His family back East taught him manners all right. And he's closer to her age than Sam was. And he's a pillar of the Baptist church. Which is not to mention his nose for buying and selling property.

One morning Ann is busy in the kitchen and watching John talk quietly at the table with her father, who nods and gets some papers, and the two drink coffee like men who know each other.

Nobody knows Abe, she thinks.

In the few months he's been here some have pegged him for a joker. The way he gets with the men. Or they say things like, "He's rough material, but rough stuff wears the farthest."

Rough stuff? She imagines him in a silky red robe. In another country. She serves him at table. He gives her the place beside him. She pushes him from his seat and takes his place and they laugh and laugh.

She glances up from whisking sugar into her muffin batter and sees John and her father across the room.

The world is too much with us....

What do you marry? she thinks. *A provider? A world? A fairy tale?*

And suddenly the Lincoln that nobody knows is before her, knocking and walking into the Tavern with his sheepish grin falling apart in confusion when he sees what's there. Who's there.

At the Tavern they all like Lincoln, Ann and her mother and father and all the children. But Mrs. Rutledge has the children out somewhere, and Mr. Rutledge looks annoyed when Abe shows up

31

looking bewildered. Mr. Rutledge looks at Ann as if she should do something. But what? The whole morning was about John. And John doesn't look happy.

Abe takes in the situation. "I forgot my...." He's all ready to lie to get out of interrupting, but he can't think of what to lie about and acts like he forgot what he forgot.

Ann puts down the batter she was beating and moves to help him. "You mean that quill pen you left when you came last month?" she says with a glance at John and her father. She goes to her father's library shelf where they keep pens in a jar and gets one for Abe. She's feels proud that she's advancing Abe's exit plan and at the same time disavowing to John that Abe comes there much.

Abe takes the pen to the door as if sent out like a servant, then feels resentful and turns back.

"Thank you," he says to Ann in a neutral tone while throwing anger with his eyes that only she can see, and she winces and burns with shame as he turns to go.

Abe's resentment seethes on his way back to his store. *How do you get to see a girl? A barn-raising once a year when everybody else wants to talk to her too? I won't go to church to see her. I won't. And why's McNeil sitting in her kitchen like he belongs?*

Damnation! It's not the time for Jack Armstrong to show up, but there he is with a handful of boys waiting for Abe to open up his store. Abe feels trouble coming and feels mean enough to welcome it. Jack is the leader of a gang of bullies called the Clary's Grove Boys, and he's been taking notice every time the showy new Offut goes all big mouth about Lincoln, how he's the smartest cuss and the best wrestler too and can lick anyone. Which is probably why Jack and the boys have taken to coming to the store and pelting each other with corn meal from the barrel and stumbling to knock the vinegar over and laughing.

Lincoln usually keeps clear and cajoles the culprits and cleans up after them but today after the boys get rolling he's just not able to make that choice and finds himself holding Jack's arm back from

32

swatting a fly with a stick of firewood that would break his only window. It's not like the store is selling so much shot and sugar it can afford to buy new glass from St. Louis. With Lincoln's hand on Jack's elbow, Jack asks him if he wants to step outside and little kids run to get everybody because the fight is on and soon Jack and Abe are behind the store with their shirts off and grabbing and pulling and rolling in the dirt.

Jack holds his own at first but when Abe starts getting the better of him his boys rush in and back Lincoln against the wall of the store and start moving in for blood. Abe's eyes flash at them coming, and he sees too that Bill Clary, whose grocery full of whisky barrels gives the Clary's Grove boys their name, is there selling drinks from a jug and Offut's there covering bets with paper money.

"If you all want to fight me, I'll take you all on!" the disgusted Lincoln rages at Jack's coyotes as they close in. "One at a time!"

Luckily, Jack's back on his feet then and calls his boys off and says he'll handle the rest fair and square. Which he doesn't, going back to wrestling with a proper start, then using his leg to trip Lincoln for a fall they all know is against the rules.

With Lincoln on the ground, Jack's boys come at Offut to pay their bets.

"Not for a dog fall!" Offut yells, folding his cash and stuffing it in his pocket and backing away. "Jack legged him and that's s a dog fall and I ain't payin!"

Jack, ever the main fixer after being the main wrong-doer, has the solution.

"It's a draw!" he shouts and he and Abe shake hands and make Clary and Offut shake hands too, and all the bettors get their money back, and the warriors set down on stumps with buckets of water the boys ran and got to wash the dirt out of the scrapes on their arms and shoulders.

That's one way to get her off my mind, Abe thinks when everyone's gone, but there he is thinking about her again. He's indignant about the reception he got... and didn't get... at the Tavern, but he doesn't know how often John calls or what it means. Are John and Mr. Rutledge in business? For weeks he thinks about Ann every time he bends the scabbed abrasions on his elbows. He's proud of the respect of the new back-pounding friends the fight won him whether he wants them or not. He's sorry Ann couldn't see how he handled himself, though he might be more careful what he wishes.

He needn't worry that Ann won't hear the story. John McNeil, who wasn't at the fight of course, and would never lower himself for such a spectacle, makes sure she knows every shameful detail he can get from the boys who were there.

Is Abe like the rest? she thinks. *A brawler in the dirt. Cider and wagers, like at a cockfight! He can read but he's a country boy. How long will he be around when his dusty little store looks emptier every day?*

"John McNeil might not be one to light no fire in a woman's heart," Ann's mother says when she and Ann knit by the glowing coals one night, "but he's an upright man. He represents something." She doesn't say how well his new partnership with Sam Hill is doing. She doesn't have to. Nor all the lots and houses he owns.

Ann nods and doesn't contradict her.

"This might be just what you need, Honey Bun," her mother tells her, and as Ann goes back and forth in her rocking chair she sees too the lingering in her mother's look that seems to say, *This might be what we all need.*

Before long the ground is as hard as Lincoln's luck with his little store, and his pride goes down and he has to work out of the store as well as in it to make his keep. He pays for meals at the Tavern when he can afford them, and while the children jump all over him when he comes, the grown-up folk... Mr. and Mrs. Rutledge and Ann herself... don't seem as warm as they used to. *Or is that me,* he thinks, *being afraid and cold? Afraid of being nothing.*

He leaps eagerly into the chance to improve himself when Dr. Allen suggests a village debate club "to bring thoughtful discourse to a frontier not yet blessed with higher learning," as its by-laws say. In the back of Lincoln's mind is next year's race for the legislature, and

34

his childhood dream of being a lawyer one day. And that ain't gonna happen, he thinks, without some schooling. Learning. Debate. Reading and study. Whatever you call it. What an ambitious person would do. Does.

He selects "Ambition" for his first oration to the little club, with its eight members... a few farmers, the town woodworker, cooper, tanner and Dr. Allen and Mr. Rutledge himself... hunched attentively on the little benches of Mentor Graham's smoky lamplit log schoolhouse which doubles as the New Salem Baptist Church.

A few of the men begin smiling as Lincoln stands to speak, expecting one of his humorous stories, but he quickly surprises and stills them with a thoughtful weaving of reason and illustration about ambition until he closes:

"Our forefathers crossed a wide and dangerous ocean because of their ambition to make a better world. Our families, and we ourselves, struggled through the wilds of this untamed continent with the ambition to find better farmland, and build better cities, and breathe free in the glorious vistas we as human beings always see shining just ahead. I take ambition to mean the yearning for something better, and the will to achieve that goal, and I say that the *yearning of ambition* is the *essence of America*. And I say too that the *right to be ambitious,* no matter who you are and what you come from, is the *essence of democracy.* It is ours for the taking. In a free and democratic world, we can choose. With ambition we rise, and without it we fall and the wheels of the ambitious roll over us on their way to a better world."

Mr. Rutledge, like all there that night, including Lincoln himself, are impressed at his success. *There's something in that boy,* Mr. Rutledge thinks on his short walk home in the dark. *I never seen it. It's too bad he don't have the means.*

Abe feels bittersweet too. *Will I ever get a chance to tell Ann? She's got to know! If she could see me like that she'd never treat me like nothing.*

He burns his lamp late in his little store and hunches over the counter writing her a letter.

Dear Miss Rutledge:

I hope you will forgive me for presuming to
address some thoughts to you when we have not
been able to speak for verry long. It is in consider-
ation of your inquiring mind that I want to share
with you some ideas that I lately addressed to the
Litterary Association of New Salem on a topec I
was in the past fortunate to discuss with yourself.
And I want you to know that on the verry night of
said address, I was conscious that my audience was
all of men whereas my previous discussion of the
same matter – mainly the idea of ambition — with
you has confirmmed my belief that women should
be, when they care to be, full participants in such
events and associations. For they too, I now know,
have ambition. And it....

He stops and reads what he's written. He hates it. He can see
himself begging for attention and approval. His flattery and puffed-
up tone. He rips the letter in pieces and throws the pieces in the fire
and watches his torn vanity flame up and die. Yes, he meant everything he said. But it's all such a lie when what he really wants is to put
his arms around her and feel her body against his and whisper the
truth in her ear that he wants her to share with the same joy it gives
him: *I was Henry Clay! Henry Clay!*

Only Abe knows the irony that the next time he sees Ann is at
the school-house site of his oratorical triumph that she missed. Snow
comes flying across the prairie and some of it settles like the people
did and a white Christmas blesses the winter, and this year even
Lincoln comes to the New Salem Baptist Church, which is how that
same little school building is dressed, with wreaths and candles for
the holy service Abe scorns but is drawn to. Telling himself that you
can go to church for Christmas without going to church for church,
Lincoln comes because he knows Ann will come, but he wonders
if the price is too high when he has to sit heron-legged on a short
school bench and see John McNeil all smug with the Rutledge family. After the service John in his long navy blue overcoat gives Ann his

36

arm as they step down from the church to the white snow romantic to some but to Abe just bitter cold. Did she nod at him across the yard before she turned to walk home with John or did he see that because he wanted to?

With a Christmas present like this, Lincoln thinks walking back alone to his freezing store, *is it a wonder I'm not a believer?* He's always across a room from her, across a yard, across the village thinking of her, and his stomach twists when he tries to think of what he'd say if they could talk.

If he thinks Ann thinks less of him these days he's right. But he has no idea that she also always knows how well sugar and shot are selling in his little store. And that he still hasn't sold that cute but forlorn little tin tea kettle collecting dust on his low back shelf. He has no way of knowing that her heart sinks like his does while his store seems to sink lower in the snow each day and bring in so little money that he closes it more and more to go out to the woods with his axe to cut a day's worth of cook stove maple to swap some farm wife for a plate of ham and boiled potatoes. He has no idea the roil of feelings set off in her when her father tells her of Lincoln's rousing paean to ambition, the topic she and he discussed over a Robert Burns poem in her kitchen and now Lincoln has had the fortune to astonish the world with his thoughts on, while she has had the fortune to take John McNeil's arm in his rich blue overcoat.

5

The winter unlocks its ice prison early and the water flows free and the big dance is on and Abe can't dance but he's going. Ann's going to be there and he has to let her know what he's done.

But scared? O Jesus. He's nothing and she's village royalty. He's homely and she's beautiful. He drives himself crazy while he walks alone through the twilit woods to the riverbank. A mosquito trumpets as it charges his ear and falls silent when he hits himself. *It's too early*, he thinks, *mosquitoes in March. But the water's high and that's why it all works.*

The big night is his. It was his idea to bring the riverboat. He knew the Sangamon was navigable even after he got his flatboat stuck on Ann's daddy's dam last year. Once free from that dam he'd taken hogs and corn down the Sangamon to the Illinois and down that to the Mississippi and down that to New Orleans. With that dam out you've got a highway.

His ironic inner voice sees the opportunity. *Ambitious, eh? They going to make you a god tonight?*

No! His thinking offends him, but he feels proud. *I'll be happy just to see them celebrate my big idea.*

Don't big ideas come from big people?

No! he thinks, but then looks around in case he said it out loud and someone heard. He's at the end of the path where the woods open out on the Grand Reception.

Across the torchlit clearing he sees Ann standing in a yellow linen dress beneath a trellis plush with shining green leaves where she's talking with a solid-looking man in a dark suit with his back turned. Abe marvels at Ann's dark red hair, not pinned up for work but swept back from her face and coiled in a bun behind her head from which one rich strand streams further down as if it has to flow.

He feels better just seeing her. It's been hard. He swats a screaming mosquito.

So what? he thinks. *So what if Offut's little store got killed by Mc-Neil and Hill's big store with its city-like world of copper cookware and trimming lace and tins of Irish tea? So what if now I'm cutting brush and splitting rails for Ike Burner and sleeping in Burner's loft with his teenage daughter and son?*

You're a child yourself, he thinks.

No, he thinks, *I've done this right. I was quiet while I set my plans working, and the ship came in and everything will change. The river will save the town. And save me. The river and Ann.*

He starts to her, but as he does a new figure steps in with her and the unknown man. Her daddy. Abe stops. He's seen James Rutledge too much the last week, mostly coming and going silently on the river bank while Abe and Rowan Herndon and others took down his dam. First they axed apart the big board-made boxes Ann's daddy and his nephew John Camron built in the waterway years ago and filled with stones every man in the village brought with ox carts and hand carts to dam the water to start the mill that started the town the way you did in those days. With the boxes opened up, the men heaved together to roll the bigger rocks to the stream-bed's edges, then raked hard to spread the smaller stones as wide and flat as they could so that where once was a barrier to slow the least quart of flowing water, now, at least while the spring freshet runs high, the 48-foot beam of the cargo steamship *Talisman* can pass.

Talisman? Lincoln thinks, as always wondering about the words. *A magical emblem or charm, like in… what? Ivanhoe? Magical? Maybe that's why the water's so high. But magic don't bring mosquitoes,* he thinks and slaps himself where the sound grows loud and misses. He sees how eerie the scene before him is, how unlike the everyday feel of New Salem and Petersburg and Athens and the other villages out this way.

Torches surround the riverbank clearing centered on *The Talisman* where it's tied at the shore, and a warm breeze stirs the trees around the clearing to wave torch-lit shadows on the big boat glowing in the firelight like an apparition. This is no log-made flatboat with two-foot sides like Lincoln drifted down the rivers to New Orleans, but an upper-deck cabin steamer, miraculously white with balustered railings on its foredeck grand enough for lounge-chairs and whiskeys while its hundred-ton bay down below could stock a frontier town like New Salem with staples and luxuries for a year. He has no idea that years to come will move his hope from rivers to canals and from canals to railroads that cross and block waterways. Now, before him is the future as he can see it, a New Salem united with the grandeur of the wider world here on the Sangamon River by a twin-stack side-paddle steamboat shining like something on stage in a drama of salvation.

Salvation! That's where he's seen this kind of setting! Camp meeting! Those orgies of remorse and repentance and castings-out and welcomings-in lit feverishly with bonfires on a tent-surrounded common ground where the lonely frontier people get a passionate immersion in humanity beyond their isolated families, heaving about with a hundred others and shouting praises that rise to the lord the way the red sparks fly up right now in the fresh spring night.

It seems fitting to Lincoln but a little frightening too to find the science of the steamship mixed with religion's dark fantasy air, and the moreso when he feels eyes on him and looks up to the bridge of the *Talisman* where Captain Bogue is waving. He waves back to the captain with a feeling like he's been caught seeing something he might should not have. Abe worked with Bogue the whole last week, piloting and clearing obstructions under and over the water, but he never saw until now in the torchlight the satanic air of Bogue's florid face framed by his silvery hair wisping up on both sides of his captain's hat like horns.

Bogue's a jolly man, Abe thinks, *and we owe him. When they ask me to say something....*

Ann's high laugh makes him swing his head to see her still at the trellis across the way. In the rising warmth of the clearing her shawl has slid down and he can see the whiteness of her upper arms. But before he can take a step to her, daddy there or no daddy, a familiar voice calls his name.

"Hey there, Lincoln." Stocky and blunt, the one and only Sam Hill shifts his cigar from his right hand to his left so he can put out the right for Lincoln. "Knew you'd be here. You and your gang are important to this. I heard you even took old Rutledge's dam out right under his nose. Jimmy must have loved it when you took the axe to his stone box, but what the hell you gonna do? The time was come and he knew that. A town that can't ship is gonna sink, right Lincoln?"

Abe's glad everyone, most everyone, has come around. You don't need to mill lumber when you can ship boards in.

"Bill Greene's corn downriver for cash," Abe says, "and gingham and boards upriver for you and McNeil to sell."

"John McNeil is a son-of-a-bitch," Sam says. "I'm buying him out and if he has any sense he'll get out of town. He got too big for his britches when he came up with this plan to navigate the river."

Abe's astounded. *John?*

41

"He's right about the river," Sam says and re-lights his cigar. "But that don't mean he can lord it like the Big Man of the City. I put him in his place and the bastard sold me his share in the store and them building lots we bought together and if he's got any sense he's leaving town but something tells me he's not as smart as he thinks he is. Or some other people either." Sam glances across the way at Ann and shoves his cigar in his mouth and turns on his heel and wishes Lincoln goodnight and strides away.

Banjo and tambourine start up and Lincoln looks up at Bogue as the older man in his silver-buttoned white jacket puts his arm around a woman in a tight-waisted red city gown with gold trim and you can tell what she is which is not his wife. Bogue catches Lincoln's eye and smiles an arch smile, and… what's that?… is he gesturing with his head toward Ann? Bogue's painted woman spins out from his arm to the distance their clasped hands allow and bows to show her décolletage and Lincoln feels the warm breeze as if it comes from her, from her to him.

Then he comes to his senses. He's got to talk to Ann. He sees the crowd now filling the clearing, all the better for his getting through without being noticed and having to stop and talk when he feels nervous. Someone has added a drum to the banjo and tambourine, not an English drum with its thin tattoo but a booming deep drum some trapper must have gotten from Indians. Who might be watching from the woods right now. Black Hawk and his people, unhappy at being pushed west across the Mississippi, are back on this side waving the war axe. But New Salem doesn't care. Not tonight. Maybe because of the wagon of cider Jack Armstrong brought, strong as he can make it. Cockfight-grade.

But now it's not cocks crowing and bobbing and clawing in a pit, but every shape of frontier character, the women like the men mostly built for work and not for pleasure but with a hell of a hell-raising start already tonight in the infernal torchlight of the clearing, dancing in their careless frontier way with scant relation to the music. When he's mid-way through the surging throng hooting over the fiddle, Abe sees, as if magnetized to turn to it, the gracefully rounding dance on the glowing *Talisman* bridge of the roguish Bogue and his glittering woman so clearly not from here. A dance in which the captain holds the woman in his arms.

As Abe slides and glad-hands through the crowd to Ann, he sees who the other man with her is. John McNeil.

If the music goes on from that moment Abe doesn't know it, alone in a silence with what he sees. Nothing exists but him walking toward Ann, her father, and John McNeil. Time has stopped and he'll never reach them. Or he'll reach them but he doesn't want to.

Are you a man or not? a voice inside him mocks. *Are you even here? What difference would it make if you wasn't?*

Weren't.

Weren't then, Mr. Eddication.

He reached them. Ann's smile is warm with the innocent pleasure she always feels when she sees Abe. At first. Then she remembers the days last week she hated him. She recalls being at the mill and looking down at him on the dam again like the first time she saw him, but this time with no wonder at a homely hero but an urge to shoot him for wrecking everything.

Her friend Parthena, a stout woman of strong will and few words, came to watch the men take out the dam. "That what they call back-breaking labor?" Parthena said. A hard worker herself, Parthena didn't look impressed, but maybe that was just resentment on Mr. Rutledge's account.

"More heartbreaking than backbreaking," Parthena went on in that way that friends get to say each other's thoughts. "What's your daddy think?"

"He's wandering all over. He agreed to the thing, but he can't bear to watch."

"Nor can I," Parthena said, turning to go. "That dam built this town."

"The steamship will carry it on," Ann calls after her, in her hope repeating what others have been saying, but she hasn't thought about

43

it really and only cares about her father. John McNeil said they had to take the dam down too, but at least she didn't have to see him tearing her father's world apart like Lincoln.

Now at the steamship's grand reception, Abe looks from Ann's fallen face to her downcast father who manages a civil glance and nod, and then to sour-faced John McNeil who lifts his head and puts his chest out along with his hand. Lincoln looks up to take McNeil's hand but maybe as part of an instinctual aversion looks not at McNeil but over his head at the banner across the trellis shouting *Welcome, Talisman!*

In the absence of such high spirits among the group below the sign, Abe turns to Ann's doleful father.

"I'm sorry your dam had to go, Mr. Rutledge."

"Don't matter, Lincoln. Not your fault," Rutledge says though he doesn't look at Lincoln and he appears like it matters a great deal, if anything does, like a broken man in his best suit for a funeral. Rutledge is short and his mumbling to the ground makes it hard to hear him under the fiddle, banjo and drum, but the others pay him the respect due an elder by straining to hear.

"Everything goes in its time, don't it?" he says. "Saw mill wasn't making a nickel anyhow. Couldn't keep the thing in blades. Still…. well…," he looks for a way out across the teeming glade. "I'd better go get my pie before it's gone too."

Rutledge steps off into the noisy crowd without looking up, even after Ann grabs him to put a kiss on his cheek, taking small slow steps the way he does these days.

McNeil's been watching Lincoln the way he often appears to regard everyone around him, with what seems like silent pride. The look-down-on-people kind. He gives you the feeling he wouldn't want to be like this if he had a choice but it's all he knows. John is nowhere near Lincoln's six feet four inches, but somehow between his square fair-haired features and his blockish build and the way he draws himself up before he says a few words, he gives the impression of being big.

McNeil looks directly at Lincoln now, and Lincoln doesn't know what to say. He's still thinking of old Mr. Rutledge. He feels like he's wronged him with dam removal, but he's not even paying the cost of it. Why doesn't Rutledge blame him? He leveled the dam and killed the mill!

McNeil looks him up and down. "Captain Bogue tells me, Lincoln, that you've been useful. You know the river's lows and highs and can trim an overhang with a mighty axe. I always say it. It's the working people of this country that will make it great."

Lincoln hates McNeil's patronizing way, but he's relieved to talk with someone who approves of what he's done.

"I wrote the Captain to bring his boat and we'd get him upstream and down," Lincoln says and he can't help looking at Ann but she only looks inquiring and doesn't play with his glance as she has in the past.

"He didn't mention that." McNeil frowns as if at the many duties of being important. "He wrote me to ask if it would be all right. I assured him the people of means in the New Salem community would do their best to prevent his sustaining any loss on our experiment."

Our experiment?

"Mr. McNeil," Ann says too brightly as if fishing for something, "prophecizes that now our corn and hogs can go downstream to market and we'll all get rich and buy the books and China dishes that come upstream in return." Abe can hear her southern accent. "Wealth and civilization will be ours."

Both men look uneasy.

"Mr. McNeil," Ann tries again, "says the future's in Chicago, though nobody here can see that far." Is she punishing Lincoln?

Maybe there's a high hillside McNeil can take us up, Lincoln thinks, and offer us all we see spread before us. Now how do you like ambition?

"Internal improvements," Lincoln says. "New Salem can equal Chicago or any place if it gets some canals and bridges so commerce can move here and back on the river. That's why I'm going...."

"Yes!" Ann says. "Mr. McNeil says 'No' means 'no courage' or 'no brains.' He says 'Yes' is what turns trees to logs and logs to...."

"Houses," Abe interrupts, glaring at McNeil, who made his money in real estate, "to sell at ten times what you paid."

The music is faster now, and Lincoln resists an impulse to grab Ann and fly into the woods.

Do it!

McNeil, about to say something, draws himself up, but Lincoln interrupts: "I'm announcing for the legislature tomorrow."

McNeil is dumbfounded at the ill-dressed and unlettered Lincoln's presumption, but Ann can't control her delight despite her grudge against him lately and her blue eyes sparkle and her grin opens wide at his stepping forward toward what he wants.

"That's wonderful, Abe!" But her heart freezes as she feels something coming and she looks at John.

"Miss Rutledge and I," McNeil says, looking down with false humility, "have an announcement to make too."

No! Lincoln thinks.

"We're celebrating the success of my venture bringing *The Talisman* upriver by announcing that we will be married."

Abe turns to Ann without wanting to, and she gasps when she sees the pain twist his face so suddenly he can't hide it.

She doesn't say, "Where have you been?"

He doesn't say, "There wasn't enough of me."

He doesn't say, "I'm going to be a lawyer." Because that would be, like everything else he's believed, a lie.

Abe moves off abruptly, and when he's gone Ann argues with John about when to take her daddy home, John ready to go but Ann wanting to stay and keep her eye on Abe, shocked at his turning and walking away without saying good bye. She's impatient with John, she knows. She doesn't want to see him. But she's engaged to him. It's the right thing to do. He's a gentleman. But she doesn't want to see him. She wants to see Abe, but she can't go looking.

Lincoln wanders dazed in the dancing whooping crowd in orange flickering light and drinks cider with Jack and the boys and loses track and then loses track some more. He wants to fight John. A duel. He has no idea that in ten years he'll ride in a carriage at dawn to a riverbank to defend the honor of a different lady, the lady he will take to the White House or is it she who takes him? *Sword,* he thinks, here on the Talisman's riverbank, having never held a sword, *McNeil on the point of my sword.*

But then he feels someone press into his left arm, then put her arm around his waist and hold him to her as they walk, and he turns to his left and it's Nancy Burner. Nancy is Isaac Burner's daughter and he's been sharing the sleeping loft at Ike's place with her and her little brother Daniel. Her hair is down and her top button open. *Is she a woman? How old is she?*

A mosquito comes at him, unseen in the night, its buzz a soaring chorus from hell, and he clobbers his ear but can't feel it. He doesn't feel the bite, either, nor does he care. *Let it destroy me,* he thinks. *Somebody's got to do it.*

Ann trembles with rage when she glimpses Nancy's arm around Abe across the way. *And the cheeky precocious girl has opened her dress at the top for men's eyes to come and go!* When Abe and Nancy disappear into the crowd Ann scans urgently for them.

If they wander off drunk and fall in the river and drown, she thinks, *I'll kill him.*

But why? For fairy tale imaginings with a country oaf?

Ann tells the impatient John that yes, it's time to go and they gather her acquiescent father and she moves her escorts homeward as women must. And leaves her heart behind. And runs back to it with her thoughts again and again as her traitor feet take her away, home, nowhere.

Pressed together in the swaying mass of revelers Abe feels Nancy lift his arm from between them and put it around her shoulder and he leaves it there and they walk on in the crowd sagging this way and that to the droning music and she gestures and he looks up to

47

see Bogue and his woman kissing on the bridge of *The Talisman* as if floating in air.

Nancy squeezes with her arm around Abe's waist to signal something. Abe knows what she's going to say. He feels the flutter of something dark. Infernal shadows shift on the Talisman's hull in the warm breeze wrapping itself around them.

She says, "Wanta go in the woods, Abe?"

And they do.

At home, Ann gets her father off to bed then covers the fireplace coals with ashes for the night. In the sleeping loft with her candle, she feels her dress tight at her throat and clutches to free herself. She's nineteen. She was proud when she altered this bright yellow hand-me-down from her married sister Jane, but now she wishes she hadn't tried to look grown-up. To *be* grown-up. She remembers the pain coiling through Abe's face. She hadn't thought of Abe that way. She hadn't thought of John that way. But what she saw was terrible. And powerful! *What am I doing? What have I done?*

6

Knowing that Mr. Lincoln is a "particular friend" of Ann's, John McNeil takes pains to be sure that she's aware of what Mr. Lincoln does and says when she can't be with him. One day John hurries to get to Ann before supper chores at the Tavern take all her attention.

With gravity he assures her as she puts on her apron that he regrets he must be the messenger, but of course she must know the truth. That morning the militia got together to march off after Black Hawk, and when they met in the bean field behind Dr. Allen's corn, Slicky Greene who sometimes works for John was there and saw it.

Apparently to pass the time while an army Colonel rode over this way from Petersburg to organize them for their departure to the war, Lincoln, true to his nature... John has heard him called a backwoods clown, but that's too severe, doesn't she think?... told a story.

"When I was a little boy back in Kentucky," Lincoln apparently said, "a lot of fellows got drunk on holidays, just like here. Well, one merry election day when the weather was bad and the roads were as muddy as a pig sty after a rainstorm, a man with a limber elbow named Bill got brutal full of whiskey and staggered down a narrow alley where he laid himself down in the mud and stayed there until the dusk when he was finally able to stand. Finding himself very very muddy, Bill started for the town pump to wash up. On his way to the pump he saw another drunk leaning over a hitching post, and this Bill mistook for the pump, so he took hold of the arm of the man for the handle and started pumping it, which set the occupant of the post to throwing up. Delighted at the abundant flow of the thing, Bill put both hands under and gave himself a thorough washing. He then made his way to the grocery for something to drink. When he came in the door, his friends recoiled backward from him and one said, Bill what in the world happened to you? And Bill said, By God you ought to have seen me before I washed."

"Oh, the boys loved it," John tells Ann, "and the ones who didn't march off with him are going around telling everybody who hasn't heard it and spreading Lincoln's fame."

He doesn't say "...like manure," but he sees the disappointment he hoped for in Ann's face and tells her how sorry he is. How sorry for any benighted soul who delights in filth.

"I have no idea," he says, "why people don't realize that what they say shows what they are."

Ann's standing at the window when John tells her that and when he's done and he mumbles good bye and goes, she's looking out into the back yard where she sees a little stand of daffodils waving their yellow heads back and forth in the breeze as if to say...what? "Yes"? "No"?

No! she thinks. *No!* Because while John talked and she tried to feel indifferent, she felt her heart drop silently through her body and down through her clothes to slip naked and red onto the floor where John stepped on it and ground it one way and another while he gloated like a backwoods conqueror when he told her that Abe's gone away to war.

7

onths later on a hot July morning Lincoln hikes back into town from militia duty in the Black Hawk War. The call to arms came in the spring when he needed it to get him out of New Salem. He'd be a hero and win her heart. Or get wounded and she'd nurse him. Or get killed and never see her again and never think about John McNeil.

On the dusty village road he sees Dr. Allen's bean field where he mustered into the volunteer army in April with a couple of dozen local boys standing in two lines to take the oath in whatever rough pants and shirts they had for uniforms. The boys elected Abe captain because he could read and write and outwrestle them. He said, "Yes, I can shoot," but he didn't tell them that when he killed a wild turkey when he was seven he felt so disgusted with the bloody mess that he never again pointed a gun at a living thing.

Not that the Indians gave them any targets. They'd get word that braves were sighted and he and his company would march this way across a forest and that way across a prairie and end-up fighting nothing but mosquitoes and hunger. They "field requisitioned" chickens after farmers ran off, shot rabbits, and made soup of potatoes. They ate raw potatoes like apples. They ate nothing and wished for raw potatoes.

Now it's a hot July morning and he's back at the Rutledge Tavern door and he wants to start over. He'll knock like he did when he first came and Ann will open the door and make him a bed and give him bread and butter for breakfast. *But this time,* he thinks, *it will all work out.*

He's scared again like when he first came, but he wills himself to knock and yell hello. Nobody comes. In the glaring July stillness he hears a splash around the side of the house and goes around and finds a laundry brush and some twisted clothes floating in a tub and farther around the house past the clothes line he hears the back door slam. It's comical. And ghost-like.

He goes back to the front door and tries again.

"Just a moment!" Ann shouts when he bangs and then, done getting off her dirty apron and tucking in the wisps of hair her laundry work had freed from its pins, she swings the door open and gets rid of her smile and selects the mild level of sternness she intends as she says, "Mr. Lincoln. We weren't expecting you." Which was partly a lie because last week Henry McHenry brought gossip that the boys were coming "afore long," after which she practiced greeting him coolly every day.

Lincoln feels ashamed and he knows he looks ashamed and he hates it. She looks like she's appraising him and she is. He looks different. Weathered and loose. Has his shirt shrunk more? She sees how strong his chest and shoulders are.

"I'm sorry I didn't write…, Ann. Or… should I call you Miss Rutledge?"

"It doesn't matter what you call me, Mr. Lincoln. All travelers are welcome at the Rutledge Tavern." She turns from him and goes across the room to the fireplace not knowing what else to do. His

52

fear makes him somber, and half of her is glad he's uncomfortable too and her other half wants to put him at ease. She glances back and sees he's coming in wearing new black leather boots and she compliments them. He says the army issued them when he signed on for extra time and they're sturdier than the deer-hide boots his step-mother sewed him with an awl on the farm. So he owes a lot to the Indians.

He's joking, but he doesn't feel welcome. But he's glad to be there anyhow, watching her put thin splits of wood on the cook fire. As if maybe she's cold. Which she is. To him.

But I'm not the one, he thinks, *who got engaged.*

"I brought you something," he blurts.

Ann stops fussing with the cook fire and turns to him as he brings something up from his bag on the floor. *How could he?* She's holding the poker and she thinks of swatting him with it but she drops the fire-iron on the hearth and takes the dried up old book from his hand and reads the cover with the joy in her face growing uncontrollable, relieved to be herself again.

"*The Tempest!* Abraham Lincoln!"

"A boy in my company found it in a burned-out cabin."

"Things survive," she says, not sure what she means. He sees how she presses the book to her chest. "I'm glad you survived, Abe."

"I had to," he says. He doesn't say, "…because of you." He says, "I'm a candidate for the legislature."

"I've heard that you are, Mr. Lincoln, and my family and I will be proud if you'll stay with us at the Rutledge Tavern on your return from your triumphant military career."

"Well, it wasn't no triumph," he says and jumps to talk politics to get away from what he's really thinking, "but it won't hurt me with voters. The truth is we only saw one Indian in three months, an old fella who wandered into camp one night looking for something to eat. The boys wanted to string him up on general principle but I said General Principle wasn't there, so I as their elected Captain would have to do, and there'd be no hangings but someone could make him eat a bowl of that poison the cook calls soup. You should have heard the grumbling about them doing all that militia for months and not getting to kill nobody."

She nods, and doesn't correct him... *anybody.* She says, "Sometimes I wished I was with you out there." She doesn't say, "So we could die together."

He shakes his head, "You wouldn't have liked sleeping on the ground." He doesn't say, "Sometimes I wished I'd get shot so you could nurse me back to life."

She doesn't say, "I'd sleep anywhere with you, Abe."

He doesn't go around the table and press her hidden warmth to him so he can feel it through the cloth and say, "What are we going to do?"

She doesn't say, "I'd do anything for you."

They're both looking at the floor in silence after all the things they didn't say, so Abe gets up and goes to the open front door and looks out and down the road and says, "Everything looks about the same," then goes and sits down again.

The table's not the same, he sees, and he's sitting on a chair, a new chair, and not the old bench, and Ann reads his confusion. "When Mr. Robert Johnson the woodworker moved into town," she tells Abe, "just about the time you left for the war, Mama marched right up, before Johnson even built his own house and said... having heard he was a Presbyterian... that she was predestined to have a real oak dining table with ladder-back chairs and if he was predestined to have customers in this town he could prove that right away, and her husband says the money will come along this summer and somehow it did and maybe that was predestined too even though daddy is a Baptist and that's all there is to that."

Abe laughs but Ann doesn't because she's thinking of what all else is different, and as Abe admires the real turned legs on the long heavy-built table she feels the dullness that comes with holding something back and changes the subject.

"Are things about the same with you?" she says, and he doesn't know what to say.

He wants to tell her about the law but he doesn't know if he believes it.

That don't matter, he thinks. *It'll get you somewhere, and right now you're nowhere.*

He surprises himself by taking his own advice. He impulsively stands when he says it as if to distract her if what he says is too foolish: "I'm going to study law."

Ann blinks and widens her blue eyes at his jump from guarded small talk to something he must have thought about a lot. He's pacing now in that way of his, his eyes shining with excitement, and the drooping corners of his mouth lift up, and a kind of intentness takes over his face.

"At the campfire one night, you know I told you we didn't see no Indians, well, I told the fellas what I'd seen that morning. I rode into a clearing at dawn and saw three dead white men there, each with a dollar-sized circle of dried blood on his head in the red morning light. It shook me up and stayed with me all day. Never has left. But that night I was saying to the fellas that at least I saw evidence that the Indians were around. We all looked out in the dark then. We didn't want none... *any...* around.

"Well, one of the fellas took an interest in my saying 'evidence' and started talking about what it is and isn't and he and I worked that definition around and around until we bored all the others and they all went to bed-down and left us drinking cold coffee by the last of the fire. Turns out this Major, he was, was a lawyer from Springfield, name of John Stuart. We hit it off. When he asked my education I had to tell him my schooling don't come... doesn't come... to a year. He said not to worry. He said I can do it... be a lawyer... and the thing is to get the books and study, lots of men do it, and he'll loan me what's in his office if I come by."

Ann knows it's true. Abe can be a lawyer. There's no way she can see now that in a few years he'll be *the* man you want to take your

55

case to the Illinois Supreme Court, but she sees how thoughtful and clever he is. How good with words. His story just now is "evidence" too of the way people take to him. Smart people.

She thinks of herself.

It wasn't just *his* ambition she thought about when her daddy came home that time and described Abe's speech about yearning for a better life. She wants something too. She just doesn't say it, and here he is saying it. Ann is congenial, anyone would tell you. She smiles a lot while she helps all the others. The corners of her mouth go as naturally up as Lincoln's go down, but her family knows well that when she sets her mouth in a darker way you better run for the hills. But that's rare, and the amiable, helpful Ann is real. She does all the sewing for the Rutledge family, even though her mother and sisters sew, because she's the best at it. She relieves her mother of much of the cooking, because she's the best at it. And for probably the last five of her nineteen years she's known better than her father how to run the Tavern but has never let him think for a moment that's how it is. Ann is the kindest person most any one of the hundred souls in New Salem has ever known. But she wants something.

Lincoln saw that the first time they talked, though he's still never said it to himself this way and might never. The closest he's come is the way he thinks of her looking at him right now: *She's like me.*

"I want to be a teacher!" she exclaims, and finds herself standing up and reaching for the broom and starting to sweep the hearth. "To teach children their letters and words!" she goes on as she whisks, "to lead them to books that take them to new worlds!" She stops and looks at the tavern kitchen that is her world, and the broom in her hands. She looks at Abe standing before her nodding with surprise and agreement as if she makes perfect sense.

Which she's not sure she does.

"I know you can be a lawyer, Abe," she says in a quiet sure voice, "if it's what you want."

He sits down now and looks up at her. "It's the first thing I ever wanted. I knew I didn't want to be a farmer. But when I was in

Indiana," he says, "and old enough to sneak away from my daddy's farm a few hours? Well, I discovered the show down at the Justice of the Peace and used to go watch people argue about who owned what land or broke what contract or broke whose nose in a fight. When the squire found out I could read, he let me read legal papers to people and take them off to the side and explain what I could. You know… summonses and deeds and wills and such, and he even let me talk for them sometimes…." He stops though he was set to go on. He doesn't want to tell her how he got scared. How he stopped going to the JP court when a real lawyer came with a fine suit and fine words to take a case one night. In the silence his eyes fall into a lost look and he gazes up at Ann as if she's the teacher and he's a little boy.

"You can do anything!" she exclaims.

Abe's face breaks out of its melancholy and into a smile, but he's sheepish and avoids her stare and hides his gaze in her broom down on the floor. He feels a kinship with that bundle of straw – feels the way she…what?… *wields* him. Blind to the immensity of his future, he cannot know the irony of his feeling small in her hands while she says he can do anything.

"I hope you're right," he says absently to the broom. Then, looking back up at Ann as if he's restored: "But I know you can be a teacher too. You've taught me Wordsworth already. 'The world is too much with us….'"

Ah, too true, Ann thinks, and what little is left of the hopeful lift she just felt drops her back into the world that's too much with her and she goes back to sweeping the ashes on the hearth because sometimes cleaning up the mess life gives you is all you can do.

"Tell me the news," Lincoln says as if to distract her, and glad for the diversion, Ann reaches for something spicy but safe as far as she's concerned.

"Captain Bogue disappeared."

"Disappeared?"

"More or less. As far as local people know. You had the last sight of him when you and Row Herndon helped him get *The Talisman*

57

back downriver, and then you come… came back to town and joined the militia and went off chasing Black Hawk. Well, Sam Hill wrote then to the Captain to come start a regular shipping route but he sent back that the river won't work. *Too skimpy* he said. Sam wrote him again but he never wrote back, and a wagoner with a load from down Bogue's way said a month or so later that *The Talisman* burned to its last spar at its dock in St. Louis and Bogue was nowheres to be found."

Too skimpy. Lincoln doesn't say… doesn't want to think… what this does to his legislative campaign claim that the river will make them all rich. "Sam wrote?" he says. "Not John?"

He waits while Ann looks down with tears welling in her eyes, then raises her face as if to announce a death and says, "John went back East."

Abe is about to shout that she's free but quickly masks his joy with care when he sees her mouth tremble.

"To bring his mother and father to live with us when we're married!" she wails, then sinks on a chair and hides her face and bursts into tears.

Abe sits heavily to absorb it. *Of course.*

"There's something else," she says.

He can't look at her. He looks at the floor as she goes on.

"He told me… something. He… took me for a walk… alone. He had his wagon loaded to leave the next morning. He said his father has debts and he, John, ran away from home to make the money to pay them. He changed his name so his family and their creditors couldn't find him and bring him down, that's how he said it, bring him down before he'd made his fortune. He's made his fortune now so he's gone back East to settle up and bring his family West. His real name is McNamar, John McNamar."

"He's a fraud!" Lincoln shouts jumping from his chair to stride back and forth. "Whatever his name is! And do we know? He lived here for years under false pretenses while he ate the bread of people he lied to. Who knows where he's gone or if he'll come back? He could be scheming another fortune in another innocent town right now! You can't be engaged to a man who hides himself!"

Lincoln cannot know that he who will proclaim again and again from platforms that he is no one but "humble Abraham Lincoln" will when the time comes disguise himself in a borrowed gray over-coat and soft red felt cap, Scottish plaid like McNeil's, when death threats on the route from Illinois cause him to sneak into Washing-ton under cover for his inauguration.

But he's indignant now, and Ann looks up at his indignation with her blue eyes bitter in a face wet with tears, her hair dark in her sorrow in the dim log tavern. She slams the words separately into the air between them: "I. Have. No. Choice!" She buries her face in her hands and bursts into tears again and Lincoln, baffled at her fierce-ness when she's so wrong, can't bear to see her for another second for fear of shouting. He can't be there. He goes to the front door, looks back at her with his face settling into its mournful cast, then turns and rushes out while she cries and lets him go.

Alone, Ann can't breathe. She gets up and throws the front door wide then shoves all the windows open and looks back and forth in the big front room and it's a prison and she hurries to the back door and throws it open too and looks out where the mill roof rises from the river out of sight down over the hill.

Abe got stuck on the dam down there, she thinks. *But he got himself free.*

Nobody pinned him, she thinks, and she sees with horror the scene in *Matty Groves* when the great lord thrusts his sword through his unfaithful wife and pins her to the wall.

Can I ever get free? she thinks, and she sits on the big gray stone that makes the step down from the Tavern's back door and gazes out toward the river with a mixture of resentment and hope and imag-ines the Sangamon out of sight down past the thorny blackberries guarding the end of the yard, down below the hill where its water flows with a brown silty shine and lacy edges, rolling into the Illinois River and the Mississippi River and down to the Gulf of Mexico and from there out into the Atlantic Ocean and on and on into all creation beyond with its continents, planets, moons, suns, and stars.

Free!

8

Lincoln doesn't get far through the village before he slumps to sit against a fence-post at Ike Burner's cornfield and Ike's coonhounds start bawling when they smell him. He doesn't think why he stops there, not somewhere else. Not that anybody cares. Nobody's out in the insect drone of that hot yellow summer morning except the dogs chained out back and baying.

Not being a hunter himself, Lincoln has always hated the hounds' loud mournful calls, but today he leans uncomfortably back on the fence-post so tormented that at first he hardly hears them. Then he wonders if they're saying what he wants to say. He sees he's by the Burners' and remembers young Nancy who took him into the woods. He heard that while he was away she got what she wanted and ran off to grow up fast with his friend Jason Duncan.

People take what they want, he thinks.

But I can't take Ann, he answers. *She's the daughter of the founder of the town and the lady-friend of the rich and I'm someone she talks to.*

She says she has no choice.
That means I'm not a choice!
Can I strangle the dogs?
No, strangle McNeil.
No.
Then what? What?
Study law. Show them.

Sure, he jeers. He looks up where the corn beside the Burner house towers over him. He makes himself stand.

Stand up to it.
The world?

I'm going to the legislature. He looks around and sees nobody. He's taller than the corn. *I'll be somebody,* he thinks.

In five years? he asks. *When she's married?*

John's not here, Lincoln thinks. He looks back to the village where he can see the roof of the Tavern after the Lukins house and Dr. Allen's place. He remembers the fighting spirit in Ann's face when she told him: "You can do anything!"

You? he thinks. He's already started back to the Tavern to move in and show her: *Me! Abraham Lincoln!*

Am I sure? he asks himself and the question although it doesn't go outside his head is so big that it seems to bang out through the fields and up against the log houses and up against the clouds and up where he looks as if he might see it echo against the whole banging blue summer sky. But the sky has nothing to show him so he keeps striding forward on the road through New Salem with his face as resolute as he can keep it, not caring if everybody thereabouts somehow hears his question too, right through the frantic complaining of those chained dogs and looks out their windows at him across their grassy front yards and sees from his desperate lunging on the road down the middle of town how unsure he really is.

9

With the last of his Army dollars Lincoln bull-headedly moves back into the Tavern telling himself Ann belongs to someone else but at least he'll get to see her. *I'm still here,* he thinks at her when they pass, *and John's not,* and she narrows her eyes as if to be careful until he passes, then sometimes when he's by her she feels his resentment that matches her own. Circumstances don't help. Frontier people get out and about in the summer when the getting is good and the Tavern is busy with boarders and travelers and family, so Abe gives up on serious talks with Ann, but he can't give up on looking. Her swaying dress, her hair and the way it falls on her breast, her buttons. He remembers again and again the daydream he had in the militia, the long hot thirsty days going nowhere in the saddle or stretched on the hard ground trying to go to sleep when he'd see himself lying with her. They have their clothes on. *That's all I'll see,* he thinks. But then he sees them closer. And closer. And he thinks, *How close can you get?*

He thinks that sometimes when he sees her around the Tavern, and sometimes she turns away and her dress stretches tight at the breast and hip, and she's gone. Will he see her, the two of them, naked? Will he see that? He doesn't know and then he starts to see it but the picture bursts into flames like something made up at a campfire.

Abe's mostly out campaigning the last of July for the August legislative election, giving stump speeches literally standing on stumps or porch steps or a hay wagon when a hosting farmer is rich enough to have one. "I am young and unknown to many of you," he says earnestly and tries to turn being nobody into a man-of-the-people advantage. "I have no wealthy or popular relations to recommend me."

The little time he's at the Tavern he feels like a nobody but helps like one of the family… chopping kindling, fetching water, mending fences and moving heavy things… and he and Ann glance and look away, and he's so shy anyway that what can he say? *You don't know who I am. How can you forget how we used to talk? McNeil is a liar! I'll be somebody!*

Ann doesn't tell him how charmed she is by the campaign statement he put in *The Sangamo Journal*, so charmed that she goes around saying parts to herself:

> Every man is said to have his peculiar ambition….
> I have no other so great as being truly esteemed
> of my fellow men, by rendering myself worthy of
> their esteem.

She admires his honesty about wanting others to like him, and his wish to really be worthy and not just seem so. How did he put it? "By rendering myself worthy of esteem.". And she admires his humility, so unlike a lot of frontier men going on about what they came from. "I was born," he wrote, "and have ever remained in the most humble walks of life."

Sometimes he feels the irony of bragging that he's humble, but sometimes he feels so humble it hurts.

He tells "speechifying" audiences he'll do big things, but feels small around Ann. He says parts of his campaign announcement to himself when he's alone between farm hayings and beef shoots and speeches on the Springfield courthouse steps. The part that comes to him the most is near the end:

> ...if the good people in their wisdom shall see fit
> to keep me in the background, I have been too
> familiar with disappointments to be very much
> chagrined.

Is he so used to disappointment that one more won't hurt him? How about a rain of them? He loses the August election. Then he hears what people said about him when he campaigned: that he was tall and gawky, that he looked a fool with his pants six inches from the tops of his boots. He heard of a judge who admired one of his speeches and then asked who the odd speaker was and was told he was "a kind of loafer over there at New Salem." *A loafer!*

Loafer or no loafer he's broke. With no more saved-up Army money to pay his keep at the Tavern he goes back to bunking with families he farms for. He stays at Ike Burner's where he's relieved but let-down too to have no Nancy mooning over him while he and Ike and Ike's son Daniel go through the chores. Then he moves to Isaac Gulliher's up the way. And on from there, shucking corn at the Greenes', splitting rails for the Allens with no way to imagine that rails he splits in despondence will someday be enshrined in the nation's museums. Broke and homeless after the election he hides in hated farmwork in places out of town where he won't see Ann.

Or more honestly so she won't see him.

But Ann sees him all the time, sees him in her heart as if he still roamed the Tavern with his big sad eyes, imagine him while she plucks a chicken for Sunday dinner, while she sweeps... as she seems to eternally... the floor. She calms her swift sweeping to his slowness. She recalls the way he falls silent in discussions, but something tells you he hasn't let his thought go, and then he turns on the other side of the room and picks up where he left off. She can see him stoking the fire with an unhurried reach from the rocking chair, never jumping up the way she does to gust off and grab the fire iron or the broom, or sail to the other side of the room to straighten a wooden ladle sneaking out of a keeper jar.

Whisking quickly again at the floor, Ann knows she'll never be as careful as Abe is, she who's busy making beds and baking bread and getting children's arms into little shirts and scrubbing tubs of sheets and trousers after heating vats of water to make everything right in a world that's gone so wrong, gone so wrong with what she did and what John did and what she's doing now to Abe. She wants to give up, but she doesn't know what that means. *Hard is the fortune of all womankind,* she sings to herself from a sad old song. *She's always controlled, always confined....*

Her longing thoughts about Abe go round and around while she churns butter one day... the way his left eye drifts upward sometimes, how he paces back and forth to think. When Russell Godbey comes by the Tavern to borrow tools she's careful to angle the old farmer to a question about Lincoln only after she's asked about all the others they know, but once she gets him to Lincoln he can't resist telling a story.

"I was comin' past Jake Bale's place the other day, and I near onto passed out when Abe surprised me bein' up on top of Jake's woodpile, just sittin' there astraddle a big top chunk of sugar maple. With a book in his hands! Big old thing! I said, What you readin' Abe? He said Not readin'. I said What then? He said Studyin'. I said Studyin' what? He said Studyin' law. Great God Almighty! Can you imagine it Miss Rutledge? Studyin' law!"

Ann imagines it. She smiles. She imagines Abe riding high, very very slowly, on a big top chunk of sugar maple. Studyin' law.

10

How often does a moment's image deceive? Harvest chores are ending, and there's little call for farm work, and the failed candidate isn't riding high on anything. After trying law for a day he turns to wandering the autumn afternoons in a sunlit meadow where insects drone in high weeds. He thinks why go on and sits on a log so he can justify his end with some real concentration on every aching flaw. When he tries to distract himself with his army daydream of holding Ann he barely gets started when the man holding Ann turns into the bastard McNeil. *Is there so little to me*, he thinks, *that I can't even imagine myself? Is my life getting so skimpy I'm the horse that lived on shavings?*

He remembers it. A carter, the story goes, was running out of money for corn and oats for his horse, so he tried feeding the old mare shavings. He got them from the wood mill for nothing and mixed in a little with some better feed. Finding the horse ate the shavings, the carter gradually put in more and more of them with less and less of the other foods until at last the horse was living on shavings alone. But then it died. Just as he discovered the solution to his problem!

What's my solution? Lincoln thinks. *And don't let it be shavings! Where's that law book you borrowed?*

Shavings! You tell me.

Or do you need the Good Book? Should you be more Christian?

Shavings! But he softens at hearing what his Mama might have said.

That's right, the devious voice says, *you've got so bitter. Maybe you should love your enemy.*

Love my enemy?

Wildflowers on tall dry stalks verge yellow all around in the slow buzzing day.

Well, the son-of-a-bitch must have something about him to love.

Like something slowly coming to an end.

Like what?

The insect whir is winding down.

Count him up, that McNeil. What do you get?

A few maples stand out, copper and red.

Lincoln hates to admit it but he does it: *He's got the woman and the money and the standing in the world....*

So if you was him you'd have that? He feels a strange kind of sense coming on.

If I were him? My enemy?

That's right. Now how do you do that? He stands and paces back and forth in the waiting day.

How did McNeil do it?

He found a partner and borrowed money and started a store.

But I'm studying law.

I can see that. The weak have excuses. It's always the wrong time. Here's what happens in time. In three or four years Ann will have a little

68

girl and boy in a two-story house in Springfield and you'll be writing real estate contracts for their daddy. If you're lucky.

If he were holding something now he'd throw it down but all he can do is throw his hands up to the uncaring sky and the insect whir kicks in again and he sees the daylight slanting and gives up thinking and goes off to cut wood before the sun gets too low and the mosquitoes take over completely.

But the thought's in him now, however he scorns it. *Become my enemy.*

He sees Ann standing before McNeil. Looking lovingly up into his face. Then he wants to be his enemy. To have the face she looks into be *his* face. He hates his face. Hates what he's become. A nobody. What he hasn't become. A lawyer. Henry Clay.

A lawyer? He can't do that, no matter what Ann says. He thinks again of all his days of so-called school with itinerant schoolmasters traveling through the backwoods Kentucky and Indiana worlds of his boyhood and he can't add them up to a year. And those were blab-schools with no schoolbooks, the pupils shouting to repeat what the master shouted: "Columbus is the capital of Ohio!" "Columbus is the capital…!" "*I* before *e* except after *c*!" "*I* before *e* except…!" Not a year of blabbing altogether. Is that the education for a lawyer?

One day he hears Row Herndon owns half a store he wants to get out of. Something he took in trade or won at poker the way debts get passed around on the frontier like horses and land and guns because debts, and debtors, are some of the few things most everybody has. But the hundreds of dollars to buy-in is too big for Lincoln, and his time keeping store for Offut wasn't pretty. And it's a fool idea anyway. *Become your enemy?*

A few days later he's hiding in the woods again because he has nowhere else to go. He likes the way time slows in the woods and it's almost magic there, what you don't know instead of what you do. He doesn't know much now. But he doesn't believe in magic. He'd run for his life if someone or something stepped through to his forest from another world the way stories said they did in another time. But that isn't what happens. Or is it?

The oaks are motionless around him again the way a breezeless heat stills things, and a few unseen birds paint the high green canopies even more still with those thin calls they make just when you think they've stopped. At the edge of the clearing where he sits in the shade the insect whir is the closest thing to motion in the little meadow before him of waist-high stalks of yellow and white and blue wildflowers.

Too listless to bring his heavy borrowed law book along, Lincoln is sitting on a log circling lazily through his own stumped thoughts when he hears footsteps in the leaves and branch-snap, and his friend William Berry, drunk again in the brown tweed suit he always wears, sways out of the trees and into the clearing. There are still a few secrets in a world this small, but where Lincoln's been hiding apparently isn't one of them.

"Lincoln!" Berry shouts, his speech slurred. "Looking for you! I bought the other half of that store Row's stuck in and he says he'll take your note for his half and you and I can be partners. What say, Lincoln? He says you can have it for a pit... a pit...."

Lincoln thinks *pittance.* Then he thinks *pity* as the whiskey-loving Berry lurches toward him with his bottle. *Where did Berry get money for a share of a store? Or was there money? Somebody took Berry's note and Row will take my note and the next thing you know somebody will lose one of those notes on a cock fight and I'll owe somebody new and you never know who owns anything on the frontier anyhow, and everything's growing and there'll be plenty of future to go around, so what the hell?*

He thinks *pitfall* as Berry, a minister's son, uncaps his green bottle and toasts as he always does, "To the Holy Spirit!" Lincoln feels Berry's cry rise in that silence that a clearing in the woods can have, as if everything's waiting, waiting for the next thing which is not a good thing or a bad thing but a thing of nature.

Is it a thing of nature too that the store in question is only a few steps away from Ann at the Tavern?

Lincoln, normally not a drinker, takes the flask his tipsy friend hands him and slugs one down with Berry for the abandon of it all, then shudders with the burn as the whiskey hits his throat while the over-warm handshake hits his palm and there in the yellowing meadow where autumn is changing the world not by doing much but just by letting things happen they've got a deal.

11

onths later it's January of 1833 and the soon-to-be
24-year-old Abraham Lincoln is backed by shelves
of cake pans and gun powder, coarse cloth and
mouse-traps. An open barrel of axe-handles sits
next to a lidded barrel of pickles. He and Berry started with the
Herndons' stock and they've got more to sell now that they signed a
note for Reuben Radford's goods when his store went out of business.
And they're in a better location thanks to moving from their original
spot to an empty building right across the road from the Tavern, in
the store that three owners ago belonged to none other than John
McNeil. "Spacious" would exaggerate the place, but it's wider and
deeper than Offut's hunting cabin of a store, and someone's brought
in a battered old rocker you can pull up by the fire in the back, and
the two windows toward the front give light to read the newspaper
by.

So it is that Abe is bent leisurely over a week-old copy of the *St. Louis Free Press* spread on the counter in front of him with a good wood-fire going, when Ann, who for a long time has been sending her little sister to do the shopping, surprises him by walking into his store on a snowy January day.

"Ann!" he says and hears his trepidation as well his pleasure at seeing her arrive in that way she has like she's taking over.

"You knew perfectly well I'd come in here if you have your store opposite the Tavern and I have to see you open up every morning and wonder what ever you do alone all day between your skimpy customers." When she pulls off her gray rabbit-skin cap, playful red curls fall down before her ears, but the hair behind is braided and pinned for her tavern work, and here she is stealing time from it. She uses her hat to dust the snow from the long fox-skin coat Abe thinks she looks good in even if he heard McNeil had it made for her before he went away.

"But I have...," he starts.

"The random woman, un-chaperoned, that I see from my window." Ann shakes her head with the shame and unbuttons the top button of her coat and condemns him as she must: "Mr. Lincoln!"

Lincoln blushes though he's not sure why, but Ann fails to get the smile she wants. She's missed his face, even... or does she mean especially?... the way he often seems to be in the hold of some gloom that's a personal challenge to her to come along and break.

"I study," he says sheepishly, folding his newspaper and gesturing with his head toward the big law book on a vinegar cask. "The ladies want molasses."

"Wouldst give them something sweet?" she teases.

"Is that what you want, Ann? You seem...."

"In need of sweetening?" Her mouth looks sour. "Indeed. I think I might go mad for the bitterness sometimes, and you haven't even heard yet what's afoot."

"Tell me, Ann."

"It's too awful. Can't we just stay lighthearted? Forever?"

He smiles because there's no one like her.

"But I do know what I want," she goes on. "I want you to take your rightful part." Here she starts sizing him up as if for costume. His brown jeans pants look perfect for his role.

"What do you mean?"

"I've seen you in my mind's eye with the women who come in. Mrs. Graham, respected by all. But Mrs. Abell too, with her cultural airs, fitted wardrobe, and the world's biggest... *eyes*... which a man like you has no defense for. Not a word! I've known you for years, Abraham Lincoln! You shy away from women but they make you talk and you let them have sugar for two cents cheaper than you wanted to sell it."

"Ann...."

"And Lizzie Burner, sent by her mother to buy flour for biscuits, knowing what you did with her cousin Nancy."

"What...."

"I have my ways. Or old Mrs. Johnson with a new story of the Christ, which judging from your loose behavior you might need. But enough. I know what I want. I want you to take your rightful part." She gets back to work. Costume? The rough brown linen shirt over the red long-john shirt seems just about right.

"What do you mean my rightful part?" he says.

"You're the proprietor, of course, but in truth as well you're a prince unaware of his high birth, and cast by the wreck of his ship as a commoner on these drastic shores." The suspenders have to go. Too old-looking.

"Drastic shores?"

"Hyperbole. An obvious exaggeration to make a point."

"Have you been studying grammar, Ann?"

"No, but I'd love to, that's the most exciting thing anyone's said to me in months, but do not think you can change the topic, Mr. Lincoln."

"I see," he says. "And I have my rightful part. And you?"

74

"Me? If you're the unknowing prince cast up on these drastic shores, I suppose I'm the daughter of the ruined duke."

"Is your father all right?"

"Of course he is. Why did you say that? You saw him at Christmas. He's better, don't you think? Less careworn, more cheerful since he built his dam back. But now he's going to…" She breaks off and bends all the way down to put her forehead on the counter as if her head can't carry all it has to bear.

He's baffled and doesn't know what to say. "Christmas was very good." He remembers it, a few weeks back, so much better than Christmas the year before. Her mother insisted on taking him in. "No lonely strays on Christmas day," she said. McNeil is still back East, and while he and Ann still don't know what to be to each other it was proper and easy eating roast chicken and gingerbread with her family and cleaning up together and singing carols.

"It was, wasn't it?" Ann says, upright again with fire in her eyes. "Father wouldn't have let mother invite you if he didn't feel better. But you, as I was saying, washed-up by a tempest behind a crude store counter, are in truth an unknown prince.…"

"You've read *The Tempest!*" His face is comes alive.

"Of course I've read it. To work now. Our characters are two. He is a young man, tall and.…"

"Ungainly."

"Ungainly? Not gaining?"

"I think it means awkward."

"But you're not awkward. You're one of the most.…"

"I look awkward."

"You have no idea how you look. Especially when the clouds of your sober disposition part and your face lights up like night gone to day."

"Indeed? As m'lady insists, though her flattery be wishful. And she of our story is a young woman, petite and well-rounded, with quick bright eyes."

"That's the spirit! Well-rounded? Like Parthena?" Ann instinctively compares herself to her best friend.

"Parthena is robust."

"And am I lacking?"

"Parthena's made for work. She's robust everywhere. You're robust where it's … good to be robust, and lacking where… a lack is a gain."

"And if Parthena is made for work, what am I made for?"

He blushes. Then finds it. "To inspire me."

"Indeed? Well, to work then, and we'll learn if I can get a rise from you. Curtain up. And…. Good day, storekeep. Prithee, hast a sup of an herb with healing virtue?"

"With ginger I might requite thee, Lady, were something spicy not foreign to your want. How am I doing, Ann?" He folds the *Free Press* and puts it aside to give himself to the drama.

"Indeed, a spicy root might quell me." She smiles at getting away with that.

"Quell you? None can do that." He smiles at getting away with that.

"I like your ginger, storekeep, with ever an edge and yet more timid than your strength might let it be. I can boil ginger to make tea, but I wonder was I… were I… to warm thee what surprise might flow. No matter though at midday what lies under cover."

Ann looks around for cues and sees the thick old volume Abe gestured at before. "I see you would study to make your empty moments full. Is that a dusty law book perched on yonder vinegar cask?"

"*Blackstone*, Madam." He stretches to lift the tome he borrowed from John Stuart and brings it before them with one hand, one of the few men with that much strength in his arm and glad to show it. "Though for its wisdom not black but gold, while for its weight truly stone on stone."

"And does it teach thee to have thy way?"

"To those who can bear it, it teaches the common law."

"The common law that we live and die?"

"Not those laws that are incontestable, but those men struggle over: property, personal wrongs, and criminal things."

"Is not dying criminal? All men protest it wrong, yet no one over-rules it."

"We are part of nature, not its masters. And we will never know the end of that."

"At least not before we die."

He puts the *Blackstone* aside on the *Free Press*. "Ann, why are we talking like this?"

Ann drops the play-acting air she's been bantering in and asks him straight in his earnest eyes: "Like Shakespeare characters?"

"Yes."

"Because we can't talk this way with anyone else?"

He grins. "That's true. Henry McHenry would think I was tetched."

"Parthena would say I need to churn more butter. It's terrible, Abe."

"Churning butter?"

She turns and walks away from him up the counter, giving the worn maple slab silent pounds of resentment with her fist as her steps creak the rough plank floor.

"Father's moving us to Sand Ridge," she says with her back still to him. "He's sold the mill and tavern and we're all going to live on a farm miles away from here on the edge of the eternal northern wastes." She turns to face him coldly from the counter's end as if to show him the distance.

He doesn't say, "I moved my failing store to be in your life and now you're leaving me."

She doesn't say, "What are we going to do, Abe?"

Ann's blue eyes narrow as if she has to tell him something that she should not, and she comes slowly down the counter back to him as she says it and her voice grows louder and louder.

"Listen to what Nannie said at Christmas. You were always at my side... remember?... and we were all singing, remember?... by candle light... and I know how my eyes were glowing... and she was on the other side of me from you and she kept looking up at me and she bumped me so I'd lean down to hear her and she whispered, 'Is Abe your fella?' And Mama heard her and looked at me and she saw my face and I knew she knew...."

"Knew what, Ann?"

"Oh, I don't know knew what!" she exclaims. Her eyes are wide with abandon and the fire he loves is rising in them. "We forgot John! Not six months gone and we forgot him! Nannie forgot him, and she made me realize I forgot him, and that made mother realize she'd forgot him too. Mother put her hand to her mouth like her teeth would drop out and she looked at me and I could see she was scared and she closed her eyes like she didn't dare see. I looked away. I didn't tell you. I couldn't. And two weeks went by and this morning I woke up and I saw it when I looked out the door."

"What?"

"Your store. You started your store where Row had it back there in the grove. But you moved it into the empty building here. Right on Main Street across from the Tavern. This is the store John had before he went partners with Sam. Now Sam's in his new store, and John's gone, and you're in John's old store. *John's store.*"

He nods.

She looks down at the long slab counter between them and freezes as if she's remembering and she says in a voice faint as a dying breath, "Do you sleep here?"

He nods.

She stares at the counter like she wants to kill it.

The door bangs open and Nannie rushes in. How do children do it? As if she'd waited in the storm outside for the worst possible moment inside, twelve-year-old Nannie pushes in through the front door with an urgent snowy wind.

When they force the door shut behind Nannie she announces her message: "Mammy says she needs you back at the house, Annie. She and Pa have to go to Petersburg and she wants you home with

78

me to look after things, and if Mr. Lincoln can take the time, if he can fix the bed that's broken Pa will be obliged. That's what she said."

Lincoln shuts down his store, no loss and maybe a gain considering his most likely customer on a blustery January day is his partner Berry come to tap some whiskey and not pay for it. Across the road at the Tavern, Lincoln looks at the bed and sees the problem. The lattice of ropes that supports the feather mattress on one of the guest beds is broken, and he can't fix it right without a tool, a rope key that tightens the ropes to a tension you can't get with fingers alone.

He remembers something his daddy said about tools. Failure as he was at farming, the man was a decent carpenter, Abe has to admit. "The man's a fool who don't use the right tool," his father used to say.

He had a lot of ways, Lincoln thinks, *to look down on people.*

But he's right, too, he thinks. *And not only do I need a rope key, I'd be a fool not to send Nannie off on an errand.*

Nannie loves the idea. She loves the snow and she loves being trusted to go for something. Ann helps her get her heavy things on again and she's off through the blowy whiteness to Lincoln's friend Row Herndon's house just up the way to borrow his rope key.

Ann feels guilty at sending Nannie, but like Abe she's eager for them to be alone again. When Nannie's gone Ann isn't sure at first what to do with their privacy that now seems so… *naked.* She looks at the unstrung bed Abe's going to work on and sees the beds beside it need made and asks Abe to help her make them while Nannie does her errand. He nods and glances at the double half-hitch knots holding the rope loosely on the bed he's going to fix.

Half-hitched, he thinks. *Sounds like what Ann and John are. But this bed in front of me isn't hitched at all.*

Ann starts making beds and Abe starts helping but isn't much help. Something gets into him, and when Ann flings the first sheet open and across to his side to lay down and tuck in Abe pulls the whole thing from her hands, shouts "Captive!" and folds it quickly and puts it on a chair behind him, then faces her smug with satisfaction. Ann tells him he's bad, but... "Captive!"... he does the same with the second. Ann squints.

She storms around the bed to punish him. "Free my sheets!" she cries and tries to go past him but he shoves her back. Truly angry now, she runs at him and tries to push him aside, but he grabs her to keep her from getting by and she's in his arms and she's struggling but her arms are around him and they're squirming and is she struggling to get loose or go into him? He bends to press her to him not knowing how this happened, not knowing that the front of his body will feel the front of her body again and again as long as he lives....

A shot.

Outside.

She grabs his arm. Their hearts stop. They look at each other. Where's Nannie?

They run to the door.

"It's probably a hunter," Abe says.

They hurry their coats and boots on. Ann is quickest and opens the door to go out and sees Nannie coming running, no coat or hat, shouting, "Blood! Blood!" They follow her racing to Row Herndon's cabin where his children are screaming and Row is bellowing and his wife Laura is lying still in her dark-soaked gray prairie dress and bloody white apron in a pool of blood spreading on the rough board floor.

The crying Nannie sobs out that Mr. Herndon was cleaning his gun and she was talking to the children on the bed and her back was to him and she heard the boom and felt something wet and turned around and there was Mrs. Herndon and blood everywhere.

"Drunk again!" Herndon bellows. "Drunk! I'll shoot myself!" Lincoln gets to Row and takes his musket from his unresisting hands and his friend collapses into himself and down onto the floor and bawls like his motherless children.

"Nannie," Ann says, looking into Abe's face as if they both know something although he feels he knows nothing, "get your coat and hat. We have to go." And Ann takes her little sister away from death, but thinks: *That death will be in me forever. It's a judgment. A sign.*

12

In the next days Abe sees Ann in the distance out his store window when she takes her bucket across the growing white January snow to the town spring, floating soundlessly like a thick coat in white air. Her face is hidden in a dark woolen scarf tied high against the wind. And everything else. He feels the distance she's put herself in and stays away. He stays away for days but then at last has to rush from the store when he sees her laboring heavy-coated toward the Tavern with firewood in her arms. When she sees him coming her stark blue eyes above her scarf go wild with alarm.

"Let me…," he says reaching, but she turns from him, hugs her burden and pushes into high drifts. *The wages of sin are death,* she thinks. Laura's death was a lesson and now it's a thorn she presses to her, like the thorn of John she gave herself and the thorn of Abe she gives herself every time she sees him. She mustn't see him.

I should have died, she thinks. *It should have been me.*

Lincoln stands confounded in the blowing snow as she moves silently away. *I thought you knew what love is.* He remembers his mother's death when he was little and she left him dead himself, moving lifelessly chore-to-chore resenting his father who didn't care and hearing only his sister Sarah trying to reach him month after month until his daddy brought a step-mother home and he buried himself crying in her apron again and again until he came back out alive. So alive that he felt love's doom again when his savior sister Sarah died in childbirth a few years later. He swore he'd never care again. But he did. He does. He did. He remembers Ann's wonder-filled eyes looking down at him stuck on her daddy's dam the day they met. Her grin flashing in quick-witted play when they talked like Shakespeare characters. Her breasts pressing into him when he grabbed her in the war of the sheets. Her voiceless, faceless turning away in the snow.

13

Now Lincoln lives in his store across the road from Ann's world in the Tavern where he doesn't dare go, where she stays inside, or comes and goes by the back door he can't watch. When he sees her through his warped window or passes her in the road she's surrounded by family, or a flock of children, or hides in conversation with her friend Parthena, the two of them looking away when they see him. His heart stops and he breathes deep and it starts again, but will it always? Do they not see him because he's become the nothing his daddy said?

He asks himself this in his dying store a few feet away from her, his store that folks seem even more to shun in the wake of the shooting just up the way, his store where he sees himself in every unwanted sack of sugar, the dusty tin tea kettle, the new ax unused in the dark back corner.

He hears Ann sing sometimes with his store so close to the Tavern, and at first he's glad he can't make out the words to her ballads, the enthralling songs his mother sang before she died young to leave him at seven with proof of life's sorrow. Is this what love is? But one day he can't resist anymore and goes out to his porch as if to shovel snow so he can hear Ann's voice as she works in the kitchen across the road.

> Oh hard is the fortune of all womankind
> They're always controlled, they're always confined
> Confined by their parents until they are wives
> Then slaves to their husbands for the rest of their lives

When the girl in the song tries to get the wagoner's lad to stay longer by offering her family's hay he rebuffs her for the freedom a man can have and a woman can't.

> "Your horses are hungry, go feed them some hay
> Come sit down beside me as long as you may"
> "My horses ain't hungry, they won't eat your hay
> So fare thee well darling I'll be on my way"

Abe can't know that as Ann absent-mindedly sings these words she sees herself running out to the barn with him and jumping on horses and escaping... anywhere!

My horses ain't hungry, Abe thinks. *Ain't,* he thinks and looks back in through his thick glass window and sees his store counter where she stood when she said it back in January. Something like, "...to study grammar would be the biggest thrill I could think of." He goes inside and puts his shovel away and the next day he walks six miles to the village schoolmaster Mentor Graham who doesn't have what he wants but sends him six miles more up the icy road where a man named Vance trades it to Lincoln for two days' labor come Spring. A grammar book.

"Kirkham's Grammar. It's the best," Mentor told him and now he has the worn leather-bound book back at the store and sets it on the counter and as he's taking off his canvas overcoat he hears Ann

85

singing again and goes out on the porch so he doesn't miss the next message in her song.

> *Twas in the merry month of May*
> *The green buds were a' swelling*
> *Sweet William on his deathbed lay*
> *For the love of Barbry Allen*

His breathing stops. *Does she know what she's saying?*

> *And slowly slowly she got up*
> *And slowly she came nigh him*
> *And the only words to him she said*
> *Young man I think you're dying*

Abe can't see Ann as she pours a handful of caraway seeds into her dough to make the bread she fed him on their first day together. Singing absent-mindedly as she does she remembers his solemn face lighting up that first day when the caraway and molasses surprised him down in the dark brown wheat and that's when it she named it *his bread.*

Pushing into the dough and then pulling it back, she can't see him listening as if he's dying in the song while she imagines giving him life with bread, and she sings on.

> *As she was walking oer the fields*
> *She heard the death bell knelling*
> *And every stroke it seemed to say*
> *Hardhearted Barbry Allen*

No! Ann hears herself and stops kneading as if frozen with her hands on the dough. *No!* Abe thinks, hating her being hardhearted, and he rushes into the store and sees *Kirkham's Grammar* and despairs.

What can I do?

"Indecisive?" The word won't apply when he sends ships to resupply Sumter, conscripts armies to suppress the rebellion, seizes rebel property, suspends *habeas corpus*, frees the slaves, and shells forts and ports and cities to drag eleven warring states back into the Union. But now he sags to the floor before the counter where the sight of his new book taunts him with his lack of a way past the wall of Ann's heart, and with the truth he already sees, that he will stack the grammar book he doesn't know how to use beneath the counter with the law book he can't get himself to look at.

He doesn't know what to do.

There's something, he tells himself.

Sure there is, the scornful voice answers. *Henry Clay will save you.*

There's something, he thinks sullenly and gets up and gets his axe and goes back out into the bitter cold to cut firewood to trade for dinner.

Across the road in the Tavern kitchen Ann brushes damp hair from her sweating face. Tears well in her eyes and turn the sight of her dough to a silvery blur. She doesn't see a tear drop into the bread as she bends to push into it again with freckled forearms below her rolled-up sleeves. *It's his bread,* she thinks behind the wet moons in her blue eyes hidden by the falling curtains of her long red hair. *But he won't eat it.*

Weeks later Lincoln padlocks his empty store for good and walks away owing more money than most men earn in ten years. His face is a mask of sadness when he's not cracking funny stories that run to the bitter side. Lizards crawling up preachers' pants to ruin sermons. Married couples mistakenly taking each other's partners in dark rooms. Everyone a fool. He's a fool in a whole new way when his friends get him appointed New Salem postmaster and the hope of the job turns out to be cruel: He's paid by the letter and how many people in town send letters when most can't read or write?

How do we sort what works *for* us and what *against*? When is our whirlpool of loss an ascent to the stars? Listen. If the post office work weren't so scarce, Lincoln wouldn't have five days a week to go fishing with Jack Kelso, New Salem's town drunk and Shakespeare-lover. And if Lincoln didn't fish with Kelso, Kelso wouldn't hold forth to Lincoln about *Othello* as the two sit on the riverbank with their lines in the water and a bottle between them, railing against the Moorish king's wrongful condemnation of his loving wife. This leads Lincoln to bring up Barbry Allen, who in her story is the cruel one. Kelso lifts his brows in surprise when the hard-hearted Barbry seems to drive the temperate younger man to reach for the bottle and tip back a swig.

"Well that ain't nothin'," Kelso says. "If you're ready for the hard stuff. If a woman like to kill you with sorrow is what you want, you can't beat the one by Keats." And the next day he brings his John Keats book with a poem marked.

> O what can ail thee, knight at arms,
> Alone and palely loitering;
> The sedge has withered from the lake,
> And no birds sing.

Lincoln sees his destiny.

> I met a lady in the meads,
> Full beautiful – a faery's child,
> Her hair was long, her foot was light,
> And her eyes were wild.

So moved he dare not read more, he thanks Jack for the loan and puts the book by to read later in his refuge out in the hilly woods where it unfolds his story.

> She found me roots of relish sweet,
> And honey wild, and manna dew;
> And sure in language strange she said –
> I love you true.

He knows the knight's mortal dream.

> I saw pale kings, and princes too,
> Pale warriors, death pale were they all:
> They cried – "La Belle Dame Sans Merci
> Hath thee in thrall!"

Lincoln walks the New Salem world for the next days living in and out of the poem's enchanted nightmare until Henry McHenry comes weaving toward him in bright noon sun with an uncorked bottle.

McHenry sees the book in Lincoln's hand and starts, "Great God almighty, Abe! I'd think you could do something useful. Rutledge moved his bunch to Sand Ridge today. Give me twenty-five cent to help him pack two wagons."

Lincoln knew this was coming but it hits him like a wagon and he can't wisecrack back nor say a word. He reaches out and McHenry hands him the bottle surprised as Jack Kelso was to see the abstainer drink. It's seven miles to Sand Ridge, a two hour walk. She's gone to the Other World, he thinks while McHenry lurches off.

The Other World.

He wanders. Changes direction. If the world wants him low, he'll go there. Down through the village he goes, down the hill behind the Tavern, down where the river first brought him.

> I saw their starved lips in the gloam
> With horrid warning gaped wide,
> And I awoke and found me here
> On the cold hill side.

Is he waking? He sees where he is now, below the village where the summer and fall have nearly dried the river, the tall grasses on its margins brown and failing.

And this is why I sojourn here
Alone and palely loitering,
Though the sedge is withered from the lake,
And no bird sings.

The dam is silent with not a drop of water coursing, here where the swift flow brought him to the dam, the mill, the miller's daughter, the enchantment....

A bird flutters up from the withered rushes and he follows its flight up over the hill where the Tavern roof rises to its peak like a castle tower and he sees it: That's where he must go. Back to the Tavern. Something will change as it did when he went there before. Something will change because that's what happens in fairytales. The third time. *Yes. Something.*

14

It's a gusty October morning and he's walking there. He's made arrangements and has what he needs. Something will happen. He can't know what.

Is the ghost of him drawn to a ghostly place? He hears the Tavern's shutters bang in disrepair now that the Rutledges have moved out of town. He knows that Ann won't answer when he knocks as she did when he came here two years ago. She won't welcome him smiling with auburn-crowned glory and he won't follow her to the bread and butter so they can laugh and declare McNeil gone forever and sway in each other's arms with intimations of immortality.

But something will change and the change lures him here and he knocks three times as he did before, but instead of Ann he gets grim Parson Onstot with the weathered god-worn face he knew he'd see as part of the deal he's made to stay at the Tavern for chores. Gaunt slope-shouldered Henry Onstot himself got to the Tavern in typical frontier musical chairs. Nelson Alley bought the Tavern from

Rutledge when he moved out but Nelson didn't want to run it and wangled Henry into renting it for the bonanza he'd make in room and board.

Onstot works a number of trades as frontier men do. Mainly he's a cooper and a preacher, rendering in the one way unto Caesar and in the other unto God as he says in his humorless way. And now a tavern keeper? Henry, so little attached to conviviality that he won't use his coopering skills to make a cask if he thinks moonshine might get in it? So it is that the Parson gestures Lincoln in as if they're both looking at the last man they'd want to share a house with and wondering how they got in this situation. Onstot would say the Lord works in mysterious ways.

And Lincoln? *Something will happen. But what?*

What, is it Ann? he thinks as he takes his socks, his second shirt and a spare pair of trousers from his satchel and puts them on a shelf in the bunk room. *What?*

He feels her there. Daily. Sees her. *She stood right there and defied me with her hands on her hips in her brown prairie dress,* he thinks, *when we fought the war of the sheets.* He sees her sparking blue eyes when he looks at the fireplace of glowing coals she stood before and told him what Wordsworth wrote.

We lay waste our powers, she said. But he has no powers. *Little we see in nature that is ours.* Except the death-like winter coming on.

Then what does it matter what we do? *What does it matter, Ann?* he asks as he picks twisted kindling from among the damp leaves beneath the trees stripped down to black skeletons behind the Tavern. *What does it matter?*

The Tavern's air of prayerful isolation grows grayer as the weather chills. On a November morning when Lincoln steps out to relieve himself he finds yesterday's rainwater in the road ruts gone silvery and crunchy. Later that day a big wind comes down from Canada and blows the last of the leaves off the oaks that crowd the forest and this is it. Winter.

Lincoln wanders through the chores of the blowing day alone, and at night finds ice etched on the window when he heads to bed in the bunk room. He leaves the lamp lit on a bedside table, and watches its flame stagger in the draft, tiny and thin in a cold dark so vast he has an urge to fill it. *With what? A prayer?*

Prayer! When I don't believe in the God my father tried to whip into me? How the mighty have fallen!

It's the night, he tells himself. The air has a strange charge he feels on his skin. It's the kind of thing there might be no reason for, but there's something insidious and he feels alone with the Parson off asleep, and something… what?… *eerie*… in the air. He jumps at a rattling sound and thinks *God!* but then looks to the offending window and feels the breeze through the leaky casement and sees it flutter his lamp and feels foolish. *Is there a God when you need him?*

The sailor thought so. He wasn't used to praying as Lincoln recalls, but when he ran into a heavy storm one night, he got down on his knees. Lord, he said, you know I never bother you. Well now here I am. And I'll promise you this. If you get me out of this alive, I swear it will be a long time before I bother you again.

Lincoln's joke doesn't free him from foreboding.

Am I that desperate? Fallen? You fall from grace, he thinks, so grace is high. I was born at the bottom. Have I gone lower still? Hell? Not yet. You make your pact with the Devil first and that gets you somewhere. You don't look fallen when The Old Man takes you up to show you… what?… from a hilltop in the stars. Hell, we don't need a hilltop, we can do it here.

Sitting in his long-johns on the edge of his bed he sees it.

He's waltzing with Ann before the *Arc de Triomphe.* Lincoln, who has never danced more than a fiddle-cranked hoe-down in leaky boots once or twice in his life, swirls in black tails to an orchestra with his red-haired angel in a long white gown. They glide among Parisian tables where platters of oysters ring spires of champagne. He'd say you were lying if you told him he'd someday eat and drink like this at inaugural balls because now he's conjuring the impossible:

93

Ann, Ann the illusion, Ann the heart-breaking longing at last in his arms.

People think hard nights start with pain, but sometimes they start with glory. As Lincoln gets under his woolen blankets he can't let it go: him with Ann in his arms. He can't let it go. He can't. It starts hurting and turning into something else.

In dark air above his bed he sees Ann instead in John's arms in the mansion they've made of the Rutledge farm in Sand Ridge, clinging warmly to her husband with their three little children in plaid jumpers at their feet on the deep red carpet. He tells himself to let it go, but he can't let it go. He can't.

He feels sick and looks to his lamp-flame. Thin. Wavering. Barely here. *Is that me? Is that how you measure? Is it worse? Do you measure by who has Ann?*

She's yours, isn't she? Has he summoned the Devil after all?

How can you stand to see her with McNeil? It won't stop.

Can you? Won't stop.

How much will you give to stop the sight?

He can't answer.

Everything?

He can't answer. Is he going mad?

How much will you give?

At twenty-four years old Lincoln is six-foot-four and the strongest man in New Salem. He lifts the big weights and wins at wrestling. If the town had to send someone against a bear with just a knife, he'd be the one. But now he's cowering.

Only you can end it, the dark voice says.

How?

He hears lines from *Barbry Allen.*

> *He turned his face unto the wall*
> *And death was in him dwellin*

Death? he thinks. *What does that matter?* He sees his father's pouting face triumphant. A glowing axe. *There's your bride,* his daddy says. He imagines himself piloting the *Talisman* aground. He sees the two stores he hollowed out with failure, people in carriages laughing at his patched pants that don't meet his farm-made boots, his torn linsey-woolsey shirt, his mole and jug ears and fly-away hair.

What does it matter?

He looks to the lamp, its dim flame struggling like the flame in his chest. *Set it free?* he thinks. *See it run up the walls and tear a hole for my soul to escape through. Yes! Dash the lamp on the floor and let the fire burn to freedom!*

No! he cries and turns to the black air above him as if desperate hope must come from nowhere and repeats the first words that jump to his tongue as if a game is all he has to save him:

"A prince unaware of his high birth cast up on these drastic shores. A prince unaware of his high birth cast up on these drastic shores. A prince unaware of his high birth cast up...."

He sees the corner of Ann's mouth when she said it at the store, not quite a smile but... *a pleasure....* "A prince unaware of his high birth...." Her knowing pleasure when she saw his pride. His innocent pride when she saw what he wants....

"A prince unaware of his high birth cast up on these drastic shores...." He repeats it, repeats it. He can't stop. He can't. He must say it.... "A prince unaware of his high birth cast up... cast up... cast up....

Then he must be asleep because of what happens.

He wakes when the door to the room slams open and a shape flies in shouting, "The wages of sin are death!" He jumps from his bed and the man, if that's what the shadow is, stumbles and scuffles and bangs and Lincoln squares as if to fight and instinctively shouts, "I'll kill you!"

The form lifts a dim lamp and Lincoln sees burning eyes as the shaking black shape shouts: "Repent, sinner! The end of days is at hand!" Lincoln, standing as if for battle but still waking into the chaos, sees Onstot with his fists raised, crying, "And will you war with God in the final time?"

Onstot turns away as if Lincoln doesn't matter, turns and slams at the window opposite Lincoln's bed and throws it open and icy air rushes in.

"Kneel!" Onstot orders and drops to pray at the sill. "Kneel as the universe crumbles at His command, for the rapture is at hand and the prince of light plucks stars to crown the souls for his celestial kingdom!" Lincoln sees it out the window over Onstot's shoulder and his mouth drops wide.

Am I dreaming? Stars are falling from the heavens… five… ten… dozens and more white lights racing down the sky.

"Repent, O sinners," Onstot grits, then shouts to the world as more stars fall: "Behold the fate of the proud!"

The stars keep falling and Lincoln thinks of dropping to his knees but can't. He wants to stand. To stand higher. To rise not fall as stars crash down by the fifties and hundreds, more… stars plummeting, rushing in shining silver lines down the black sky.

But as they fall a flutter rises. Inside him. A lift.

Something's up there. Something beyond the stars still impossibly streaming like shattered glass down the horizon… falling… falling… but beyond them… behind them… stars steady, not falling. He stares and sees that while some stars fall, some stay, and the staying stars waver in place, flickering as if with a lift of knowing pleasure. Are they calling? Calling! Yes! And there he sees a spark-made face, Ann's face, among the stars that won't fall, and he rushes out the back door into the frost-hardened yard to lift his face to her face in the crystalline air with tears of joy on his cheeks until he brushes them and they fall on crusted ground like seeds of hope, like falling stars that go down and down while we go on and on and on, and he stands looking up at Ann's face among the stars and laughing and laughing and laughing.

15

When the sun comes up the next morning the grim Parson clunks a tin cup of coffee on the table before Lincoln as if he blames the free-thinking fool for personally ruining the end of days. Lincoln picks up his coffee and the older man glares at him and growls: "We're sinners in the hands of an angry Lord!" and goes off grumbling.

Lincoln smiles to himself and walks to Sam Hill's store to get the book, *Kirkham's Grammar*. He returned the other book, *Blackstone*, to Stuart in the summer saying sheepishly that he didn't have time to study law, a pretty weak excuse given his skimpy postal hours. But he never did get rid of the sorrowful *Kirkham*, and he's glad now, and in the dim back of the store he goes to the roll-top desk that is his post office and finds the book in its pigeon hole next to the one that holds the old blue sock he keeps his postal receipts in. *My cash and my dreams* he sometimes calls the sock and the book to himself, the cash too slender but tended weekly, the book rich in promise but ignored.

He pulls it out carefully, *Kirkham's English Grammar in Familiar Lectures*, its chapped leathery presence radiant in the new-found expectation of his eyes. He admires its faded tan deer-hide cover, warped a little in the back, its title stamped on its spine in worn gold ink, the whole of it glowing like a grail. Where did he read about the grail? *Ivanhoe?* A radiant chalice of sacred knowledge? Wait. He recalls his luck with *Ivanhoe* magic. *The Talisman.* A talisman is supposed to be an amulet with special powers. It worked in *Ivanhoe,* but in his life *the Talisman* went down in flames at its dock in St. Louis. He takes it back. *Kirkham* isn't a grail. It's a book and a good one. Mentor says so. Lincoln brushes the dust off the thing and slides it into his big coat pocket and takes it back to the Tavern to find out why.

Now, he thinks as he gets his coat off and gets his book out in the Tavern's big front room, *I reckon I better open it.* He hesitates. It feels… so… *momentous.* Onstot's not there, and Lincoln puts the book on the table in front of the dwindling fire and finds things to do instead of sitting to read. He finds some sticks of maple in the wood box to build up the fire. He takes out the ashes. He sweeps the floor and remembers Ann sweeping. He remembers when he felt *wielded* like her broom. He throws the broom in the corner and tells himself not to be a baby. He finds the ladle and a cup and gets a drink of water.

He thinks, *The less you are, the more you have to do.* He sits down on a wooden chair across the dining table from the fire, with *Kirkham's Grammar* on the table in front of him. He pulls back the cover, a flyleaf, the inside title page, four pages of recommendations from school officials, a page of author acknowledgments, a table of contents, a preface including "Hints to Teachers and Private Learners," and finally reaches the "Introduction to Lecture One":

> Grammar is a leading branch of that learning
> which alone is capable of unfolding and maturing
> the mental powers, and of elevating man to his
> proper rank in the scale of intellectual existence;—
> of that learning which lifts the soul from earth,
> and enables it to hold converse with a thousand
> worlds.

A thousand worlds! Astounded, he rises from his seat before the fireplace to re-read the last words with his arms outstretched like the preacher at the Baptist Church when he was a boy: "...lifts the soul from earth... to hold converse with a thousand worlds!" He shakes his head in wonder, sits down and reads on.

The first lecture sounds deep into Language itself. Before our crucial but artificial languages of words, Kirkham concedes, there is a natural language all animals use:

> Natural language consists in the use of those
> natural signs which different animals employ in
> communicating their feelings one to another...
> This language is common both to man and brute.

The language of natural signs, Abe thinks, and sees Ann's face in the sky behind the falling stars. *Signs that different animals employ,* he thinks. Including people when they can't... so he reads it... can't use words. When they can't speak the same language, or other things are in the way. Like when Ann sings or hums? She can't say it right out, but says it in signs. It's approximate, rough. What does she mean and not mean when she sings *"Barbry Allen"*? *Does she know? Is she the Barbry who can't love William who dies of the longing he can't say?* Lincoln tightens at the feel of a casket building around him.

Or does she mean something else? He stands to pace. Can they free themselves to speak? How did she say it in the store? *The chance to study grammar would be my greatest thrill...?* It sounds crazy but she's like him and he'll lure her with it. Grammar. So proper for people of means, but... what?... in their laboring village... impractical?...

foolish…. *Eddication!* He feels a flutter of someone at his back and remembers as he turns how she leaned into him when they struggled over the sheets. No. No one's there. Of course.

But he feels her presence and recalls her eyes shining that golden day then so terribly dimmed by Row's death. As if something in her had died. Or killed, or been guilty… or what? But last night said that didn't matter. She was above him… reigning, presiding, constant, no matter what fell. Was it natural language? He would show her. He raised the book before him. With *Kirkham!* Lifting the spirit to hold converse with a thousand worlds!

But he has to get to her. In Sand Ridge. Remote Sand Ridge. A random set of farms a seven mile walk from the village. Not a place you happen to go to. How can he spend time in her neighborhood? His friend Jimmy Short's tiny cabin is nearby. Judge Bowling Green, the justice of the peace, lives out there, but miles in the wrong direction.

Elizabeth Abell. Mrs. Abell.

Buxom and motherly Elizabeth Abell is a forward-thinking woman, and a forward one too, who seems to think of Lincoln as a kind of project. The education provided by her wealthy Kentucky family makes her, she seems to believe, the perfect person, maybe the only person in this wilderness, to reshape the rough edges of the young woodsman who obviously wants to improve himself. She often reminds Lincoln that she needs a man to do chores while her husband is out of town so much on business. "And," she makes a point of saying, "I can give you the comforts of home."

A few days ago, as she does every year, she invited him to join her family for Christmas, a visit she said with big eyes would be a special gift to her as her husband could not be with them.

He sees why he can't accept her invitation. *I'd be taking advantage of her,* he thinks.

Or might she take advantage of him?

He looks down at *Kirkham:*

The path which leads to grammatical excellence
is not all the way smooth and flowery, but in it
you will find some thorns interspersed, and some
obstacles to be surmounted....

He closes the book and finds Mrs. Abell's invitation card and writes on the back that he will be honored to attend.

16

Bennett Abell is from a privileged Kentucky family like his wife's. He "married her rich," as they say but then gambled and drank away most of both of their fortunes before Elizabeth made him move away from Lexington and build a substantial house in the Illinois woods with what they had left. It's a real frame house like in Lexington, if a small one, not a frontier house of logs. It's got rooms, downstairs and up, with plastered walls, not one big open space downstairs for every waking event and a half-story gable upstairs full of beds for whoever doesn't fit down. If you want to brag ancestors, these folks would beat you, even if the others in Bennett's family might not acknowledge him anymore, but the problem of what predecessor portraits to hang was solved by Elizabeth's decree that every available wall would be faced with books.

Having provided his *belle* with the best estate she sees she can get, Bennett Abell now tugs his broad-brimmed black hat low and pulls on his tight black leather gloves and lights a cigar and drives his two-horse carriage off to do something shadowy for most of each month, leaving his wife alone with two sons and a farm house full of books. Some feel sorry for Elizabeth Abell and say she didn't know what she was getting into, but then who does? Suspecting Mr. Abell of dark commerce, people have ideas why Elizabeth looks sometimes superior and sometimes sheepish. But she gives to the poor. And she displays her most patrician graciousness every time she reminds the reticent Lincoln that he must visit her when he comes to Sand Ridge.

She also invites him for special occasions, as for instance the Christmas invitation he accepts that year with a scheme he hopes will get him casually closer to Ann. So intent is he on his thoughts of Ann that he hardly notices that Elizabeth Abell's note celebrating his acceptance hopes he will be prepared to carve and perform other manly duties in Mr. Abell's absence. More important in his thinking is making sure that word he'll be at the Abell home just up the way gets to Mrs. Rutledge, who kindly had him in for dinner last Christmas, so she'll know that he's taken care of and won't worry. That same word of course goes to Ann, who is not as relieved as her mother is for Lincoln's sake. Not at all.

Not that she wants to see Lincoln. That's not the problem. Or not the only problem. She thinks of Elizabeth Abell seeing things only she, Ann, should see, like the way Abe delights in pressing the back of his fork to pick up the crumbled crust left on a pie plate then smiles as he lets it melt in his mouth.

Christmas comes and goes without much incident. Once when the Rutledge family is standing around the fireplace singing carols after dinner Nannie looks up at Ann as if she wonders where Mr. Lincoln is, or is that only Ann's fantasy? And at the Abell household there's a moment after the boys have gone upstairs to bed when Lincoln is humiliated by Mrs. Abell's giving him a gift when he has no gift for her. It's a book of Byron, *Childe Harold's Pilgrimage*. Excited as if the power of the library on the Abell walls has symbolically come to his hands in the form of this book, Abe is embarrassed too, because here he is again, the lesser one, and he wants to run away but he has to sit beside Elizabeth on her horsehide sofa to share the light of the lamp on the stanzas she insists they read together to get him started.

Lincoln has heard of the book and is eager to read it, but he's surprised at its aggrandizing a young man who was noble, but:

> ... spent his days in riot most uncouth
> ...Sore given to revel and ungodly glee;
> Few earthly things found favour in his sight
> Save concubines and carnal companie....

"You know you needn't go out in the dark and cold when there's a place for you here," Mrs. Abell says when he's about to leave. Apparently absent-minded because she's tired, his hostess starts taking down her long dark hair. When Lincoln explains that Uncle Jimmy's expecting him at his place out the moonlit road, Mrs. Abell excuses him, but makes him promise that he won't be shy in the future about accepting what she has to offer.

He's about to open the door with his hat in his hand when his courage surges and he turns to her and says, "Well, you've been so kind, there is one thing I might ask."

Lincoln's been learning surveying. Sangamon County Surveyor John Calhoun told him that fall that if he could get the surveying skills in hand the growth of civilization thereabouts would bring him all the roads and farm and house lots Calhoun can't keep up with in the New Salem area. Lincoln had never thought of surveying, but why not? *Why not,* he thought, *one more occupation for a man who's talked of lawyering but not done much about it, who knows how to farm but dreads it, knows how to run a store but can't keep one alive past three months, and knows how to be a postmaster but can't make a living at it in a village where no one writes letters. And besides,* he thought, *George Washington was a surveyor and then became so powerful the sight of him could make an Englishman shit!*

So he tells Mrs. Abell, who loves self-improvement, that he's been burning late-night oil bending over Gibson's and Flint's surveying treatises with Mentor Graham, who's a sometime surveyor and mason as well as the village teacher. By days, Lincoln says, he's out scrambling through late winter brush doing things wrong before he navigates a second way across a snowy swamp to do it better the second time. There's something in it that's right for his nature, he says, something about defining something by bounding it north, bounding it south, bounding it east, and bounding it west.

And now Calhoun has some confidence in him, and an assignment for a month or more has come up right here in the hills between Sand Ridge and Petersburg. But it's a two-hour walk with heavy tools from where he's staying in New Salem village....

Yes, Mrs. Abell brightly answers his unasked question, he must move in with her and the boys for a while. Lincoln smiles, pleased to be welcomed closer to Ann. Mrs. Abell smiles, grateful to have Lincoln coming closer to her. As if to seal their agreement she steps boldly to him and goes up on her toes with gentle balance to give the surprised young man a parting kiss on the cheek. *He'll understand,* she thinks, *when we read French novels.*

And so Lincoln moves into Mrs. Abell's comfort in Sand Ridge. And so it is that early every day he travels slowly past Ann's house when he goes out to map the new road and locate parcels abutting it, using his rods and chain and compass to find and set landmarks in snow-hidden marshy meadows and tangled forests where only Indians and drunken trappers have gone before. In the dusk he slogs back past Ann's house on his weary way to the Abells'.

One morning in his second week he sees Ann working outside, hacking with a hoe at a thawing porch-side flower bed. He hasn't thought about what he'd say if this happened, or maybe he decided and what he decided just clears out of his mind when she's suddenly there and all he can do is grasp around in his head in panic.

"Ann!" He marvels that he instinctively calls to her in that familiar way, the way they decided to always talk to each other. Before that

106

changed. He's more muted now: "Ann, I thought about something I wanted to tell you."

"Yes, Mr. Lincoln. What is it?" Pleasant but constrained, she rests her hoe but holds her ground ten feet from him across the little front yard. They are two people who know each other, nothing more.

"I've got a copy of *Kirkham's Grammar,* and I intend to study it."

She wants to throw herself into his arms. She wants to bloody his face with her hoe and run off crying. She blinks and turns away and gives the ground a hack.

Lincoln goes on. "I read something he said about thorns."

"I'm sorry to hear that," she says to the ground and goes back to working it.

"Well, the thing is, thorns are natural." *Natural,* he thinks. *Do they speak a language?*

She remembers the day she pricked and burned her skin picking berries escaping Sam Hill. And here comes Lincoln with more thorns.

"Mr. Lincoln," she stops and look at him coldly, "I don't think...."

"Please just let me tell you what happened."

She closes her eyes and sighs and opens her eyes and looks at him expectantly, and he sees the unspoken message. The sign. *This better be good.*

He leans his ranging rods and a heavy gray satchel of other gear under a roadside tree and steps toward her on the patchy grass at the front of the house without getting too close.

"I get awful scratched up in my surveying work."

"I heard you've been doing that." She doesn't tell him she gets all the news. Nor that she doesn't like everything she hears.

"So one night I came home…"

She knows where he means and looks down at her hoe.

"…and Mrs. Abell said, 'Lordy lord, Mr. Lincoln, your trousers are shreds. If you get me some buckskins I'll sew them on your pants and you can climb with no pain through the thickest brush to where the sweet water flows.' And she did. Look!"

Ann glances as required, but in truth she doesn't want to see his pants with leather patches that she could have made better.

Something is wrong, he knows, but what? And what can he do but plunge on? "Well, that made me think about the thorns Professor Kirkham says are natural when people study grammar and how we can get through them by helping each other."

Ann lifts her hoe and slices hard into sod. "Stop by if you need a cool drink, Mr. Lincoln." She hates herself for turning him away, but she lets go into her bitterness as if it were his and not her wrong that she has to punish, and says without looking up. "We hate to think of you needing help to get through the brush to where the sweet water flows."

He doesn't know what to think. She keeps slicing grass. He doesn't know what to say. He shrugs and gets his things and mutters goodbye with false cheer and goes.

Ann looks down the path whose bend has taken him. *Kirkham's Grammar*. She never thought a book could make her so sad. Jealous. Left out. She tries to picture a tanned deerskin cover but sees a heart the size of a book, deep red and cracked by a jagged lightning line.

That afternoon, out on a twisting parcel of land that won't give up its corner, the sweating Lincoln sits on a log and thinks maybe he should give up. Give up on the torture of the difficult parcel, give up on Ann, give up on being a lawyer and his other puffed up dreams.

When he thinks how contrary she got this morning, he feels contrary too.

Maybe you should celebrate, the voice in him says. *Maybe you won this morning.*

What do you mean?

She was exciting when she got hellish.

He's surprised at that thought, but there's something to it.

And why do you suppose she got hellish? the voice that knows so much says.

He sees it. *She was jealous! Why else would she hate me for being nights with Mrs. Abell?*

108

Yes, and having her help you through the brush to where the sweet water flows!

She offered me her own sweet water to get even!

Lincoln stares as he thinks, mesmerized by a strong green blade of grass coming up three or four inches through the last half inch of snow in front of his log. He doesn't understand Ann. Or himself. He sees one nobody-nothing blade of grass making its skinny green comeback in the cold. He gets up wearily and goes back to the iron rod he seems to have once again placed in the wrong location. A clump of earth comes up with the point of the rod when he pulls it, and down six inches or so in the ground he finds it: the shaved wooden stake his notes tell him mark the corner where his hard-to-get parcel meets the road. The corner he's been looking for.

Sometimes you're doing the right thing and you don't know it, he thinks. *Is it a sign? Natural language? Luck?*

17

It's late when Lincoln gets back from the woods that evening and the boys are asleep upstairs in their half-story bedroom next to the one that Lincoln uses, and Mrs. Abell is waiting anxiously by the lamp with the book in her lap. *Childe Harold.* Reading it alone while he was working she found some lines that alarmed her. She opens one side of her maple drop-leaf table and brings him ox-tail soup and bread from the kitchen and sits down at the table with him to read to him while he eats:

> Strange pangs would flash along Childe Harold's brow,
> As if the memory of some deadly feud
> Or disappointed passion lurked below:
> But this none knew, nor haply cared to know;
> For his was not that open, artless soul
> That feels relief by bidding sorrow flow;
> Nor sought he friend to counsel or condole,
> Whate'er this grief mote be, which he could not control.

Mrs. Abell tells Lincoln wordlessly by the way she looks up between lines that she sees him in the poem, and his eyes looking at her lose focus as if he sees that she's seeing him naked and he closes his eyes to escape. *Does everyone see me this way?* He resists an urge to fall on his knees and crawl to her and fold himself into her ampleness and sob out every sorrow. Instead he nods with grudging recognition.

"It's the wrong book!" she exclaims and closes it. "This is Byron's book of melancholy, and surely not all he has to give us nor we to relish. We must read *Don Juan!*" She puts the first book down and picks up the other.

"Here is a tale to sweep us away in madcap liberties!"

Liberties, Lincoln thinks, with only a vague idea of what that might look like. And his hostess opens *Don Juan.*

The next time Lincoln approaches Ann working on the now softer ground of the flower bed in front of her house, she sends her helper Nannie off and he knows that she wants to talk. Signs, he thinks.

"And does your stay continue with Mrs. Abell, Mr. Lincoln?" Like a lot of others on the frontier, Ann likes to get right to important matters. She's kneeling on a board to keep her knees from the wet black earth while she uses a finger to etch a shallow line then shakes tiny seeds down the indented line from a folded paper.

"I reckon you can say it that way."

"And what other way can you say it?"

"My work in this part of the county still needs me."

"Oh. Then I hope your calling to work is not diverted by too robust a hospitality."

Lincoln smiles inside at how complex and subtle Ann's code is now that he's getting used to it. She's teasing him about having a work-ethic and being hedonistic at the same time. She's alluding to Elizabeth Abell's ample figure and blaming the Abells for being rich. And she's giving him a chance to disavow interest in Mrs. Abell or make the mistake of admitting he enjoys her.

He looks down the road to where it makes a bend and from here you can't see what's around it. He wishes he were around it and on

111

his way instead of having to figure out something to say that won't get him in trouble. He keeps losing with Ann. But she wants to talk. So let there be trouble.

"We read a good bit." *Let her think about that.*

She'd had her suspicions. "Really, and what does one read with such an accomplished lady?"

"We read around."

"Reading around? Is that like beating around… the bush?" It's the old Ann again with spite like lightning in her eyes.

He says it right out to provoke her: "Byron, for one."

"Byron! Has he not been jailed for what he writes?"

He's glad he's scandalized her and now sees a way to make his case noble too. "For the crime of poetry?"

"Is it against the government? Or worse," she adds as if there are only two choices and she's already chosen the second, "against morality?"

Lincoln blushes as if suddenly caught at a *liberty,* and Ann sees his distress and wants to stand up and comfort him. But she wants to hurt him too.

Suddenly feeling the weight of the iron he carries, Lincoln puts aside his rods and throws his bag of chains off his shoulder to clank on the road. Now if only he could run. He clears his throat. "It's just an idle thing here and there," he says.

"Well, I have no doubt that's true. I don't know the man's poems. Father wouldn't have him. If the post would even deliver Byron. But I know his reputation. Bad odors carry so."

"Could the man be flawed but the writing be good?"

"Perhaps. But would only flawed people read it?"

"Maybe so," he says with a grin at his own proud humility. "Maybe that would have to be the case."

Ann shakes her head slowly as if unable to comprehend anyone's accepting their imperfections. She doesn't know what else to do but bid him good-day, which Lincoln finds a relief. He feels satisfied with himself until he takes up his tools and goes around the bend in the road and stops at a patch of Forget-Me-Nots where the dark forest bank slopes down to meet the road. He knows these tiny blue flowers, his step-mother's favorites, and he sits heavily beside them and hides his face in his hands, his hurt heart overthrown by their innocent celebration.

How has life turned him and Ann into battlers when their hearts want to beat together? *Like the two men who fought,* he thinks, and he recalls the story as he walks.

There were two men, drinking and arguing, who went at it so long and hard in their intoxication that at last they went at it with fisticuffs, which because of their condition resulted in each man's fighting his way out of his own overcoat and into the overcoat of the other.

He'll think wistfully of this story when North and South face each other with cannons and bayonets years down the way. Right now he sorrows at the waste of the fighting, which later he will sorrow that he has to bring on. He doesn't hear Ann singing low back around the bend…

Confined by their parents until they are wives

… as she folds and pockets the little paper her seeds were in and picks up her gardening trowel and cleans it off.

Then slaves to their husbands for the rest of their lives

Getting to her feet she realizes that though she tried her best to put Lincoln on the spot, she went through their whole encounter on her knees, and she vows as she walks heavily up the porch steps and opens the screen door that she won't do that again.

Even if on her knees is just where a shamed secret part of her wants to be.

18

Weeks later Ann comes out the door as Lincoln approaches early in the crisp morning when the ground is still dewy and the worst of the heat-loving bugs aren't out yet. She's waited for him and though she carries a trowel for show she isn't coming in truth for the garden but for him. The work she's done on the flower bed at the front of the house is a trifle compared with the big kitchen garden she tends out back, and the decoratives she's planted out front don't need help. *She* needs help.

"Ah, Mr. Lincoln!" she exclaims with sharp-edged gaiety in her eyes. Her line is ready: "You must tell me who says the words." In a show of casualness, she looks down as if to see where some weed might need her trowel while she enjoys her little triumph.

"The words?" Lincoln puts down his things and tries to calculate what she's asking. If you've been walking a few miles with a heavy load, even the cool of the May morning is hot enough for you and he takes off his hat and wipes the band. With her hair pinned up he can see the stern set of her jaw as she bends and stabs the soil. *Maybe there are times,* he thinks, *when lying is best for everyone.*

"The words when you and Elizabeth…," she says with a grudging glance, "I believe that's how we must use names in the case of such an intimate connection… when you and Elizabeth Abell read the words for the things for instance that the sixteen-year-old Don Juan does." Just casual conversation, the bounce in her voice says as she trowels up a few weedy sprouts. "The things he does with the ardent older woman."

Lincoln breathes deep and blushes crimson and is glad Ann spared him looking at him when she hinted at obvious sin. He can tell her he doesn't know what she's taking about, and tell Mrs. Abell tonight that they must be careful not to reveal their reading secrets. His eyes search back and forth as if for a way out as he recalls how uncomfortable he sometimes feels sitting close on the sofa with Mrs. Abell when they take turns reading *Don Juan*. But he admits that it's exciting too. Even though it makes him feel somehow… *unprotected.*

"What makes you think…," he begins.

"Ah, Mr. Lincoln," Ann interrupts, fussing with her weeding. This is all so casual, she wants to imply, but she lifts her chin with a righteous surge as she goes on with a pout in her voice, ironic and not casual at all. "You must never forget that although I am dispossessed at this time of some parts of the fiefdom that was once and is ever my due, I nonetheless have friends in the right places to know what books others buy and carry hidden in deep baskets from the postal office in a town not their own lest the whole world know what license they indulge in."

Ann's elaborate speech again makes him stop and parse out her meaning. *She* should be the lawyer, he thinks. He looks down at her pretense of gardening and shakes his head slowly at the wonder of her. And the frustration. And then it comes clear. Ann's friend Arminda Rogers is the daughter of the Athens postmaster Colonel Rogers, and, as Lincoln knows, Elizabeth Abell has her "sensitive"

115

books sent to that office in the next town over so people in New Salem don't see what she reads. But Arminda knows.

Arminda Rogers is Ann's "educated friend," a former school teacher ten years Ann's senior who has adopted the younger woman as a loved and charming "project."

As formidable a frontier scholar as she is a loyal friend, Arminda could relish nothing better than to help her protégé take down this Mr. Lincoln she hears is lately so proud of what he reads.

So Ann knows what Byron book has gotten to Mrs. Abell, but the presence of the book doesn't necessarily mean that she and he read it together. He can lie. *Attack*, he thinks. *She's inviting you to.*

Not knowing what else to do, Lincoln says with the best he can manage for a smirk, "And do you also know what Don Juan does with the Empress Catherine?"

Ann, who planned this encounter to embarrass Lincoln, finds herself looking up at him and blushing angrily as she falls into his trap. "She, the scandal of Europe who took into her *boudoir* horses and dogs? I had no idea that she's involved in Byron's rhapsody of sin! Arminda told me the merest things. And do you read aloud of the Empress's lechery?"

Go on, he tells himself, *move it back to her.*

"Is it what I read that bothers you so? Or who I might read it with? *If* I were reading it." He's surprised at how legalistic he sounds, but it seems to work as it stops her for a moment.

Ann, forgetting her vow not to kneel this time, sees that she's on her knees at the edge of her flower bed. Heedless of the dampness in the ground, she throws her trowel down and pulls furiously at weeds as if compelled to clean up the world that others soil.

She stops. With a sternness so quiet she could be talking to herself, she says without looking at him, "It is very important whom one does things with."

Invite her to read it with you, something in him says, but that has problems. This is a woman who won't even have a grammar lesson

116

with him. *You don't know until you try*, he thinks. And could he get the book out of Mrs. Abell's house?

You can do pretty much anything if you ain't afraid, he thinks, and he hears his *ain't* and he's ashamed of that and afraid of his fear.

He's afraid to speak. Afraid things will get more out of control.

"What do you mean?" he says softly, honestly hoping Ann will help him find understanding when it's all such a damnable mess.

"Sometimes," she says, picking her trowel back up, "you can't say what you mean."

"No matter," he asks, "who you're talking with?"

She looks up at him. She thinks. *If it makes a difference who you do things with, does it make a difference who you talk with? Can it change things? Some things?*

She looks away. She thinks of all she hasn't said and she aches with its weight. She feels she might fall. She can't. Can't.

"Some things you just can't say," she says, and hates becoming hard when she just wants to be strong.

"There's a story…" he starts, but she won't have it and stops him without looking.

"Please!"

Lincoln's feelings are harder now too, and he blames her like she seems to blame him. *That's what you do*, he thinks, *when you get hard. The Devil probably blamed God for his fall from heaven.*

Maybe I've lost all I can lose, Lincoln thinks, and he feels too hard to care.

"Well then," he says to Ann, "I reckon I'll move on." He picks up his things and mutters a formal farewell and Ann returns it stiffly and bends to her flowers. His eyes go to her white hand spilling fresh black soil around the line of little heaven-blue blossoms whose seeds he saw her planting in April. He's surprised and not surprised that they're the same flowers he found in the forest after the last time they talked. Forget-Me-Not.

It takes all his strength to turn and start walking. When he's around the bend there they are again as he remembered. His Forget-Me-Not's here. Hers there. Like a sign. *But of what?* he thinks. *What?*

He doesn't see Ann on her knees back around the bend, leaning forward over her flowers, oblivious to their names and colors and meanings, with her trowel on the ground and her body shaking and her tears falling into the dark loose earth. He doesn't hear her crying in the confusion behind her eyes, *Come back!* ... words for him and for the past she can't change and for the self she was before everything she can't say.

19

It's summer and Lincoln has moved again as he does so commonly you'd think he's used to it but he never is and he wakes and sees corn coming up out the barn loft window and wonders where he is. And why. Surveyor, post master, rail maker, fledgling politician living here and there, he finds himself thinking of John Malone who woke up unsure too.

Malone they say had a pair of big steers to draw his cart the night he started late for home with a few drinks in him. And a jug in his hand to light his way. When the wheel of his cart hit a root his yoke came apart, and off his two steers wandered into the woods, leaving John slumped asleep in his cart. When he woke the next morning he said: "If my name is John Malone, I've lost a pair of steers; if my name is not John Malone, I've found a cart."

Lincoln peers all directions out his barn loft window to locate himself. The sight of his old store down Main Street across from the

Tavern reminds him he's at Dr. Allen's again. Close to the post office he still maintains along with his new surveying. Between jobs he'll get the Doctor's firewood in, maybe starting today if he overcomes the urge to flee back to sleep in the drowsy morning. His rough linen shirt hangs on a nail too far up the post to reach from bed, so he stretches for his trousers in the pile next to his shucking-stuffed mattress on the rough board floor. A mouse scoots away as he tugs his pants. *It's better than a house loft out here in the barn,* he tells himself. *If you don't mind a little company.* Then his stomach tightens; There's *Kirkham's Grammar* in the pile.

Burn it? He thinks, half joking and half just lost as he has been for so long about what he's doing with that book. He can hear his father: *How many books did John McNeil read?*

Lincoln's not going to burn a book. Yes, he's had the thought in desperate hours, but the planting he swapped for it cost him too dear... or is there another reason? What good is it now that it's flopped with Ann? He doesn't know why he always takes it with him when he moves and does nothing with it but hate it as a sign of hope gone to... what?... something gone.

It's not like he needs better grammar to make his way. His survey in Sand Ridge together with a handful of other roads and lots he did over the winter and spring have now made him the official Deputy County Surveyor. And tomorrow he'll start his big summer assignment, one the County Surveyor wouldn't give to someone he didn't trust, the postal road on the other side of the river, from Colonel Rogers' post office in Athens to Sangamo on the way down to Springfield.

As he washes up in the basin on the hay bale that's his only furniture besides his mattress, he remembers parting with Elizabeth Abell a few nights ago. They were reading with her two boys asleep when she broke off. Don Juan was being stalked in an English castle by an older woman coming to his chamber disguised as a hooded friar and Elizabeth stopped there as if she'd remembered something and stood up. She put *Don Juan* aside and took from her bookshelf something she wanted to read from the newspaper and sat down again on the sofa so close that her thigh touched his and they both pretended they didn't notice. He guessed he could give her that on his last night of staying with her.

"It's a Byron poem. Printed in *The Cincinnati Chronicle and Literary Gazette*," she said as if the newspaper's approval made everything all right, and they looked together at the newspaper in the lamp's shadowy yellow-orange glow.

"So, we'll go no more a-roving," she read, and she kept reading aloud and he read along silently as he looked over her shoulder:

> For the sword outwears its sheath,
> And the soul wears out the breast

He was looking down over her breast so bountiful it obscured the newspaper on her lap as she read down the page and through the last four lines:

> Though the night was made for loving,
> And the day returns too soon,
> Yet we'll go no more a-roving
> By the light of the moon.

Her breast touched his arm as she turned her florid face to him at the poem's end with appeal in her big dark eyes. "It's sad," she said looking up into his eyes, and he knew she didn't mean the poem. He knew too that she didn't mean what *he* was sad about, that sadness she'd found in him when he came to her and for all he knew he would take with him for the rest of his life when he left.

But maybe I'm not just sad anymore, he thought. *Maybe I'm hard now.* And then he thought: *Hard men take women like this.*

And he did.

He didn't know how but he fumbled into Elizabeth Abell at first with her knowing help and then with a vengeance on the world that her robust body took for passion but had nothing to do with her.

121

Now, in his sun-lit barn loft a few days later, Lincoln remembers what he did with Mrs. Abell the way a drunk remembers something he did that he keeps hoping will turn out to be a dream.

It reminds him of the man who offered a stranger in a carriage a drink of brandy. No thanks, the stranger said, I never touch it. A little later the man offered the stranger tobacco and was disappointed at the same response. The man kept to himself with his smoking and drinking then, only looking at the traveling stranger from time to time with disapproval. When the time came for them to part, the man told the stranger he felt sorry for him. It's been my experience, Sir, he said, that a man with damned few vices has damned few virtues.

Was what he did good? Can vice be good? Sometimes? Good for you?

When he's dressed he pulls *Kirkham* from the pile on the floor. He remembers the last time he saw Ann, the last thing he said to her. "I reckon I'll move on."

Am I moving on?

His mind moves on of its own accord, thinking: *The man's a fool who don't use the right tool.* And he knows what he's going to do, though he doesn't know why.

He goes to his village post-office, so called, the roll-top desk with two dozen pigeon-holes for sorting at the back of Sam Hill's store. He doesn't deliver as far as Sand Ridge and wouldn't want to see Ann right now anyhow, so he'll wrap his gift in brown postal paper and leave it for someone from the family to pick up with the rest of their mail the next time they come. He writes a note to go with the book:

Dear Miss Rutledge…

he writes, over the objection of something inside him telling him not to do it.

122

Clearly I must apologize for my presumption upon
your attentions when you have other necessities
and plans. As I wish verry much for you to live-out
the advancements in life of which we have spoken,
I insist that you accept the gift of this guidebook
to the excellence in speech and writing that will
help you winn the standing in life that you aspire
to and deserve.

Handsome language! something sarcastic in him teases, *this man
should be in the legislature.*

There's an election in August, he thinks earnestly. *Why give her the
book? Why give her anything? The strong ones take. I see it. My language
is good but I've got to study.*

Wait, he thinks, *first I think of burning it, now of keeping it to
study?*

That's right, he thinks. *Keep. Take. Win. Win the election. Study
law. Show her.* There's a pause and he adds: *I think you know now how
good that can feel.*

He knows what that means. *That's not who I want to be.*

Even though you're nothing as you are?

Nothing. His father's taunt. Lincoln stiffens and goes back to his
letter and writes honestly, "I hardly know what to say in closing."

But something in him knows. *Tell her you know you don't deserve her because you know how small you are. An illiterate Kentucky
dirt-farming father's drunken spewing of lust in an unchinked log cabin
in the bear-filled woods. And tell her she's taught you to be cruel. Tell her
that thanks to her you've started taking what you want....*

"I wish you happiness in the path you have chosen," Lincoln
writes. He has no idea how bitter that will be to Ann: "...the path
you have chosen"! He stops. "Path" gives him an idea and he stops
writing and starts outside and the voice inside him shouts a final
warning: *Nothing ruins a life like caring too much about others!* So full
of intention that he doesn't care what's true and not true, he steps
outside where the day is heating up and heads for the margin of the

123

cool wet woods across the vacant yard next to the store where he finds what he wants.

As he stands up from his mission on the dewy ground, he sees a grave marker he hadn't noticed in the high grass between the woods and the backs of the village stores. This is not surprising, as the custom of the time in towns too young to have well-established graveyards is to bury folks in sight of their houses. A few tilted gray stone slabs in the back yards of every village mark the rest of those who not long before had no rest in their contest with the wilderness. He doesn't go over to investigate more closely, but for some reason, maybe just because he needs to make a message of it, the gravestone's size and shape reminds him of the marker he stopped and read on his passage here three years ago:

> Life is not forever
> And neither is death

And love? he thinks as he goes inside to finish his package. *What about love?*

He posts his mailing in the pigeon hole marked "Rutledge." Why? He'll later tell national leaders who want a more definite plan than he can make, "My policy is to have no policy." Sometimes you must take a step without being sure why, take a path without knowing where it goes. Has Ann driven him to acting without calculation, he whose temperament tells him to take every possibility and measure and map it and bound it north, bound it south, bound it east and bound it west?

20

A week later Lincoln is deep into his work on the biggest survey of his young career. Athens may just be a small town across the river, but surveying its road is no small-time matter. Surveying the post road from Athens south is a federal contract to map part of the route down toward Springfield, a fast-growing city angling to replace Vandalia as the state capital. Lincoln couldn't have gotten the job without the blessing of the Athens postmaster Colonel Rogers, who's quite the man. Rogers was a militia leader back in New York State and out here on the frontier is the kind of educated and decisive man people look to for leadership. His post office and general store is the hub of Athens, which is beating New Salem in growth thanks in part to its being surrounded by wide sunny farmland instead of dark woods.

The air over that farmland is parched and dusty where Lincoln chains across a sun-struck cornfield just south of Athens on a June afternoon. He pulls his ranging rod out of the ground and walks it up the way to plant at the end of his laid-out chain, every one of its long links 7.92 inches, its hundred links exactly 66 feet. The tall iron rod is an old English one with worn bands of red and white paint that Mentor Graham sold him, and he wields it playfully like a staff.

And I, he thinks, *am Abraham. The shepherd and father of my race.* He imagines the float of a long biblical robe. *Abraham of the two wives. Or was it three?*

When I have not one.

He stops at the limit of his chain, but instead of driving the pointed rod into the loose soil to mark distance and direction, he rests stands it on the ground at arm's length and tilts his head back to focus upward at its rounded end. *Two meters tall,* he thinks. *Six feet and going on seven inches.*

Which gives me something to look up to.

Surveying. He likes the art of it, the craft. Giving the world shape and definition. Measuring.

He's been at this new survey for a week, starting from Athens and working by now a couple of miles down toward Sangamo Town and Springfield, and he doesn't see a lot of passersby in a day, so he's surprised to suddenly see a young boy running down his corn row with a neat little light blue envelope.

"From Colonel Rogers!" the little boy shouts as he was no doubt instructed, "Special Delivery!" And off he runs as Lincoln opens his mail.

It's an invitation, and Lincoln feels fortunate to have an invitation from Colonel Rogers, whom he doesn't know well but who's been good to him at a distance appropriate for a busy man of affairs. The Colonel wears a dress coat over his ivory-handled pistol, and is always rushing off to look after one of his stores or one of his farms or one of the deals the governor needs to go the way only Rogers can make it go.

But there's a challenge too in the Colonel's summons to a cool 4 o'clock lemonade in the Rogers' parlor. Since his wife's death the Colonel's daughter Arminda, Ann's friend, presides over his domestic establishment in the finest frame house in Athens, and Lincoln is embarrassed at the thought of seeing Arminda, who will surely perform the hostess role, and whom he knows has conspired with Ann about his scandalous reading.

There was a time when Lincoln might have found an excuse to avoid seeing Arminda, but he can't do that now. He's running for the State House again in August, as a member of the Colonel's party, the Whigs, and he needs the Colonel's support. He'll do what he must even if he can hear that voice he doesn't like inside him gloating that he's finally seen the light and is pitching himself into scheming as he should. Lincoln firms his resolve up through the day and as he sees 4 o'clock approaching from the drop of the sun he arms himself by thinking he can endure Arminda's distaste for an hour if that's what it takes to win the Colonel's blessing.

Lincoln looks woeful in his familiar way as he approaches with his clinking tools up the steps of the Rogers' white frame house at Athen's wide main intersection. He's never met Arminda, not traveling in her lace table-cloth social circle that Ann was lucky to be adopted into. Her father Colonel Rogers is not only a political figure of note and the Postmaster of Athens, Illinois, just across the Sangamon River from New Salem. He owns the Athens general store. And he always has horses and farms to sell. Learned and traveled and well-enough connected to get a far bigger postmaster job than Lincoln, the Colonel has a lot more books than Ann's father. And a daughter who's been to college.

"So you're the famous Mr. Lincoln!" There's only bluff honesty and no trace of irony when Arminda greets him at the open door with the gracious smile that's a ready resource for a woman of her standing. She resembles her father the Colonel, he notes, sturdy and rounded and self-assured.

A substantial and feminine woman of her time, Arminda, as they say, "dresses" every day, never chops wood, attended for more than a year the Jacksonville Female Academy, taught school in a more obedient classroom than she knew any man to run, is comfortable with

ballroom dancing and whist, and has been known to take French –
but only French – brandy. The lady of her house since a fever like the
one that took Lincoln's mother, took her mother more than a dozen
years ago, Arminda has nothing fluttery or fretful about her. She has
nerves of wool, she likes to say, though as Abe sees she favors silk for
wearing, but then what could be more appropriate for the daughter
of Colonel Rogers?

And what could be more ladylike than Arminda's warm welcome of her rough-clad guest into the front hall, wall-papered with
blue and white *fleur de lis,* as if in such a gracious world there are
no bygones to let be bygone. The whiskered Colonel comes nimbly
downstairs pulling his coat on over the bobbing white handle of his
flintlock pistol, greets Lincoln in a hearty way, and apologizes for
having to hurry off. Duty calls. The baffled Lincoln hears the family's two-horse carriage brought up out front. The stump-tough but
smooth-mannered Colonel pulls on his deerskin driving gloves and
says he knows Lincoln is whipping the post road survey just like
they'll whip the Democrats come August. Rogers submits to Arminda's farewell kiss on his cheek and after raising his brow in mock sub-
mission to necessity and giving Lincoln's hand a parting shake he's
out the door and soon gone with the sound of well-trained trotters.

Arminda acts quickly to get things in hand, starting with the
uncertain Lincoln himself, whose hand she takes with a liberty he
doesn't expect, but clearly she's possessed by a particular excitement.
Lincoln sees how pleasant she looks in her silvery brocade with the
commonness of her face enlivened by her winning mood.

"How fortunate we are," she confides as she draws him into the
sitting room, "that you come when an old friend of yours is in town!"
Lincoln misses what Arminda says as he marvels at where he is. No
frontier log building with a sleeping loft and shed-like additions, this
is a full two-story frame house, roomier and more tasteful than the
Abells'. He's heard enough of such places to imagine that across the
hall from this walled-off room is a more formal parlor so important that no one ever goes in it, and behind the two front rooms a

dining room and a walled-off kitchen down the hall at the back of the house. The spacious front corner room Arminda's brought him to has its plastered white walls hung with portraits and landscapes between three bright windows. One interior wall has a brick fireplace, before which sits a mahogany library table, Arminda's darling, which her "helper girl" polishes so its deep notes sing. Four dark spindle-back side chairs from Virginia surround the great table. A heavy carpet-like rug brightens the floor in the middle of the room with blues and silvers. A sofa covered in a thick blue and white floral pattern like the one on the hallway walls sits under the front windows, flanked by two matching armchairs that complete the other side of the room.

Gesturing to get the distracted Lincoln's attention, Arminda stops him before the library table where he sees on the deep red wood the leather-bound book lying waiting to be opened.

"Yes," she says with her grin overflowing, "Professor Kirkham!"

Lincoln is relieved at Arminda's playful behavior but puzzled about what she's up to and why she has the grammar book he sent Ann. He wouldn't be surprised if she told him her father left on her instructions, but she doesn't do that. Instead she pivots back to the doorway and with a dance-like sweep of her hand for presentation, exclaims, "And yet another old friend!"

Ann walks in with her eyes downcast in determination. She holds the wide skirt of her floor-length black cotton Sunday dress at both sides, makes a proper dip of greeting, then looks up at Lincoln with just enough of a nervous smile to say the next move is his. Her rich auburn hair is swept back in a restrained formal bun, but tiny fires light her eyes.

His slack-jawed amazement wins her over. She grins as if she has no choice, and makes an offer: "Shall we study?"

The three sit at the table, and Lincoln feels he has to say something so he says the only thing he can think of even though he's afraid it's wrong: "So…. We can… help each other?"

Arminda looks at Ann. "Ah yes," Ann replies. "With the thorns." She picks up the Kirkham. "Thanks to the road-builders, and…" with a glance at Lincoln, "the surveyors who make the road-builders possible, there were no thorns between my house and here. But I must admit that for the longest time the very thought of the thorns was daunting." She pauses, then says as if to herself: "All of them."

"But then," she says, "I recalled what you said, Mr. Lincoln, about our helping each other. And there's no doubt that's true, although there might be danger in what bedfellows we choose to take help from."

Did I say bedfellows? She lets her word choice, ill-advised or not, sink in, then goes on. "When I had the good fortune to receive this book in the mail… thank you so much, Mr. Lincoln… I found there was a sign in it for me…," and here she pauses just an instant to give Abe a look into her flashing eyes before going on, "maybe many signs. But I took the book up wondering: Does the Professor who tells us of the thorns tell us also of a solution? Of what we might do with the help we can get?"

She lifts the book to read at a place she's marked.

"Here's what you might remember he said:

> The path which leads to grammatical excellence, is not all the way smooth and flowery, but in it you will find some thorns interspersed, and some obstacles to be surmounted….

"Two paragraphs later, he writes:

> You are aware, my young friend, that you live in an age of light and knowledge;—an age in which science and the arts are marching onward with gigantic strides."

130

Ann closes the book and appears to rest her case, but Arminda, ever the teacher, wants to hear more, and her inquisitive expression asks Ann to explain what she makes of all of this.

"What better to take one over thorns and obstacles," Ann nearly shouts her discovery, "than gigantic strides!"

Lincoln, the practical-minded boy from the woods, is so used to thinking in physical terms that he sees the strides of his own long legs, the most gigantic strides, it might be, in Sangamon County. But what good are they?

"Bravo!" Arminda salutes Ann's discovery, vague as it is so far, but Lincoln, lost in himself, wonders if there's even a small step he can take toward Ann without her blocking his way?

"There's more," Ann says with a satisfied smile. "I've not only thought of gigantic strides. I've made one."

As if suddenly waking, Lincoln realizes he hasn't seen Ann this full of life since the icy January day that Laura Herndon died. Her vitality is magnetic, and he remembers times he's touched her, held her.

"Tell us, Ann," he says quietly. "Please."

"It's thanks to the newspaper," she begins, and turns to a little stack of papers on the table. *"The Cincinnati Chronicle...,"* she says as she unfolds the paper with a look that seems to Lincoln almost impish, "has chosen to aid the spread of literature in the crude fledgling culture of our western states by printing poetry. Including poems by Lord Byron. One of which," she says with a so-there glance at Lincoln before finishing with a tone of proud finality, "I have read."

"You?" Arminda says and frees Lincoln from having to... or being afraid to... say it. "You, the antagonist of all Byron stands for?"

"I steeled myself," Ann explains, "against the immorality I feared on the chance of finding some wisdom worth the cost. Will you listen to what I found?"

Lincoln feels panic rising. What if she reads the poem that Elizabeth used to seduce him? Is that what Elizabeth did? He begins to say that maybe they can all read it privately later, but Ann ignores him and begins the poem and Lincoln looks at Arminda, whose eyes say that she too must recede and let Ann have her way. And Ann does:

> When we two parted
> In silence and tears,
> Half broken-hearted
> To sever for years,
> Pale grew thy cheek and cold,
> Colder thy kiss;
> Truly that hour foretold
> Sorrow to this...

Good God, Lincoln thinks.

Ann reads the poem in obvious cadence, landing hard on the rhymes at the end of each line, but with a sincerity the other two find themselves leaning to so they don't miss a word.

> Thy vows are all broken,
> And light is thy fame:
> I hear thy name spoken,
> And share in its shame.
> In secret we met—
> I silence I grieve,
> That thy heart could forget,
> Thy spirit deceive.
> If I should meet thee
> After long years,
> How should I greet thee?
> With silence and tears.

When Ann's done, her silence makes her listeners uncomfortable in a way that hearing the poem did not. Lincoln rages inside: Is she speaking to me? To John? Or imagining one of us speaking to her? The poem doesn't fit anyone exactly but has parts about all. They parted and she grew cold. He and she. She and John. He doesn't know. But *light is thy fame?* Disgraced, or just little known? Does she know what Lincoln's done? Or is it John whom no one knows? Who deceived the world about who he is? Or does Ann feel disgraced? She who's so moral she thought Byron a sin?

He sees no answers in her face. Not even a coy look that says she's withholding one thing more. On the contrary her eyes flash boldly as if with the urge to give something away. Her whole face, her body, wavers torch-like, and her eyes shine wet, and what she must say rushes out.

"Don't you see? This is how we live! All of us! Disappointing one-another. Losing what we love and living with what gives us sorrow. Clutching to us our secrets and regrets."

Yes, yes, they nod.

"But that must not be!" She stands and waves the book. "Thorns! Thorns! My gigantic stride was not just to read a poem by Lord Byron. My stride was a leap… where? I don't know! I'm in the air. Will I land safely? I don't know! But I will not live with my thorn-torn soul slowly bleeding out in sorrow the grace we came here with and must carry… or will it carry us?… beyond!"

Ann sits and both of her hands go to her open mouth too late to stop the passion she can't believe she let out.

Arminda stiffens, sighs. Ever the teacher, and proud of that, she realizes that her protégé knows something that she herself has never learned. But then again, she thinks: *Who has learned things like this but those who have to?*

Lincoln smiles consolingly, admiringly, at Ann who's still too shocked by her outburst to accept his consolation. She's sitting beside him and he wants to put his arms around her but doesn't dare. He feels she's said something wise although he's slow to know what it is. What freedom she wants. Or is it not her wisdom but her passion he admires? To want anything that deeply and to say so!

Does this mean she'll tell him now? Tell him her secrets and regrets? He imagines seizing her forearms in a strong grip and looking in her eyes and demanding: *Tell me! Tell me you'll marry me and get rid of John. Or tell me I'm a fool and I don't have a chance! Tell me!*

133

Can she see his secret as he looks at her across the table? Can she see his broken heart?

The two women are looking at him.

"Then," he manages, "... then.... are we right to live our strong feelings openly instead of... *reserving* them?"

"Enough!" Arminda intercedes with a bright tone to offset the harshness of taking control the way her father's daughter would, and does. Who knows what might happen if they don't have decorum?

"We are right," she admonishes, pushing back her chair and standing and starting for the kitchen, "to live out openly our thirst for lemonade. And *Kirkham!*" she calls as she reaches the door, "But don't you dare open the book until I get back!"

Knowing Arminda won't be gone long, Ann says quietly to Abe: "I have something to show you," then reaches in her pocket for a neatly-folded embroidered pink handkerchief and opens it before him to reveal the treasure of a dried sky-blue Forget-Me-Not.

"This," she says, "I found marking Professor Kirkham's explanation of 'natural language.'"

"Communication without words," he nods.

"Signs," she says while Lincoln touches the little blue flower with his eyes and summons the courage to look at her face. But the sign he hopes to find there is eclipsed when Ann suddenly turns as he does to Arminda's bustling entrance with lemonade and cookies and a new idea.

"I heard you say 'signs,' Mr. Lincoln," she says as she puts her tray down, "and I think in doing so you show us the way. But for an old habit of speech here and there, you two are both so good with language already that a systematic march from rule one to rule one hundred will not be our most productive path. Perhaps we need a higher authority to find a higher way."

"Whatever riddle are you speaking?" Ann likes the playfulness she feels is coming.

"I propose," Arminda announces, "to have the chance opening of the book to any page determine that we study the principle which that chance opening discovers. The ancient Romans found guidance that way in Virgil, the Christians used it to tell fortunes from the Bible, and we can use it ask Professor Kirkham what we need to learn."

Lincoln, still looking at the Forget-Me-Not, asks in that droll way of his, "Would the theory then be that what one finds in a book is not altogether by chance?" He doesn't look at Ann but imagines her looking at his flower and smiling.

"Who will open the book?" Arminda calls.

"Mr. Lincoln I believe should have that honor," Ann says to reward him for their private joke, and Lincoln, who likes honors as much as he likes gingerbread and doesn't get enough of either, accepts the book as she slides it along the table. He's sorry she doesn't hand it to him so their fingers can meet.

Cheat, he thinks. *Ann's new at this and I'll do better with her if she does better at it. Go to the front of the book where it's easy.*

But he won't. He closes his eyes and grasps and spreads the book's leather covers front and back so he can't feel the number of pages, and with his eyes still closed pushes a finger between the open pages and to an unseen spot on a page and opens his eyes and reads:

EXERCISES IN FALSE SYNTAX.
NOTE 1, TO RULE 12.

A noun in the possessive case, should always be distinguished by the apostrophe, or mark of elision; as, The nation's glory.

"Wait," Ann says. "Sin tax?"

Uh oh, Lincoln thinks.

"A cost we pay," Ann asks, "for doing wrong?"

Abe and Arminda laugh, then wonder if they should have when they see Ann blushing.

Arminda smiles gently, "No, dear, *syntax* is Greek."

Abe can't stop himself: "And the Greeks don't pay for doing wrong."

135

Arminda can't resist: "If they do it, it's right."

Ann understands now that she's being had and joins in: "Is that why Lord Byron goes there?" And they all laugh a hearty laugh at the lovelorn lord and move on to the definition of the term as the set of rules for how words make proper sentences. Then they take up the possessive case.

Lincoln reads an example of false syntax for correction:

That girls book is cleaner than those boys books.

And the explanation:

Not correct, because the nouns girls and boys
are both in the possessive case, and, therefore,
require the apostrophe, by which they should be
distinguished; thus, "girl's, boys'" according to the
preceding NOTE.

"But," Ann complains, "we can't *hear* the apostrophe, so we don't know something's wrong unless we see it there or not!"

"Exactly!" Arminda pounces. "The standard for spoken language is not so exacting. You and Mr. Lincoln speak well. But in writing, we must be more proper, or our "sins" are on paper for all to see. It's not important for chopping rails or washing clothes, but if Mr. Lincoln is to be a legislator and you to continue your fancy of becoming a teacher, you must write more properly than you speak."

"Properly?" Ann says as if holding the term at arm's length and looking it over. "And why must we be proper?"

Arminda is taken aback. Propriety is an assumption that civilized people don't question. "Well..," she says, searching her brain where not a whole lot comes to help, "I suppose so people will think well of us." She might be further surprised if she could know how much Lincoln believes without question in this idea, while Ann's face betrays that she finds it offensive, and her hand unconsciously goes to her hair which she feels so primly swept back she wishes she could shake it loose in a torrent.

"So I must burden myself," she says, "to show others what they expect to see?" Lincoln changes the subject by pushing the book across the table to Ann so she can scan the examples, and Arminda leans her head in over the book with Ann and takes the three of them through the uses of apostrophes to form singular and plural possessives.

Ann of course becomes quick at this as at anything she must do. But she stays captured too by her inner quarrel with propriety. When they've done with possessives, she spies and points to a last example:

"Aha!" she cries.

Thy ancestors virtue is not thine.

"This might puzzle a reader," Arminda explains, "about whether one or more ancestors are in question."

"Yes, but for its weightier matter," Ann counters, "does it suggest that virtue might change over generations?" Again Arminda is struck at the way her pupil is inquiring. But is she enjoying her uncertainty more than she should?

"The worse for you, my dear young lady," Arminda frumps with a partly-humorous reproof as she rises with the feeling that they've done enough for one day, and Lincoln starts gathering his things to go. At Arminda's teacherly suggestion he copies some rules about person, number and gender from *Kirkham* so he can write practice sentences as Ann will also.

They agree to meet to study *Kirkham* again while Abe is conveniently working here in the Athens area where Arminda's sitting room is theirs and Ann has a place to stay the night when she comes from Sand Ridge. The blessing of their togetherness fades as Abe bows his farewell and Ann curtsies and reminds herself grudgingly: *It isn't proper for a lady to give herself away.*

Was that resentment I saw in her farewell? Abe wonders as he walks from Arminda's house. *Should I have done more to win her? Did she want me to take her in my arms? Or was that the last thing she'd want?* The sun goes down as he walks home to New Salem. Once he'd held her… the way a man holds a woman… the day they acted like Shakespeare characters, then played a war game with the sheets and he took her captive, surrounding her with his embrace and feeling her warmth against him, *in* him. But then Row Herndon shot his wife, and Ann's affection for him died and he never knew why.

But now?

As he walks into New Salem village in the twilight, he imagines Ann in his embrace again. So soft against him. But strong. She looks up at him. There's no resentment in her face but radiant light as she shakes her flowing hair and laughs and says, as if it were he and not she who went away: "*There* you are!"

21

As Ann gets ready for bed in the Rogers' guest room that evening, she repeats silently in her mind: *A possessive noun should always be distinguished by the apostrophe.*

To be proper, she explains to herself. *About who owns what.* The song that obsesses her, *The Wagoner's Lad*, starts singing in her head:

> Hard is the fortune of all womankind
> She's always controlled, always confined
> Controlled by her parents until she's a wife
> The slave of her husband for the rest of her life

My ancestor's virtue is not mine, she asserts as if to argue with the song. They had to live in olden times she can live her way now. *I must now, mustn't I?* she thinks as she climbs into bed.

My ancestor's virtue is not mine. She puts out the candle on her bedside table. Arminda's plump featherbed is cozy, but in the dark

Ann isn't as sure of herself as she was in the light. *Do I even have virtue?* She feels wounded by the idea of propriety, its imposing rule. What others think. Would think. Worst, the women. She imagines their disapproval, the women of the village, their shapes tall, blockish or tiny hidden in long dark prairie dresses as they line both sides of her path with a gauntlet she must survive, their faces concealed in hood-like bonnets so you can't see who's who, which doesn't matter, does it, because propriety is the same for all, and anyone who doubts it can see the bitter fire of the absolute in their relentless eyes. She must run through their blows and curses. Run! She runs, now stung and now stunned by their blows and sometimes slowed but determined to keep going, to escape to the forest where proper ladies don't go and she must go alone, afraid that she'll be alone in the dark and she is but she runs and runs in that forest which is not proper for a woman but is her refuge, until at last she sleeps, sleeps the restless sleep of the guilty, the hunted, the warrior who knows she must fight again the next day just to be who she is.

The next day she's captivated again with grammar, proprieties and all. But is she fascinated with grammar or beset by it? Back at Sand Ridge after a bumpy wagon ride, she sees now that it takes an apostrophe as well as molasses to make the *beans'* sweetness right. It's the *carrots'* and *tomatoes'* weeds she pulls, and the *socks'* holes she darns by the *fire's* glowing light.

In the hours between chores she studies a *sentence's* parts: *The subject acts,* she learns. *The subject's object is acted upon.*

The object is acted upon. One night she's saying that to herself between the house and barn on her way out to the cow when a sudden wind throws itself at her and nearly shoves her down. *As if I'm an object!* she thinks, and goes back on her way making little of it… the grammar, the wind.

When she's done throwing hay down and making sure the cow has water and can get to her salt lick, she goes out behind the barn and gazes skyward over the meadow. No sooner does she see the clouds speeding full of silver moonlight than another burly wind, stronger in the open behind the big-timbered barn, throws her sideways so she has to grab the barn door. It heaves at her again after she backs against the barn, its surge clattering the leaves in the trees and groaning through the eaves of the barn and drumming at her ears.

Natural language? she thinks. She doesn't feel the wind wants to hurt her. But to put her on notice. As if with... *a claim.* But what? She runs for the house lest its roughness catch her in the open again and she goes to bed partly glad to escape the wind, and partly hoping it will come to her dream, *tell her.....*

The next night the wind comes again. And the next. *Is it always like this? Why wasn't it back at the Tavern?* But wait. She remembers the daffodils moving gently in a breeze there as if to tell her... something. But the bold rush of air in the nights at Sand Ridge isn't gentle, and is far from silent but more like a shout and some nights she yells back at it, yells into its noise so loud that no one can hear her blaring truths she doesn't dare tell... her wrongs, the web she's caught in, pinned....

It's all there! she thinks one night when the wind's grand clamor out behind the barn calms down to a silence she can think in. *It's there in the grammar!*

"A transitive verb," she says aloud as if to the waiting wind, "*takes* an object."

She pauses and the wind is silent and she goes on. "A man *takes* a wife."

The wind rises as if it might answer but she defies it. "Is that it?" she shouts.

It pushes at her but she resists. "Is that it?" It worries at her skirt and sleeves as if to answer, and blows her long hair wild but she doesn't care.

"Tell me! Is that the rule? Is that what's *proper?* What *must be?*"

22

With a plan to meet again for grammar, Lincoln's back at surveying the Athens post road in the big heavy summer sun. His days are marked by careful measures, but his sightings of Ann are not so scientific. When he wakes on his corn-shuck mattress her face hovers in the sky out his barn loft window as if she's watched him in his sleep. He sees her when he's tramping with his chain and finds a raspberry bush and stops to feast and she's picking on the other side with red ringlets framing her blue eyes and freckled nose, smirking to tease him: *Where have you been?*

He remembers how hard it can be for her to keep still. Back when he saw her more. She *goes.* In the middle of something, she gets up and turns around to see what she must do. It's almost a dance the way she spins a half-turn, stops, then moves forward across the room to get the candle mold on the mantel, or changes her mind and turns back because making candles can keep and whoever she's talking with really must come first. Even if they *could* be more interesting. She *goes* when she gets nervous. Something needs her attention and if it's not before her then it must be behind her and it will not escape. She didn't rush back and forth in their grammar meeting, but he knows the force she can use for a giant stride. But Byron! Her condemnation of secrets!

He stops smiling. He's seeing her again. They're talking. Grammar. She's not fleeing him now. His old unworthiness takes hold of him. *Am I fooling her? Fooling the world?* Conditioned to think there's something wrong when he does well, the unworthy part of him makes a list while he gathers his tools at the end of a surveying day.

I've got the County Surveyor and the Athens Postmaster thinking I know what I'm doing with a compass and chain when I'm making up geometry as I stumble through the woods scribbling down numbers when the mosquitoes let me. I go out to give speeches for the election next month and when I get up on stumps the wild boys roar. They like my mix of high-toned Henry Clay talk about building a nation and low-down raccoon jokes so they know I'm like them. I had my way with Elizabeth Abell. And now I've got the red-haired princess reading Byron.

This too shall pass, he reminds himself.

He doesn't like it. Is he taking advantage of people? Deceiving them? Is he riding high and about to fall? *This too shall pass....*

But what about John McNeil? he asks himself. *What's Ann hearing from John?*

If he's going to fret here's something more than imagined trouble. Ann is engaged to McNeil and Lincoln doesn't know if she's heard from him in the two years he's been gone. He's got to find a way to ask her. They'll meet again soon with Arminda. And Professor Kirkham. ...*to hold converse with a thousand worlds.*

First person singular, he thinks and looks around at the darkening woods where there's nobody else for miles. *Just me. Alone. Ann and John are singular when you say them separately, but more when you say them together.* He sees them holding each other and hates it. *They. We.*

143

But I'm he, I. Alone. While he winds up his chain to go home he hears in the forest stillness, a lone bird call. *Me. Me. Me.* He shoulders his weight and turns to go. *Me. Me. Alone. Alone.*

The next Saturday Lincoln gets a swaying and jamming wagon ride to Springfield with a neighbor. He's got a speech to make that afternoon, some of it set and some he'll improvise. He's a common man, they'll know that from his suit and the way he talks. Or his lack of a suit. He doesn't own a formal jacket. Like most country people hereabouts, he's got what he's got. As for what he doesn't have, there's so much of that, and of what he owes, that he's glad he's not in debtor's prison.

The sight of the campaign audience crowding the boardwalk next to the Courthouse, mostly in overalls with a few suits here and there, pulls him out of himself. An ease comes on him when he gets with a group about politics. Talking with Ann used to be easy too, but he can't think of that now. Gatherings on village greens and clumps on sidewalks like the ones he's walking through now want the jokes and stories he chooses to make his proposals look good and his opponents look bad. He remembers people's names and shouts hellos. He makes his way with many a slap on the back up onto the Courthouse steps and he starts and the gift of it rolls.

"Some of you know my face," he says, "though I don't envy you having to see it. I got into a carriage one day and the man in the seat opposite me pulled out a revolver and leveled it at my face.

"What's wrong, neighbor, I said. He said he'd made a vow that if he ever saw a man uglier than himself, he'd shoot him. Well, I said, then you'd better shoot me. If I'm uglier than you, I don't want to live."

He interrupts the men roaring and waving straw hats. "But we're not here to talk about my poor lank face, neighbors, but the face of the earth and how the government, *your* government, can put a smile on that face and on your face through a program of railroads and canals to bring the goods we need in and send the goods we make out and turn every hard working village on this prairie into a Chicago, a

New York, a glowing city with houses and roads and schools for all, and all at no cost to you through the proceeds of the sale of public lands as we spread civilization westward...."

As he goes on he thinks, as the best speakers can, in a second part of his brain about what the first part is saying. He's never known why he's good at this. It just happens, mostly, and yes he prepares with history and examples and the words of political friends to support him and the words of rivals to laugh at. But even after his years of speaking to come, he'll never know how starting with one year of *eddication,* as his illiterate daddy scornfully called it, and a youthful taste for imitating preachers, he grew able to hold listeners as he will years from now when his speeches in marble halls win him the presidency, unite and lead the northern states, and define democracy forever. He'll never know how things just come to him like today when he finds himself telling his crowd that one of his blowhard opponents is like a storm of lightning and thunder that makes people pray for more light and less noise.

"Pray?" someone shouts up. "You talk about praying when you're not a believer? They say you're not a Christian, Lincoln! The Bible tells us there's a heaven and hell, and you need to tell us where you think you're goin'!"

It takes him only the time for a knowing nod, then a smile. "I'm a humble man," Lincoln says, "so I don't presume to ask for heaven. I'll be grateful if the people of this district will send me to the legislature!" In the laughing hullabaloo he wishes, as he does again and again on the stump, that Ann could be there to see him master the crowd. But he reminds himself again that he can't think about her now, nor trouble himself either with McNeil who tries to push his way into his thoughts and makes him feel very far from mastery.

A man with a confident voice steps up to interrupt him on the Courthouse portico. "Stop being so damned compelling, Lincoln, and let an ordinary man get up here!" It's John Stuart, his Springfield lawyer friend since the militia, coming up out of the crush. John's his fellow candidate on the Whig ticket now and after he takes his turn speaking, he leads Lincoln back to his office for a little talk.

Having been to Stuart's before, Lincoln's used to the feel of the lawyer's office but it still holds enchantment for him. Maybe it's the books. Everywhere you look. A glass-fronted bookcase of legal volumes on every wall. And a stack of books on the roll-top desk at the side and another on the table in the center of the room where they tower over ink pots and metal-nibbed pens in a jar and the older quill pens and the knife to sharpen them. It's a heady place for a man who loves books and has never gotten enough of them. Ann would like it, he thinks, the room of books. Though she'd probably be glad not to have to read these particular ones, which aren't for reading anyhow, but *using*.

The tools of the trade. He imagines having books for tools instead of rods and chains and axes, venerable books like the thick leather-bound volumes in front of him with gold titles stamped on red or black panels on their spines: English case reports, digests of law, volume after volume of statutes and treaties. There's a bookcase of U.S. Supreme Court cases, and one of state court cases from Illinois and bordering states.

"If I can be a lawyer, you can too," Stuart says as they sit at the table, and Lincoln tries to believe his friend despite the mountain of study all the books imply. Lincoln, who long ago realized he doesn't like the effect of whisky enough to put up with its burning taste, fends off the brandy Stuart pushes across the table. He's intoxicated enough just being here, nearly dizzy at the combined allure of the books and the fear they put in him when he reckons himself by their power. The power to make him the man he wants to be. That he told Ann he'd be. That he needs grammar for. *The grammar that brings us together. The little we get together.*

Stuart sips his brandy and claims his friend's attention again.

"Well then, that does it," Stuart cajoles, "If you won't take my whiskey you've got to take my *Blackstone*. Again. It's the place to start." Exactly what Stuart said when he loaned him *Blackstone* be-

146

fore. Stuart, slighter of arm than the woodsman Lincoln, needs two hands to slide the grand authority at him, but slide it he does and Lincoln sits with the book before him again: *Blackstone's Commentaries on the Laws of England, Volume 1.*

Is this the start to taking those mountains of legal volumes down? As Lincoln opens the big leather-bound volume to muse on its grainy time-spotted title page, Stuart looks at the woodsman's hands. His long dark fingers with weathered knuckles taper to uneven nails. Purple veins and scars mark the backs of his hands, and heavy calluses protect his palms like you'd expect on a man who works hard-scrabble farms.

Lincoln doesn't miss what Stuart's doing. *Evidence,* Lincoln thinks. *Always looking for evidence.*

Lincoln's compared himself to Stuart plenty and he thinks he'd trade. He'd trade the length and strength of his arms that toss heavier men at wrestling to have learned Latin like Stuart did or had even a year of college like this professor's son.

But Stuart's a deal-making kind of lawyer, the kind Lincoln would like to be, and he sees all the sides he can. Stuart says, "Lincoln, you've got hands like a river man... how do they say it, *half man and half alligator*... but you use words like a preacher. Or... if I dare say... a politician...."

Lincoln raises a big hand to stop his friend. "Could I go too far, Stuart?"

"In what way?"

"Well, sometimes when the speaking is flowing and the people look up and nod and laugh and yell, "Give em hell, Abe!" then I keep going, I go further, I crank it up and..., sometimes I wonder if I'm like the river boat whose whistle was too big."

"Meaning?"

"There was a boat, they say, on the Illinois River, and the man who built her had a feeling for whistles, he loved the river boat whistle sound, and he made her the biggest and best whistle anybody ever heard. The boat was handsome and proud and people loved to hear her coming, which you could do for miles. But the damned vessel couldn't really deliver anything. It turns out that the builder put so much of the boat's space into her whistle, she didn't have any room for cargo."

Stuart laughs. "Take the book," he says. "Study it. The law teaches limits. It'll help you learn your place. You and law were born for each other."

Lincoln thinks: *You and the law were born for each other. Exactly the kind of thing Ann would say.* And he stands and lifts the *Blackstone* to him and it weighs, really weighs, even for a man as strong as he is, but he's got to lift it while Stuart stands there with all his assurance and Ann, he imagines, sits by her fireplace in Sand Ridge thinking he can do about anything he wants. *If she thinks of me. She must!*

And so the surveyor goes out squeezing his determined grip on the law book with its thick old dark leather cover and green and gold marbled page-trim. The book is his, Stuart tells him as he sees him out the door, as long as he needs it.

With the *Blackstone* under his arm outside on the rough plank sidewalk, Lincoln recalls the day he and Ann joked about *Blackstone* and Ann bantered them into Shakespeare characters and Row Herndon shot his wife and Ann stopped talking. But times have changed, and Ann's back in his life, and the law book's back too. No matter how much work it threatens to be. He said he's going to do this. He won't let her see him shorn.

Given the weight *Blackstone* adds to his long walk home, Lincoln is relieved when Ike Cogdal, come to Springfield for the speechifying, pulls his wagon to a stop in the muddy road and offers his favorite young politician a ride back home to New Salem. Having seen Abe with books before, Cogdal isn't surprised when Lincoln no sooner sits next to him on the wagon seat than he opens the big old tome and reads in a mutter under his breath while Ike drives the jouncing twelve miles back to New Salem.

But it would be a mistake to think that Lincoln considers only the law of real property on that bumpy ride home through forest and meadows dimming in prairie twilight. In fact his mind keeps going to Ann who's become another kind of law. The law that he wakes up each day to a world with her in it. Even if he can't always see her when he wants. She's there. As surely as the sky is.

23

Lincoln and Ann and Arminda meet again at the big mahogany library table in the Rogers' parlor. Although Arminda usually has her Irish girl in the kitchen, she lets Gracie go for the day when she has Ann and Mr. Lincoln call, both for the sense of privacy and for the chance to show off her own touch with cakes and meringues. So it's her pound cake and lemonade they have on the table when it's Ann's turn to open *Kirkham* to a random page.

Ann pauses with the closed book before her.

"I found an example," she says.

"An example," Arminda repeats.

"An instance of the improper language we discussed that slips by in speech but we can see in print. It leaped at me from the newspaper. Here in the *Sangamo Journal*. May I?"

The two lift their brows in puzzled assent.

"It's a quotation from a speech by a legislative candidate."

Now Lincoln doesn't like it.

"His name," Ann says with a smarty-pants smile, "is Abraham Lincoln."

What can he do but hope she'll be kind?

"Really," Ann says with an earnest look at him. "Do you mind, Abraham?"

"My record," he replies with a look of very political good will, "is available for all to see and discuss."

"Here it is then," Ann says, and introduces Lincoln's defense of his running for office despite what some critic implied is a shabby appearance. She says, "The newspaper quotes the candidate defending his form of dress as a form of freedom, beginning by saying: 'Had I have known that the nature of a man's clothing was a qualification for office....'" She tries to keep from looking at Abe's shirt, which is neat but has a torn chest pocket she's wanted to sew for a year but hasn't wanted to try his pride about.

Lincoln looks away, already embarrassed at thinking about his appearance and apparently about to be convicted of bad grammar to boot. He shifts his unwieldy legs in his worn trousers under the table but that's no help. *Sin after sin to pay the tax for,* he thinks. But his foot unwittingly touches Ann's and the bump somehow brings her out of herself and she wonders what she's doing. Is she punishing him for being free when she isn't? Free to wear what he can and get away with it when she's chained by propriety, or cowardice, or... what?... need? By caring too much for the opinions of others?

Arminda saves the day. "Yes, *had I have known* needlessly adds *have* after *had* when *had* would do the job on its own: *had I known.* But I find it most fascinating that this Mr. Lincoln," she says looking up from the table to exchange a knowing smile with the others, "is being called down for his appearance when his chief campaign proposal has to do with something he calls 'internal'... not external... 'improvements.'"

Now they're on his ground. "I'm sorry," he says, intuiting Arminda's thought, "but in this case internal improvement doesn't mean the opposite of surface appearance. It means improvement in transportation. If government invests in canals and roads and bridges, the industry of the people can take produce to market and bring in goods to buy. Illinois corn will feed Pennsylvania manufacturers, and the print shops of Philadelphia will send us books and New York the wing chairs to read them in."

New York, he thinks. *New York is where McNeil is. Why would I want to make transportation better for him to get here and marry Ann? Has she heard from him? Is he gone?*

"It means," he says, suppressing his bitterness and sticking to his principles, "creating and maintaining road and rail and water routes internal to the nation, the countryside." He leans back in his chair and stretches his legs out under the table and crosses his ankles and rests his case, pleased to have a clear position on this kind of local issue when local issues, and not the national dramas his idol Henry Clay gets to contend about, rule his political world.

Ann senses Abe's relief, and his refuge in his astuteness relieves her guilt for putting him on the spot, and she sits up in her seat and joins him on the train to internal improvement. "And," she cries, "the mills of Massachusetts will send linen and brocade to dress us ladies… *we* ladies… like ladies instead of kitchen maids!"

But no sooner has Ann spoken than she feels she betrayed herself. Better dresses are not what she lives for. Her idea of an internal improvement comes not from trains but what? *What? Giant strides.*

"I've got a spot in *Kirkham*," she announces, and opens the book to a place she has marked, cheating thereby although neither of the others knows or cares because both are delighted to move on. One of the words in a passage leaped out at her while she leafed through the book. It was the word *passions*, but she doesn't reveal that, just reads:

FIGURES OF SPEECH.

Figures of Speech may be described as that language which is prompted either by the imagination, or by the passions.... The following are the most important figures:

1. A METAPHOR is founded on the resemblance which one object bears to another; or, it is a comparison in an abridged form.... Thus our blessed Lord is called a vine, a lamb, a lion, etc., and men, according to their different disposition are styled wolves, sheep, dogs, serpents... etc.....

"I remember," she looks up from the book to remind him, "that we talked about natural language, the way signs convey meanings that people can't say in words? But here is another way to express what common language cannot. Is this what happens in *Barbry Allen?* Are the lovers shown in metaphors?" She sings a verse near the end, intoning slowly to make the words clear:

> *Barbry Allen was buried in the old churchyard*
> *Sweet William was buried beside her*
> *Out of sweet William's heart there grew a rose*
> *Out of Barbry Allen's a briar*

"Is *he* the rose at the end," Ann asks, "and *she* the thorn, and are they at last together in that way?"

Arminda turns her head to hide her blush. She doesn't know the details of Ann's emotional life which both ladies have thought it inappropriate to discuss, but she feels her young friend venturing to danger. Has her fancy for giant strides prepared her to speak of her affections, or is she unaware how near she might be to some confession? Arminda neither wants to be a party to such a confession nor a restraint upon it, so she stands before Abe can answer and excuses herself to go out back to fetch ice from the spring-box. She diplo-

153

matically lets her friends know that the ice has been difficult lately and will certainly take her a half an hour or more.

Abe too puzzles at Ann's daring in quoting "Barbry Allen." And it's a strange happy ending she chooses to tell: *Yes, the rose grows round the briar*, he thinks. *When Barbry and William are dead!*

"Is there something in the book," he says to Ann as Arminda goes, "about *fully happy* figures of speech?"

"Oh yes," Ann teases, pretending to study a page and find something. "Here it is: 'political speakers say for instance that if they are elected a great harvest will come…' when they don't mean a harvest at all."

"I know that one," Lincoln conspires. "And the seven lean cows will vanish and seven fat ones will appear!"

Ann shakes her head slowly in wonder. "No one talks like you."

"Or you," he says.

"I'm sorry I embarrassed you."

"I don't care about that."

"What *do* you care about, Abraham Lincoln?"

Here's his chance to ask if she's heard from John. Or should he turn the question back on her and ask what she cares about, or who? Or is it *whom?* Whichever it is, he can't say it. But there's something he *can* say.

"I care about you, Ann."

Tears fill Ann's eyes and she reddens, but she won't look away from his gaze.

"Can your care help me make giant strides?"

Frightened, he jokes: "Nay, t'would be needless when m'lady is already beyond me."

"But storm clouds beset me…," her brimming eyes are fixed on his worried ones, "…midway between heaven and … far far worse!"

He leans to her intently. "Then I'll lift you!"

"Yes!" she exclaims and pushes her chair back to rise before him and he rises to meet her and she smiles what he sees as a dangerous smile but her arms are open and he's done with fear. They embrace with an intimacy they've only known in distant longings or the touches of play and never as now unashamedly drawing each other to them to feel and know each other's bodies. Her warmth is euphoric, but he pulls himself from it to slide his hands down her back and grip her waist and lift her above him where he sees her astonished pupils wide like two round theaters with their blazing blue curtains of day pulled back to reveal in black circles of night… is that him? He swings her up to kneel on the table and takes her hands.

"Look where you've come," he appraises her elevation, "with your giant stride!"

"You can't leave me up here alone!"

"This is how I first saw you. Above me, as you'll always be."

"Where I don't deserve to be," Ann says and leans down so their faces are level and he sees himself now in the flames behind her tears and he feels a warning but he can't be warned. They embrace and she presses to him.

Abe feels a tremor of change and leans back to see Ann's face. Shining waters are high in her eyes again and her quivering lips whisper, "The world has brought me to my knees." She hides her face on his shoulder and he knows that she wanted to joke but it didn't work and now she feels captive to what she said. He knows what he has to do. He helps her down from the table and into her chair and her face falls onto her hands and her tears flow.

"Tell John," Lincoln says with quiet certainty, "that he must release you from your promise."

Ann speaks coldly. "There is no John."

"But…."

"John is a ghost," she says to the table with an edge of anger. "I'm engaged to a ghost. Is this a figure of speech?"

"Please, Ann. Write and tell him that you want him to be happy but in his long absence you've learned that you can't make him so. That you're sorry but you know now that you must marry me."

Ann lifts her head to look at him astonished. "Is that a proposal?"

155

He doesn't believe what he's said. He wants to explain but can't. He breaks free and abandons himself. "Yes! Will you marry me?"

Ann stands with both hands to her mouth, turns from him and erupts in a storm of tears as she rushes from the room and leaves Abe alone with the doom-like ticking of the big dark clock on the marble mantel.

What did I do?

The room has no answer. He sees the melancholy setting sun in the Hudson River scene on the wall. He sees the centerpiece on the table. A delicate little white basket the size of a tea pot, it's the kind of decorative touch women set store by and men don't see. But he knows it. It's Ann's little basket and she must have carried it the miles from her front garden in Sand Ridge, filled with... look at them, snug in the little wicker nest her hands wove and painted white... dozens and dozens of tiny blue flowers the shapes of stars. *Forget-Me-Not.*

24

That night back at Sand Ridge Ann feeds the cow late then goes out behind the barn. The moonlit branches of the border oaks bounding the meadow stir as if the wind has something to say. She's ready. Let the squall shake the branches and come down from the trees with its rage.

But as the breeze comes her way from the high far leaves and stirs closer it gets softer, and softer, and poetry, sweet but painful, rises in her.

> Thy vows are all broken,
> And light is thy fame:
> I hear thy name spoken,
> And share in its shame.

Can the wind share my shame? Can anyone? Can anyone break the hold of the past that owns me?

"Carry me to him!" she shouts to the wind, reaching out to be taken the way she opened her arms to Abe that afternoon. But the wind won't lift her. Nor does it bring more words, no poem or song to tell her why she opened to him then closed and ran. But little by little tonight she feels, and then little by little accepts, the gentleness of the wordless wind in natural language quivering the sleeves and skirt of her dress, and combing her hair with soothing touches the way her mother used to, and reaching in through the buttons of her dress and caressing with invisible fingers the wound she feels is never ever going to heal.

25

When Abe wakes the next day he forces off thoughts of Ann for thoughts of politics. It's Sunday and after church in election season folks get together at a nearby farm for a drink of cider and some campaign talk. But as he walks to where he'll speak at Island Grove, Ann refuses to stay away. Lincoln feels testy about having to succeed with the world today when he was such a failure yesterday with her. His insidious inner voice is at him.

Your speech didn't win that little election, did it?

She'll get free of McNeil!

I don't know about that, the dissenting voice says confidently, *but she's keeping free of you, isn't she?*

It's true and he resents it but shoves it out of mind. He slows to a more composed pace on the forest road. Heavy heart or not, he'll meet a crowd in minutes, and he's got to do better today with a laughing crowd than he did yesterday with a crying woman.

And damned if there's not a beef shoot before the speeches. And he hurried to get here! The shoot always brings out a crowd, Edmund Taylor tells him as he accepts the annoyed Lincoln's I.O.U. for the dollar each candidate owes for the prize.

Lincoln looks across the crowd and sees the browsing steer – a fat ox – tied up nearby. He feels tied up too now, but there's no way out, and soon his friend Row is there with a musket for him and he's priming and charging and loading and ramming and trying to find a way to look relaxed. Between greetings and guffaws with the men he surveys the competition and sees off on his left a pair of bearded trappers all dressed in buckskin against the thorny thickets of their lives and slouching against the rail fence with their un-cocked long guns at their sides. Over past the milling straw-hatted farmers on his right another group with rough linen shirts and canvas vests slumps on Row's porch with shoulder-slung powder horns and pouches of shot, hunters who make their living shooting game. *There's your marksmen to hit the nail on the board at fifty yards!*

The thought stops him.

What a way to drive a nail! *The man's a fool that don't use the right tool.* There might be a way to build something with a gun, but for hitting a nail he'll take a hammer. And for getting elected?

He takes Row's gun back to him and says it's ready to shoot and would Row mind standing in for him while he looks into something that's come up. Only after he's stepped away from his puzzled old friend does Lincoln remember the time he took Row's gun away to keep him from shooting himself.

The day he lost his Laura and I lost Ann. But Row's made a fresh start. He's got a new farm, a new mother for his kids. And I trust him with a gun.

But I tried a fresh start with Ann she ran away.

He puts the thought of her away again. *Can't think of her. Can't not.* Nervously explaining himself to himself, he wanders past the house toward the privacy of the woods as if to answer the call of nature but in truth to avoid the shooting and think about what to say.

About the time the beef shoot's over and somebody's leading away the complaining prize steer, Ann's mother leaves Ann off in Row Herndon's crowded dooryard and takes her wagon to a quilting bee down the road, unable to say no to her Annie but shaking her head as she drives off because she knows what happens at these bottle-passing events. She trusts Ann to navigate, but she worries. And all the more because she feels her daughter is mid-air these days with no idea of how to come down.

Ann makes sure Lincoln won't see her in the crush of people milling between Row's house and barn. She's covered with a shawl mostly hiding her face and she leans on a fence in the back row of homespun frontier folks come to hear the candidates. Somewhere in the early going when the less-favored Democrats are holding forth from the hay wagon, a group of rough boys unleash a fresh jug of firewater and the hooting and shouting start up good.

Ann willfully stands her ground to make a private space for herself in the jostling and yelling of country folk and the plunging here and there of Row's chaotic chickens, feeling both weak as a woman out of place and strong because she's daring this male world with only a few other women in the audience, and they of the pipe-smoking sort, who don't look like they're fleeing from propriety like she is but might never have seen it.

Unruly farmers jolted on corn whiskey go after Lincoln when he makes that slow way of his up the rough board ladder onto the hay wagon to start his speech: "Words and more words don't run the world!" one voice yells. "We need to know what you can do. We got to know you can make a hand before you get our vote!"

Lincoln looks over their heads to the wheat field beyond. "Boys, if there's a scythe in the barnyard let it be my partner and you fall in line and keep up with the dance!" As if transformed from his usual "slows" he jumps down from the hay wagon and takes off his jacket and trades it to Row for his cradle scythe and strides through the three or four dozen wide-eyed and laughing watchers and into an acre of wheat and makes the round of the field laying a neat swathe

161

low and then turns to the few sweating stragglers mowing behind him and asks if they'd like to have another go.

"No! No!" they shout. "Give us the jug and take the votes!"

Back up on the wagon with everyone but the Democrats smiling, the sweating Lincoln rolls his sleeves back down and buttons them for propriety and says, "I'm humble Abraham Lincoln and a lot of you know who I am. I don't pretend to be anything I'm not. My daddy raised me to farm work…" Here he doesn't say as he'd say in private, "but he didn't raise me to like it," but just keeps going the way these things just come. "I have no wealthy and powerful friends to recommend me, just good people like you. Ask old Mother Johnston over at Concord if I chased her down two miles to return the penny I overcharged her on molasses for making gingerbread. And you know how important gingerbread is! Ask Bill Greene who helped elect me Captain of militia when we went to chase Blackhawk even if all we ever fought was mosquitoes, ask him if I stand by my men and my word is true. Ask Postmaster Rogers across the river in Athens why he chose me to survey the post road from there to Sangamo Town. Or ask my old friend Row Herndon here who piloted and trimmed back the branches and boulders with me to bring the steamer *Talisman* up the Sangamon River and prove that good farmers like you can have a way to ship produce to market and bring back the iron tools and the calico for dresses to give you and your families a better life.

"Yes…" he goes on, knowing he's come to the tricky part. If he can sell this next part he's going to the State House, and if he can't he's going to keep on being humble Abraham Lincoln. "Yes, some say the *Talisman* shows the opposite. It never came back because the stream is too low. Some people say No. Well, friends, you have the choice. You can vote for someone who sees the obstacles to a better future and says No. Or somebody who sees the ways past the barriers and says Yes."

He remembers talking Yes and No with Ann and McNeil the night of the *Talisman*. *Did I get the idea from that bastard?* He wishes Ann could see him waving the plunder now.

Ann can hardly keep herself from joining the voices yelling, "Yes! Give us Yes!" but her heart stops a moment when she sees improbably across the farmyard, as if the distance magnifies it, the way his right eye looks clear and hard at the world directly before him while his left eye lifts high to see beyond.

"I say Yes, my friends," Lincoln's on with his parade, "and here's how. We learn from our experience. We don't go down in the ruins of what doesn't work and perish, we stand and get a feed of Mama's pork and beans... and maybe some of Grandma's gingerbread... (*Hooray!* someone yells), and we say – just like you do when that fence post keeps falling over and you dig it down deeper or change its location – and we say: 'How do I do better next time?'

"A canal, my friends. A canal! Every shallow spot of the Sangamon River, and every unforgiving twist of its winding course... remember that fence post, deeper and in a new location?...can be replaced with the deeper and straighter channel of a canal put here as an Internal Improvement by the federal government with the proceeds of its growing sales of federal lands and at no cost to you and me!

"A canal from Springfield to Beardstown! And the farmers of Springfield will send corn and wheat down the Sangamon Canal to Beardstown on the Illinois to join the Mississippi and the high-paying city market of St. Louis! And the wheelwright of Athens and the cooper of New Salem will welcome shipments of metals up that canal from Alton so their arts can roll hundreds of wagons across our red saw-grass prairies! And the hard-working, right-thinking, smart-voting people of Huron and Petersburg and right here in Island Grove will ship corn and hogs and casks of molasses ("For gingerbread!" someone shouts) right back down through that canal and down the Illinois River to the wide Mississippi and on down to New Orleans itself where what we grow here, we humble people in our humble towns, will win us the praise and grateful financial returns from the

163

wider world of the American nation that a canal in a program of Internal Improvements will bring!"

A voice calls above the hooting, "Abe for President!" Does he hear it? Years later he'll tell a Washington visitor, "Yes, I dared to dream this dream of the White House and what has my dream become but ashes and blood?" We crave without cost and later we pay, but the future can't scare Lincoln today so he laughs on his way to his first elected office as he ends a happy vision in a racket of yelling and beating on buckets and butter churns. Abe climbs down to be mobbed by the farmers and trappers that he and the white lightning have inspired, and off at the edge of the crowd Ann makes her way back to the road past shoeless boys in the dirt with marbles, and rough-looking woodsmen gambling on dice in what they can find for shade. She meets her mother in the wagon where the farmyard meets the two-wheel track of the road.

When her mother starts the horse and looks over at Ann sitting silent on the seat beside her she sees that her daughter isn't there. Her keen blue eyes her mother has seen focus sharply on the chores before her are gone. Distant. Oblivious to her surroundings on the bouncing wagon ride home, Ann sees Abe, sees him anew now and sees the others seeing him. She's learned now that it's not just her. It's him. The way his pensive face comes to life when he talks about who he is and what he believes in, and the sorrow frozen in his everyday gaze melts away and his eyes unlock and dance and his face unlocks and opens... there's no other word for it... opens as if the heavens are parting and something from another world is coming through to this one... not just the vision he's talking about, but the joy of the vision as if music and tumblers in bright-colored tights spilled it rolling down the street in the world's biggest parade... and the goodness and the promise of it, and of him, shines on everybody lucky to be there in the golden light.

26

L incoln's last weeks of speech-making and bone-banging wagon rides to shake hands and remember names in tiny settlements of three or four houses blend with sweaty hours pulling chains across dusty fields to keep his surveying going and pay the bills. In nights of survey exhaustion he fears he'll lose the 1834 election like he lost the one in 1832 and have to survey the rest of the brambled universe in the sun for the rest of his life.

Or it's waking that's painful and not going to sleep. Many know the drowsy waking that destroys our rest by recalling our sins and secret shames that others can't know who don't have branded inside them the weaknesses that make us who we know we are. Lincoln drowses on an August morning in a reverie: Austin Gollaher saving him from drowning when he couldn't save himself, things he and his cousin John Hanks did with sheep, the wife-swapping doggerel he wrote in his anger when his sister married Aaron Grigsby, the night he went in the woods with Nancy Burner, his damned-fool falling into Elizabeth Abell, city girls laughing at his high-water pants in New Orleans, his father beating him for using big words....

Banging. Someone's banging on his door, the door to his barn loft at Doctor Allen's. Whoever it is must be standing on the ladder and pounding up at his plank trap door as he yells : "Wake up, Lincoln! Wake up! You won the damned election!"

Lincoln yelps in celebration and the owner of the voice clomps off... it sounded like Ann's cousin John Camron who clerks the elections... then forces himself up realizing there must be a mistake. Those boys at Camron's where they had the voting yesterday don't most of them read, much less count that good, and he'd been there most of yesterday and the liquor was flowing. Both parties poured whiskey where men in coarse pants and muddy boots milled in the yard, and then spilled out more for those waiting on the steps to the porch. As if that wasn't enough, more tin cups went around up on the porch itself where voters raised their hands to take the oath that by that time they might or might not understand.

Lincoln pulls his trousers on and looks for his belt. Is he still dreaming? He takes his first pair of trousers off, and puts his other trousers on, his good ones in case it's true. He hurries to Camron's and sure enough that was Camron himself who'd brought him the news and it's true! He's going to the legislature! Camron's hung-over but he can see well enough through his sore red eyes to know he's never seen Lincoln's sad face so like the sun in blue sky.

Word came back at dawn from the other precincts, Camron tells him as he pours himself a drink... for medicinal needs. "You were the second vote-getter 'mongst the four who won, just fourteen behind Dawson out of nearly fourteen hundred votes! You beat John Stuart by two hundred votes!"

On the short walk from Camron's back to the middle of town Lincoln feels his face grinning and sees his arms swinging, far the from the way he remembers coming into town on this same road three years before. Suddenly self-conscious, he tightens his walk and

166

puts on a serious face in fear of giving offense. But another grin awaits him at the post office where he finds an elegant little blue-edged envelope from someone who got out earlier than he did that morning. Inside is a delicate note card inviting him in Ann's spirited script to "The Third and Final 1835 Meeting of the New Salem and Athens Grammar Group" when it convenes on "Saturday Next" to celebrate the "Elevation" of "Member Abraham Lincoln" to the Illinois State Legislature. The quotation neatly scripted across the bottom to set the theme is not from Kirkham. Nor Byron. It's this:

> When a fence post don't stay, we don't give up on
> it, we find a new place and dig down deeper.
> Abraham Lincoln

Abe can see that someone told Ann what's in his stump speech. But what she took from it! She wanted to take giant strides. He remembers her crying out, "Lift me!" and he did. And they crashed to earth. And now are they to dig down deep? *What the hail?* as the weather-weary farmers thereabouts say. And now her playful invitation, singing a very different tune than the wail he remembers her running off with. But he's won the election, his mood is good whatever hers, and he writes to accept her invitation.

He thinks as he goes back to his loft for his tools to start the day. *I beat Stuart! Me, Abraham Lincoln. I'm going to be somebody. And Ann knows it.* Reckoning this time by who he beat, he doesn't remember his shame after the last election when he gauged who he was by who he lost to... or any of his other shames.

Me, Abraham Lincoln!

27

Things start stiffly on Saturday at the Rogers house where Lincoln arrives in his aging ivory linen shirt to find the two women in rigid gowns, a red floral brocade on silver for Ann, and a garden of dark green flowers on coppery silk for Arminda. Their hair is formal too, pinned high in fountains of braids in honor of their victorious statesman whom they repeatedly call The Honorable Abraham Lincoln. Arminda looks almost aristocratic with her hair pulled back from her high forehead and her high Germanic nose, while the ever-restless Ann looks more like a visitor in the stately guise she must have borrowed from Arminda and taken-in quickly for the occasion.

Lincoln wants to enjoy their attention but being as short on formal graces as he is on formal education, he feels in his everyday shirt and trousers like he should go outside and hold somebody's horse. While the women set places at table with white cloth napkins and silver-plated flatware that Arminda long-ago cajoled the Colonel into buying from New York by way of Cincinnati, Lincoln waits as instructed "at his leisure" on the *fleur de lis* upholstered sofa across the blue and silver oriental rug from their table setting and recalls that the legislature they're sending him off to will make him spend time with well-dressed people with proper manners every day. People who ride in carriages, not wagons. He thinks of the story of the man being run out of town on a rail who said if it wasn't for the honor of the thing he'd just as soon let it go by.

He's sure he's sitting "at his leisure" the wrong way and folds and unfolds his legs several times but can't find the composure he knows he's missing. Nor is there leisure for him in the gilded Rogers ancestor on the walls. Nor in the northern New York mountain scenes whose dark sublimities can't make his legs stop feeling storklike while every way he moves them seems to make his pants look even shorter.

He thinks of the story about the hotel in New Orleans that bragged that no one could die on its grounds. That, it turns out, was because at the first sight of mortality the staff took the expiring person out to die in the gutter. *But dying's not the problem today,* he thinks. *It's surviving when the living gets too grand.*

He wonders how Ann can possibly feel, she who ran away crying when he asked her to marry him but is setting out shining silver now. Will she keep a cordial distance like her bright stiff gown radiates? Is she an Ann he doesn't know? But then why does she keep looking at him as she bustles about with the hint of a grin like she's got something she can't wait to say.

He's relieved to see the easy-going Colonel come down the stairs with his white pistol handle waving in its holster just when Arminda has at last brought the angel food cake on the china platter, not the pewter, to the white-covered table. In a rare moment of settling-in, the Colonel sits down to eat his cake with gusto. He's got to maintain his robust figure he jokes, then true to form is soon up and pulling on his silk-lined tweed jacket. He tells Lincoln they're expecting great things from him, by which Lincoln knows he means favors for

169

the elders who think they got him elected. His carriage clatters up outside, the Colonel puts on his hat and snaps a farewell from its brim, the door closes, his team outside stirs and then starts, and the Colonel leaves behind as he always does the feel of importance and efficiency the world knows him by.

"Now," Ann says brightly, "we can play!"

"What on earth do you mean?" Arminda says. "We have grammar to study."

"Exactly," says Ann. "And I have a game to study it with."

Arminda rolls her eyes and Lincoln rolls up his sleeves, relieved at things turning less formal, and to tell the truth tired of studying grammar. He sits in front of the platter and asks if the children get more cake when they play the game.

Abe cuts cake for the first time with a real cake knife on a china platter. *Angel food,* he thinks, and wonders how Ann's wings can ever escape from her back when her red-on-silver brocade seems hard as armor.

"…so Mr. Lincoln's quotation," Abe hears Ann saying, "will be the focus of our study: 'When a fence post don't stay, we don't give up on it, we find a new place and dig down deeper.'" She stops. Abe is digging deeper into slicing the cake, and he hears Ann quote his informal "don't" and is afraid she's going to pick on him again for his mistake, while Ann is proud that she's about to use his words this time to make up for how she used them before, and Arminda is fluttering her eye-lids with an amused expression, confused between Ann's playful spirit and her own intention to seriously honor Lincoln's electoral success.

Ann, sensitive to the two others, starts feeling uncertain too. All right. She'll give up taking turns parsing the words from Abe's speech. But she must have something, and she's about to say what, when Abe hands the plates of cake around.

"O dear!" Arminda exclaims as she cuts into her cake with her silver-plated cake fork, "I've just remembered that I must go in a moment for a chore at my father's store."

170

"Arminda!" Ann complains, "if we can't play my grammar game..."

"Can I atone for my bad grammar," Abe says, "by eating more cake?"

"No, my dear Abraham," Ann says gently, "that would be eating humble pie."

The tenderness in Ann's voice confirms for Arminda that it's time to leave her and Abe alone, but when she stands to apologize again before going, Ann objects.

"I'll sacrifice my game for the occasion, but we must at least enjoy its grand finale, which has a special role, Arminda, for you. Will you help us if we do it quickly before you go?"

Arminda gives an acquiescent bow and sits, and Ann brings out her planned culmination.

"We must determine whether Mr. Lincoln's quotation is ordinary language or figurative language. And why. Here it is again: 'When a fence post don't... and we'll turn aside from the 'don't' as something that fit the situation... when it don't stay, he says, we don't give up on it, we find a new place and dig down deeper.' And, Mr. Lincoln," she says to Abe, "as players with previous exposure in this matter, we must let Miss Rogers have the first try." Abe doesn't know what she means, but nods.

"Arminda?" Ann says. "Ordinary language or figurative?" And she sits back pleased with herself and picks up her cake and fork.

"Well, if he's talking about fence posts it's ordinary language," Arminda reasons immediately, "but if he's talking about something else as I hope he was in a proper political discourse, then the fence post must be a figure of speech that stands for a different matter."

"Exactly!" Ann says. "Oh, Arminda, Mistress of Grammar, you're too clever. As it happens, when he said this Mr. Lincoln was not talking about fence posts at all, but canals and other transportation improvements!"

Lincoln sits up. "You sound so certain. Did your father repeat my speech to you?"

171

Ann flares red as she says it but can't stop herself. "I heard you myself!"

Arminda stands unnoticed in the rising conflict and gathers plates for the kitchen. A veteran teacher, she goes off pondering Ann's having designed, purportedly, a game for learning grammar in a playful way. She reminds herself that she and many others have long helped children learn the alphabet by singing the letters in songs, but she's jealous. And proud of the girl. She might make a teacher yet.

"You watched me speak?" Abe asks Ann between shock and disbelief. "But I would have seen you."

"I hid. What else could I do?"

"Your daddy would have brought you to a speech if you insisted."

"Can you blame me for wanting to be alone with you?"

"In one of them rough and wooly crowds?"

"*Them* crowds?"

"*Those* crowds."

"It was worth it. You spoke as if there was no one but you and me. Light came from your face. I saw your heavenly smile open wide. I heard you say we're not bound by our mistakes. You didn't just talk about changing rivers to canals, you talked about changing our lives!"

Lincoln stares at her eagerness and feels his heart surge.

"Will you walk me home?" She says it as if she's been waiting to. "If you say yes, I'll change back into my *real* clothes and leave Arminda a note and we can go."

Astonished at her, and at himself, he wants to say, "Marry me!" but he tried that before.

"Yes," he says. "Of course."

Ann smiles and goes upstairs.

I'll be alone with her, he thinks when she's gone upstairs. *In the woods.*

Excited and afraid, he feels so urgent that he has to do something. What? *Go up to her. She's seen through propriety. Arminda's gone for an hour. Go up to your red-haired angel. Are you a boy or Lord Byron?*

172

Lincoln goes to the stairs. Fear stiffens his knees and slows him. *What am I afraid of? Failing with her? Succeeding?* He plunges the other way across the little vestibule to the front door and rushes outside and down the porch stairs. He wants to run but he wants to be with Ann. He'd feel good running. Or wrestling. He wants… *something… physical.*

When Ann comes to find him she's casually dressed and ready for their walk but puzzled. She doesn't want to ask why he's pacing back and forth in front of the house in the heavy noon heat of an August day.

28

be breathes better when they start walking down the slope from the houses of Athens village where just like in every town, people shove in together then hide from each other. But he feels hemmed in again when at the bottom of the hill they start walking between fields of August corn high like green palisade walls on both sides of the road. In a summer still long to come he'll recall this confinement when he feels imprisoned in Washington at the big damp White House with swampy fields around him and complaining cattle and half-built federal temples. He'll pull his beard-bound face from brooding in his office and grab his ten-year-old Tad and shout "Let's break out of jail!" and hurry the boy past the guards to the toy store on Fourteenth Street for tin soldiers and kites. Kites to find the wind that's free *to go.*

"I admired your figure of speech," Ann says, apparently not as affected as he is by the narrowness of their lane. Having been restless too, back at their "reception," she's relieved to be out of stiff brocade and swaying down the dusty road in a light cotton dress as sky-blue as her eyes. The short sleeves of her dress show her arms, pale up high where they're usually protected, then darker and splashed with freckles down lower where they get more sun. The curved neck of her dress has no high buttons at her throat. Her hair is unstuck from its ornate pile of braids and swirled and loosely pinned beneath a wide straw bonnet.

Abe looks down while they walk, still stewing inside although grateful too that surveying will save him from shucking that towering corn this fall to earn his keep. "I admired your admiring it," he replies. *But how does she feel? About me?*

"It helped me feel better about what I have to."

"And what is that?"

"You know."

He's frustrated but doesn't say it. Urges collide in him and then merge and he says, "I know another figure of speech. I never used it, but I worked it up. Do you want to hear?"

She nods, trusting him to say something right for the situation and not wanting to say what she was going to have to say.

He looks down as they walk, formulating. "I'll show you how the speech would go."

"Ladies and gentlemen," she throws both hands to the sky as she shouts it, "the Honorable Abraham Lincoln!" Abe smiles at her introduction, then sobers his face and lifts his right arm to declaim and lets fly to Ann and the high August corn as they walk.

"Voters of Sangamon County! I first came to this country passing through on a river barge of produce for New Orleans, and I got that boat stuck on the Rutledge dam in New Salem. That's right. You know that dam. It did good in its time. New Salem grew up around that dam. Would any of us be here without it? Settlers came where there was a dam-powered mill to turn logs to boards to build houses, and to grind their grain to meal to eat and put in sacks to trade for pigs and gunpowder and axes.

"It was a good old dam but I learned a lot about what it could and couldn't do after it stopped my little river boat back in 1831. It was a good old dam for its time but when the time came for boats to move freely on the river, when people needed water flowing freely more than they needed its pent-up power, and when other nearby mills could do its job, then that dam's time was over.'"

"Yes!" Ann cries, carried away again by his preaching and stopping in the road to proclaim to the corn and the sky: "Like John McNeil's time is over!"

Lincoln is shocked, then believes it because he wants to, then grins. *Can it be?*

"But," Ann adds as if remembering herself, "let's not talk about John. Even in figures of speech. Forward!" she says and marches with her eyes set straight ahead.

"Not even," Lincoln says, falling in with her stronger stride, "to say he's a sour apple?"

"Not even that," Ann says with a smile and slows her pace. "Let's talk about you being a lawyer and I teaching school. *Your* being a lawyer? *Me* teaching…? *My? My* teaching school?" *Do I sometimes believe in what's proper and sometimes not?*

"It's a Plan," Abe says and she hears the capital "P."

"A Plan?"

"It's always been a Plan," Abe says. "Don't you think? A Plan from beyond. How I was stopped by your daddy's dam, and we saw each other, and I came back for you."

"But I got engaged."

"So our love would be tested. The things that don't work at first are part of it. I bought a store to try to be John, but my store failed so I had to be myself."

"But I ran away when Laura died. You and I were flirting and Row shot her. Dead! Wasn't that God's judgment?"

"What God would kill an innocent woman to keep us apart? That was life and it tested us, and look, we're together!"

"But you don't believe in God."

"Exactly. Ann, even the people who believe in God only believe when he's useful. My daddy went to the Pigeon Creek Baptist when the preacher said God's against slavery because that meant more land for Daddy and less for slave-owners."

"So where does the Plan come from?"

"I don't know. Where does it?"

"It's a mystery."

"Perfect!" he declares and points up ahead. "We're coming to The Mysterious Woods." And Ann looks up and sees it, the road flanked by high green corn delivering them into the shade of a forest that will take them to the meadow on the Athens side of the river and the bridge to New Salem. He's happy when she puts her hand to his arm to make him pause so she can think. She craves the shade's relief from the sun's hard glare, but she's timid about the forest, which her daddy has sheltered her from. *Everyone knows,* she thinks, *that the forest isn't healthy for ladies.* But now nothing can stop her from going.

"Yes!" she says and takes his hand and starts striding. Abe, who grew up in Kentucky woods where panthers roamed, feels at home as they step into the forest and holds her hand protectively and feels honored to do it.

"The Mysterious Woods." Ann repeats Abe's playful naming slowly, then stops to look about as timidly as if she were entering a cathedral. Or an ambush. She remembers when she ran to the woods in a dream.

Is Abe's pleasure in the woods contagious? Or is Ann so secure with Abe that she suddenly feels as many do that the woods have a gift to give. "Yes!" she exclaims as if something's gotten into her. "The Plan!" She breaks from his hand to run to the roadside. "Look!" she cries, "Forget-Me-Nots!" and down on her knees she takes off her bonnet and picks tiny blue flowers and tucks them in her russet hair.

"So you agree," he says, marveling at her bedecking her auburn hair with blue stars the color of her dress and eyes. "It's a Plan?"

She hears his invitation to discuss it more. "You think too much, Abe," she exclaims, standing and looking at him while she lofts a

177

handful of flowers above them like confetti. "We must *do!* We must do what we want!" She runs down the lane before him.

"Come!" she cries, "we must do everything!"

He runs! At last! And he's to her in a few steps and she takes his hand and they both slow down to walk together. "A woodland scene!" she says. "We must have a woodland scene! Look!' She points to a grassy clearing edged with ferns in the shady oaks. "It's perfect! How do they make these places perfect?"

He doesn't know. He wonders himself at the graceful grassy surround a few steps off the forest road. And he can't say no to a woodland scene. Nor can he say no, nor does he want to, when she instructs him to "recline romantically beneath a tree" while she does something else for a "woodland moment."

"I see what we must do," she says, going behind the thick oak he reclines against. "But you must not see." She takes out the comb that binds the bun of her hair and shakes her hair loose and lets it fall around her face and flow down the front of her dress, and some of her Forget-Me-Nots cling in her tresses and some float to the forest floor.

She calls to him where he sits wondering what she's doing. "You look so worried, Abe. You look that way so much. We must cure you. Your face must give light the way it does when you give speeches." And she begins to gather something into her bonnet from the ground behind the tree.

"Say those poems of yours," she says, "the ones you recite by the fire and make mother and daddy cry," and he knows the melancholy poems she means because these are about the only ones he knows.

"*The Banks O Doon?*" he says.

"O yes!" she says enthusiastically, "that one's so sad!"

And he rolls it forth and its false-hearted lover has no more fear for her than the hard-hearted Barbry Allen she also feels clear of today.

"Yes!" she says gaily as she works at her secret task. "More sad poems! *The Last Rose of Summer!*"

And he declaims the Thomas Moore poem become a favorite
song of the time's tenors who trade painful loss for beer in taverns,
the one that ends:

> So soon I may follow when friendships decay
> And from love's shining circle the gems drop away
> When true hearts are withered and fond ones are flown
> O who would inhabit this bleak world alone?

"More!" she shouts, off at the other side of their circle of grass
and still busy with something between the ground and her bonnet.
"More sorrow! More!"

"Why Should The Spirit Of Mortal Be Proud?"

"Yes! Wonderful! Turn day to night with that one!"

Given license, Lincoln stands and orates his favorite poem about
death, all fifty-six lines in fourteen stanzas, starting with:

> Oh! why should the spirit of mortal be proud?
> Like a swift-fleeting meteor, a fast-flying cloud,
> A flash of the lightning, a break of the wave,
> Man passeth from life to his rest in the grave.

And ending:

> 'Tis the wink of an eye, 'tis the draught of a
> breath,
> From the blossom of health to the paleness of
> death,
> From the gilded saloon to the bier and the
> shroud,—
> Oh! why should the spirit of mortal be proud?

His treasured coins of mourning spent, the standing Lincoln
looks at Ann who's come up to him hiding something behind her
back.

"Sit down, sit down," she says, "or I'll never reach you."

He sits and leans again against his tree with no idea what she means. She's out of sight now, behind him again and chatting to distract him as she moves in.

"What is it that Pastor Cartwright says when he baptizes? 'I convert thee to new life…?'"

Abe, a man of speeches though a hater of Cartwright, knows: "He says, 'Be thou converted from the world of sin!' But why…."

"Yes!" she shouts as she readies to pour. "Be thou converted from the world o' dreary to light anew!" And she lets go and Abe looks up to see acorns showering on him while Ann's face shines steady and smiling up beyond what falls as her face held steady that cold night behind the falling stars.

He smiles and says, "I think your spell is taking hold."

Finished with her baptism, Ann steps before him to gleam with satisfaction, saying, "What do you mean?"

He stands to join her and looks with no inhibition at her loose hair draping her breasts. When he sees her hair unbound he feels unbound too.

"I remember a happy poem," he says, his head bent, his face close to hers.

"Dear god I'm powerful!" she says. "Recite!"

He does, boldly staying close and speaking low, with his eyes on her lips:

> Jenny kissed me when we met,
> Jumping from the chair she sat in.
> Time, who love to get sweets
> Into your list, put that in.
> Say I'm weary, say I'm sad,
> Say that health and wealth have missed me.
> Say I'm growing old, but add,
> Jenny kissed me.

"Jenny?" she asks skeptically and puts both hands to his chest and shoves him playfully away.

Uh oh.

She's relentless. "Who would that be?"

"She's an… imagined Jenny," he says. "I've never…."

"Really?" Ann says, stepping close again and lifting her face to his.

"Not yet," he says, excited by her teasing eyes.

"Maybe you'll be lucky someday!" she exclaims and turns and runs into the forest on the darkening road, and what can he do but chase her? He's surprised at how fast she is when she really runs, making the racing star of the New Salem men work his legs and lungs to catch her. He's winded when he does, and he takes her hand to make sure she doesn't go anywhere.

Catching her breath, she doesn't say, "I've never been kissed either." She turns aside a dark thought about John and squeezes Abe's hand and looks at him as they walk and asks if he liked their woodland scene. To him she's a thing of the woods herself with her dress wrinkled and her hair long and loose and dotted with tiny stars.

"I did," he answers to reassure her while he thinks of saying, *I want you to baptize me every day,* but he's distracted and looks up above them where rain is starting to patter on the covering trees. Louder, it comes louder, the shower turning quickly to a pelting, and water comes streaming down on them through bobbing leaves. They huddle beneath a great-canopied tree but the shoulders and sleeves of his linen shirt darken and cling, and Ann's dress and her hair down her back cling too. They look at each other getting soaked.

Pressing her bonnet to her head, Ann shouts "Come!" and plunges running again down the forest way as if when there's no other way to make things better you can do some good by just *moving.* Confounded for a moment, Abe soon feels without understanding, that this is her, this is destiny, and starts running to get to her and isn't sufficed by catching up but must show her what it's like to be left behind, so he reaches her and passes her on the road and races on. When he's nearing the end of the woods he pauses and turns to look back and Ann comes passing him flying with her blue eyes flashing and her hat in her hand and goes splashing out of the forest as the

181

rain comes fast on the harvested field already ripe with a new crop of mud. Again he runs to catch up with her, knowing nothing about the gauntlet of grievance-filled ladies inside her she races to escape, and he shouts: "Is this how it will always be?"

She stops and turns with no answer and sees the light in his face in the pouring rain. She flings her arms wide and they're around him and he pulls her close then slides down to embrace her knees in the mud of the field and looks up and says: "Will you marry me, Ann?"

"Of course!" she shouts and splashes to her knees in the puddle before him and her lips find his and they abandon themselves to each other and to the storm. At last Ann stops and pulls away with the smile Abe knows as her Knowing Smile, her eyes teasing from the frame of her rain-dark hair.

"Was Jenny's kiss like this?"

"Nothing," he smiles and shakes his head slowly, "was ever like this."

Their embrace takes them to a place where there is no rain and Abe gets to his feet and lifts Ann to join him and lifts her feet from the ground and swings her around and around until he sets her down and she clings, drenched, like he's saved her from the flood of her life.

He wants to run again. He wants to lift Ann and carry her, carry her running all the way to New Salem and put her down in the town square, though there is no town square and he knows that, and say, "Look what I, humble Abraham Lincoln, have got!"

It won't hold up, a voice in him warns. *You know that.* Lincoln hugs her tighter.

Don't care and you can't be hurt, it says.

Living is hurting, he thinks.

I tried to warn you.

Not to live?

There's no answer.

"The rain's not a judgment?" Ann says, leaning wet in his arms in the field in the slowing rain with her face innocent as a girl's.

Seeing he missed it, she asks again: "Say the rain's not a judgment, Abe."

The rain's stopping now and he sees what's happening over her shoulder as he holds her close.

"There is no rain," he says, and leans back so he can see her face as he gestures with his head to what's behind her.

She's puzzled, unsure what he's saying.

"If there's a judgment on us," he says, "it's behind you." And she turns and sees the rainbow on the horizon.

He says softly, "Will you still marry me?"

"I do!" she shouts and spins to face him grinning.

It feels natural to have her say that, and he puts his arms around her and feels comfort, not risk. As if he were home.

"I do?" he says. "You'll owe sin tax for that. You need a verb in the future tense, not the present."

"Not if we start right now!" He feels the warmth of Ann's smile on his chest as she presses her face against his pounding heart. *It's all impossible,* he thinks. *And real.*

By the time they reach Ann's house in Sand Ridge with the sun going down they've decided. She'll write to John McNeil: *Surely you'll understand my feelings after your long time away with no word... better for both of us... release each other from our promises....* They won't tell others until John knows, and then they'll get married and have three fat babies. He'll be a lawyer and she'll study at the Jacksonville Female Academy and become a teacher. Their national book will be *Kirkham's Grammar* and their national flower the Forget-Me-Not.

As Lincoln ambles happily from the Rutledge house to bed-down at Jimmy Short's instead of trudging back to New Salem in the dark, his discouraging voice can't resist a last go on the dim forest road: *You know you're heading for trouble.*

He thinks of his surveying tools always about to be seized by the Sheriff because of what he owes, and the money he's got to borrow tomorrow on top of his national debt to buy a damned suit for the legislature. He's going to Vandalia, two days of stage-coach bouncing across corduroyed roads, where he hears the boarding houses are icy and some of the stares are bound to be cold when he gets there from the woods with his messy hair over his too new suit and lord knows what manners. And the mess with McNeil and Ann will worry him every day. *Maybe there's always something right,* he thinks, *but for sure there's always something wrong.*

Who, he thinks with a grin, *isn't heading for trouble?*

Ann looks up into the dark above her bed that night. At first she can't stop smiling about Abe. She thinks of waking little Bobby and Nannie to dance in circles with them. Then she remembers John and a cold fist squeezes her heart and pins her where she lies.

29

onths later the winter of 1835 is ending and the iced-up streams are running and Lincoln is bouncing in a rattling stagecoach on his way home from his first legislative session at Vandalia. He looks back at learning the State Assembly: swapping votes, doing favors to get on committees, jumping out the State House window to ruin the quorum when the votes are against you. Off-days he watched lawyers at the courts and reckoned what it takes, and he likes his chances. Some are blow-hards, some are small-town politicos with boss-like swagger, some put on a scholar act, and some just bumble through. If they can be lawyers, he thinks with no more disrespect than they invite, he can too. It's all in the books, like Stuart says. The principles. Then there's the forms, and the truth is he's been drawing up documents for his neighbors for years but never counted it really law when he copied a template for a contract or deed. He did a will too, and a mortgage for Jimmy Short's brother Josh. Now he's sized up the men and how they use the books and forms.

A few he envies. Stuart of course, the handsome son of a college professor, and Steve Douglas, a cocky five-footer who knows books and people. Lincoln already feels the rivalry he can't see the future of: in the legislature, at law, in epic debates for a Senate seat, and finally the race to be President. But he knows you don't want to size yourself up by Douglas, a giant no matter how short he is. Lincoln's glad Ann doesn't know the man.

Ann… Ann…. His politics fade and his worries sharpen as the two-day stage-coach moves him farther from the legislature and closer to Ann.

Will I ever get to be alone with her?

And then…? he thinks, but it's too big for him, so he tries to stop thinking about it and looks out the window for something new. His old militia daydream of lying with Ann comes back as it did many times in Vandalia and he gives up to its warmth but as he and Ann get closer and closer and start shedding their clothes, they dissolve into the mist that hides the landscape.

They must be almost there. The stage stopped at the New Salem tavern in the fog a while ago, and now they're between the village and Sand Ridge. With nothing to see outside but wet gray air, he's stuck with what's in the cabin of the lunging stagecoach.

I'm in the stage, he thinks. *A carriage. I, Abraham Lincoln, am riding in a carriage. In a suit.* Yes, he borrowed two hundred dollars from Coleman Smoot to buy a formal outfit before the session. And yes, he learned to put on the airs that go with the suit. With Stuart's help. Gloves when a gentleman is not eating or drinking, gray the safest general choice, stand when a lady enters or stands, offer your arm every time you can, and never refer to another person by his or her first name in public. "Oh, and for God's sake, man," Stuart said, "*never ever* let me see you eat from a knife again!" A hefty business traveler from Peoria sleeps on the cracked leather stage seat opposite him with his arms around a satchel of eggbeaters and vegetable-peelers.

Soon. He can feel her warmth.... *Can it be?*

Lincoln looks cautiously at the sleeping salesman to be sure he won't take a prying interest, then reaches in his pocket for some papers and unfolds her letter for the third or fourth time already smiling.

> Dear Mr. Lincoln:
>
> I write this not knowing if things remain yet with you in the manner of our last communication before you left New Salem for Vondalla and your exciting new life as a legislater. My feelings are the same. Nothing has changed, nor can it change while the same stars shelter and hold us in place and the same breezes stir our skin.
>
> Although talk of breezes can only be figurative language in reccent days when there has been no breeze. The weather here is cold and still and damp. Mother says the moist air keeps her skin from parching. Father says when water doesn't flowe, sickness flowes. I say still waters run deep and recall with gratitude the deep thoughts you and I have discussed, and ever will. While the same stars, etc.
>
> Please write soon to tell me how the whether is with you, and that you will soon be governor and senator and all the rest. Especially if you continue to wear that fine new suit. Please send the comments of your friends about the suit, but not the flattering remarks of the women at your hotel which would make me jealus. But perhaps if you tell me how much you think of me, I will forgive you for their thinking much of you.
>
> Knowing that you will keep private this letter in which those who know of my engagement might wonder at the expressions of our deep friendship,
>
> I am, your
>
> Ann Rutledge

He recalls when he first read this letter and flooded with happiness at having it, and having her affection, which is such good fortune he sometimes can't believe it. But he remembers too getting angry because Ann said nothing about changing her standing with John. But then his feelings changed yet again when he realized that even the month or more they'd been apart by the time she wrote that letter was not enough time for her to have heard back from a letter she sent by the horses and stages and riverboats of the U.S. Postal Service to John far back east in the farmlands of upstate New York.

Lincoln looks to be sure the man clutching his leather bag of tin cooking gadgets is still asleep, then unfolds Ann's second letter that came two months after the first.

> Dear Abraham:
>
> You will see from the above that I bow to your letter's admonishmant that we must know each other through our personnal names in our personnal and not public communications. I consider it a high honor to be on such a basis of personal address with a gentleman living in a world with, as you wrote, "much flourishing about in carriages" and "the taking of tea in real China cups on grand verandahs."
>
> Such personal address, it goes without saying, makes it the more important that our letters are kept from the eyes of others as long as I seem to be in an arrangement which gives exclusive claim on such familiarity to another.

She hasn't heard from John! Or has she heard but can't say so? "I seem to be in an arrangement...." "...seem...."? Has John excused her from her promise to marry but it's not diplomatic to be public? But our letters are not public. And where's the cheer she would have if she were free of him?

He reads on.

188

And oh, the burdens of such pretenses! Oh dearest
Abraham, if only I could adequately tell you of
my distresse at our world of confinements. Secrets,
hidings of private from public, limitations in
what we may and may not do and say. Even bold
Arminda and dear Parthena, wise as they are but
surroundid as I am by those who expect other than
I am, cannot resist the claims of propriety. "My
ancestors' virtues are not mine," I think. Should I
want them to be? I who do not even feel today as
I felt yesterday, and hundreds of yesterdays before
that when I did not stand up to dimand the virtue,
the *new* virtue, and the fate that I cannot be happy
without?

Am I confusing you? Forgive me, please. And
forgive me again if I am not all I should be and not
doing all I should do. And forgive me a third time
if I silently cry out as I do aloud only at night to
the wind (yes, you will knowe my secrets) behind
the barni "Where is my tall woodeman to lift me
for the giant stride beyond these thorns?"

Reading this in the carriage he's alarmed as he was when he first
read it by the firelight in his Vandalia boarding house. But again he
finds comfort, as Ann surely wanted him to, in her closing.

In parting I must command you as the daughter
of the troubled duke must command the secret
nobleman who is no longer a secret now that he
dresses in a fine coat for his daily legislations and
assorted flourishings. You are not to feel distressed
for one moment at my complaintes. I won't allow
it. These are ills that will, like all ills, pass. Especially now that you will before long be home to give
me, in the further unfolding of your nobility and
your encouragment of my own, the strength I need
to do what I must do.

He will help her. He will. *But how? I must wait until I'm with her.*
I'll know what to do. I will? She will.

189

He looks out the window and sees a familiar old tree through the gray blur of mist.

No wonder I'm worried shut up in here with nothing to do. Nothing but worry. Which does no good. About John, my mountain of debt, Ann. Everybody's heading for trouble, he remembers and loosens and smiles. *But some get to find it in a woman's arms.*

Lincoln gets himself and his bag out of the stagecoach in front of Ann's house in a light rain seeping through heavy gray air. As if watching for his coming, Ann flings the front door open and runs to him and throws her arms around his neck. "You did come! You did! The wind told me you would!"

He squeezes her flutter as if to stop and keep and protect her, and she sighs comically as if he's pressed all her air out, then breaks away while he stands like a speechless dolt until she pulls him by the hand. "Come in out of the rain!"

Come in out of the rain, he thinks. *So simple.*

Inside, Ann slams the door behind them and orders his boots off. "But don't you touch that jacket," she says, admiring him. "Oh, Abe, you look like Henry Clay!"

The great Henry Clay? Humble Abraham Lincoln? The Honorable Surveyor from Sangamon County? Who am I? For the months in Vandalia he kept a formal front all day but that won't work here. Nor will his nightly role as a teller of earthy stories to the boys drinking cider by the boarding house fire. No lizards up ladies' dresses for Ann.

Ann gives him his cue. "You look like you should orate in a suit like that."

"Precisely, your honor!" he declares and strikes an oratorical stance with his right hand soaring before him like Daniel Webster in a newspaper illustration. *"What I Learned In Vandalia,* by The Honorable... But Still Humble... Abraham Lincoln."

"Uh on," says Ann. "Should I get coffee?"

Abe's punctured but he gets the point and relaxes. As Ann turns to go the kitchen he sees her figure that makes his remnants of worry disappear: her back, the way it narrows to her waist, her hips.... He

190

missed the bright clear sight of her in Vandalia, remembered her more poorly as time passed, imagined her when he was alone, and now he's captured by the profile of her breasts and her auburn hair falling to hide her face when she bends to get the pot from the fire. She turns and meets his eyes and his heart leaps with fear at being found out, but she smiles.

Thinking to clear space for the coffee things, Abe turns to the table near the fire but finds a white cloth speckled with silver threads folded there.

"Are you working on a dress?" he says.

"A dress? Don't men know anything? That's a gown."

"Do they allow gowns in Sand Ridge? Does the gown have a carriage?"

She threatens him with the cookie jar in her hand. "This cookie jar doesn't have a carriage," she says, "but it can make its way to your head, Mr. Lincoln. That's Parthena's gown for marrying Sam. A friend of hers in New York sent it on after her own wedding, but Parthena's more woman than that city girl so I've got to let it out here and there. Then when *she's* wore it… I mean *worn* it…." Ann stops to remember something. Or forget it.

"You should wear gowns all the time, Ann."

"Of course, m'lord," she says and performs the closest she can to a ball-room curtsey in her deep blue prairie dress with a cookie jar in one hand and a pewter plate in the other.

"I mean it. All the time. And drink coffee from real China cups. And you will. I know I can be a lawyer now. I saw who gets away with it. And the politicians! A few are high class, little Henry Clays, but a lot are backwoods preachers and self-taught drunks with big mouths and pistols." He feels good now, feels his strength, and he knows where he's going and what's in his way, and he says it: "Have you heard back from John?"

Her eyes narrow as she thinks.

"Objection!" she shouts as she lifts a tin coffee mug high to an airy tribunal.

"Objection? I thought you were the judge. Are you opposing counsel?"

"I'm everything, Abraham, you know that. Whatever's needed to keep you in line. Now you've just got here and I want to enjoy you. Don't make me think about... other things. Can we talk about... him... later?"

"Sure, Ann. You just know...."

"I know men have been banished for contradicting a woman's will."

Abe is impressed when Ann talks like this. He likes it and doesn't like it. "Banished?" The rain's rhythm on the roof speeds up and he goes to check if the front door's tight. "Not in a downpour, I hope."

Ann moves Parthena's gown and brings coffee and molasses cookies and they sit at the table and Ann explains. "The essence of a banishment my dear unknowing prince cast up on this drastic shore is that the banisher cares not a fig for the discomfort of her banishee and in fact hopes he'll have a hard time... shipwreck, hunger, highwaymen, thin thin gruel... so he'll act better when he comes back."

"He gets to come back?"

"Of course. If she doesn't want him to come back she has him hung."

"I tremble."

Ann gets up and lifts the filmy silver-flecked gown to her front for him to admire. "You'd tremble if you saw me in this gown. It's French."

"French?"

"Do you see the top?" she says and smiles her dangerous smile. "Well.... It just about has no top."

Hyperbole? he thinks. But he turns red imagining. She's distracted him from John. And everything else. She sits back down and he moves his chair closer.

"We're alone," he says. *Can virtue and vice be one?*

"For a while. Mother and father took the children to Camp Meeting two days ago, so they'll likely come back sometime tomor-

192

row. When your letter told me when you hoped to arrive I used every known excuse to get out of going there for salvation."

"So we'll be alone for...."

"For a different salvation...." Now Ann blushes. "Have you ever been to Camp Meeting, Abe?"

"It's against my religion, your honor."

"Parthena says Camp Meeting should be called Mating Camp. She says when spirits get lifted, skirts get lifted."

"Right in the tent where forty families are sleeping?"

"Or pretending to sleep."

"Have you done that?"

"Abraham!" She jumps up and picks up the wedding gown from the side table and takes it to the bed under the front window and turns her back to him to spread it out front down so she can go to work on the back.

"I mean," Abe says, blushing and apologetic, "have you listened while you pretended to sleep while...."

"I might have a hard time opening my gown if you're going to keep asking naughty questions."

Did she say that on purpose? Should I say, "I wouldn't want to keep you from opening your gown"? He doesn't, but the thought makes him watch her more keenly. He watches her sit on the bed next to the gown, follows her fingers reaching inside to turn over the seam, sees her slide her seam ripper under every fifth or sixth stitch to lift through the tight thread and part the soft cloth. Wisps of her hair fall free from its pinning.

"This is the brave part," she says. "Opening something precious when you're not sure what will happen." She looks over as if to gauge him then back at her seam.

"I listened to Parthena," she says without looking up. "... and Sam."

"Parthena and Sam?"

"At Camp Meeting. I saw them go in the bushes, then I heard them moaning. I was so ashamed! Just hearing it. That was before

Sam asked me to marry him. If she'd moan with him I knew she loved him, so when he asked me I had to say no."

Abe is astonished at hearing why Ann didn't marry Sam, but then too, knowing Ann it makes perfect sense. *Because Parthena loved him.* He can't get comfortable with Sam and Parthena twisting and moaning in the bushes a few feet from the preacher thundering inside the revival tent. Would he and Ann…? He changes the subject.

"But then you said yes to John."

"Stop! No John! You mustn't make me think of him!"

Abe's frustration overwhelms his caution and he blurts as if to strike back: "Well, if people are having all that fun at Camp Meeting now, what are *we* doing *here?*" Then he's afraid she'll hear the complaint that his joking tone couldn't hide. And she does.

"That's a very good question, Abraham Lincoln. To think that I gave up my conversion, my salvation, not to mention my possible spirit-lifting skirt-lifting, to be here with you under the pretense that I was feeling too poorly to go to Mating Camp when really I was feeling too wonderful because the wind told me you would come and you did come and that's why we're here."

Like most men Abe loses fight when he thinks he's wanted.

"Shall I take off my jacket and get comfortable," he asks, "or would you like me to orate while you sew?"

"Oration! Oration! By the Honorable etc., etc., and… etc…!"

Yes, Lincoln thinks, *declaim all the way from her inspiring everything good you've ever done to your loving her so much you'd never deprive her of a good skirt-lifting. And tell her if she has the courage to start into something precious when she doesn't know what will happen, you do too.*

He stands and tugs his Henry Clay jacket down straight and elevates his right arm to the Daniel Webster pose. But he can't do it. The ancient sadness of his everyday expression comes into his face and then a kind of resolution, and he takes off his jacket and hangs it on the back of a kitchen chair, aware of her watching and wondering. He pulls another chair from the dining table and turns it around so

194

he can straddle it and lean forward on its back toward where she sits on the bed in silent surprise.

"Tell me about the wind," he says.

Ann looks at him, then back at her seam.

"You'll think I'm crazy."

"As crazy," he asks, "as the smartest most beautiful woman in Sangamon County falling for a homely gangling boy who borrowed a year's earnings to buy a suit for the legislature where he went in fear that suit or no suit they'd see what a bumpkin he really is?"

She grins and looks back at her work. "But that's why I love you."

"Because I'm a fool or you are?"

"Because you're brave."

"I get my courage from you."

"I have no courage. I get it from the wind."

"Tell me."

"I will, but first I have to take something back. The wind didn't really tell me you were coming. I used to think it talked to me. And maybe it does. Is it natural language? Or is it me?"

She takes him back through it, how first she hated the wind she had to push through like an enemy to feed the cow. She tells him how she told it to kill her if it thought she needed another problem. She tells him how it shouts that it doesn't care and she shouldn't either. How she talks to it alone behind the barn, sometimes trading loudness for loudness, that everything it shouts has to be, and when she shouts back she casts out her hurt, the pains of the great vile hateful things and the tiny little bleeding things, the scarred heart that weighs a mountain and the finger she put a needle in. Sometimes it's a team of horses bolting for the edge of the earth and she calls to it to take her. She tells him how it sings... sometimes sweet consolations... sometimes howling marches to help her meet what has to come. "But at least," she says, depleted at the finish, "when the wind sings, even something awful, I'm not alone."

Now Abe is alone, so far from all she's said, with no way to reach her. He thinks of holding her, thinks of holding wind.

195

Ann, who stopped her thread-ripping when she let go into talking about the wind, looks down and finds her place on the seam and goes back to opening the gown. She stops to smooth back some strands of hair come down in her eyes and senses Abe's distance and wants him back. A line of poetry jumps into her head.

"It's like in Wordsworth," she says. "What is that poem? You remember. '… a presence far more deeply interfused' or something. Can you get it?"

Abe fetches the Wordsworth from her father's little library, easy to find because when he moved his family here from the Tavern, Ann's daddy hung his bookshelf right where it's always been, side-by-side with and in the shelter of his wife's precious china cabinet. As Abe pages into the poems, they agree it's *Tintern Abbey* they want, and Abe finds it and scans to the lines she's trying to recall, about, the poet says, a "presence." He reads:

> Whose dwelling is the light of setting suns,
> And the round ocean and the living air,
> And the blue sky, and in the mind of man;
> A motion and a spirit, that impels
> All thinking things, all objects of all thought,
> And rolls through all things.

"Yes!" Ann cries looking up from her work. "….a motion in the living air… rolling through…!" Their eyes meet and she sees the liveliness she inspires in him when she gets inspired, but she looks away. She peers closely back at the gown as if she must study what she's doing, her eyes as precise on the tiny threads as her blade must be.

"Have you ever just wanted to give up to something?"

Despair? he thinks. *The lamp flame luring me to burn my way free?*

"I gave up to you," he says. "The night of the falling stars."

Ann pauses her seam-ripping again at this idea as big as something the wind might say. "The stars fell," she says. "You told me. But what did that have to do with me?"

196

"There were hundreds or thousands of stars like streaks of silver shooting down like a rainstorm, the stars that rule the night dying and plunging in what seemed like the end of the world. But then the falling ended and it wasn't the end. Because up where the falling stars had been there were some stars still steady, fixed and true. And your face was there, high in the fixed and steady stars, smiling as it always will be."

"My face?"

"Always."

Ann nods quietly as if she knew that and goes back to work thinking what a pair they are, she with her wind and he with his stars. *What do you marry?*

"You're such a dreamer," she says. She looks at his profile then, with his left eye going off the way it does, the one that lifts where the stars are.

He looks back at her. "It's just the facts, your honor."

How little he knows himself, she thinks. "Then tell me a dream," she says. "I need a dream."

Abe stands impulsively to pace his way to their future. In his mind he leaps past the thousands of dollars he's in debt though he knows the reckoning will someday have to come.

"It's perfect," he says. "Abandon yourself to this," and he looks down as he starts pacing, but his face is alight. "I've got one more year in the legislature, but then I get elected for another term. I survey all god's… what am I saying?… survey all creation to support us. I fight to get Springfield named state capitol instead of Vandalia, and then when I study law… I've still got Stuart's *Blackstone*, and he'll loan me more books when I'm ready… I can clerk in his office in Springfield when the assembly's in session. I hang out my lawyer shingle, we get you to the Jacksonville Female Academy to become a teacher. We build a big house on a leafy street in Springfield and have three fat babies… a governor, a senator, and a judge… and we fill up the house with Forget-Me-Nots and when obstacles and sorrows come…" here he stops and plants his feet and looks at her for the

197

stirring conclusion, "... we remember that at first it looked wrong when your daddy's dam stopped me on the river but that was for the best, and years later it was best when I proposed in the rain and again and again things looked a mess but we laughed and said who's not heading for trouble and it all worked out in the end."

He sees Ann's rosy smile of a little-girl-found, then sees her smile dim to the frown of a little-girl-lost.

She stares at the tight seam she faces and shakes her head. "He won't let me go."

"Who?"

"John. He's a demon."

"A demon?" Abe doesn't know that he believes in demons.

"With a cloven hoof," she says, trembling with it. "I see it now. He has me enthralled and won't let go!"

"He can't let you go because he doesn't have you, Ann. He's not even here. He's been gone for nearly three years. He's nowhere. He's McNeil, McNamar, McNobody. Have you heard from him? You'll never hear. He's gone and you're free!" He doesn't want to argue but what can he do?

"There you go again!" she shouts with tears flaring in her eyes. "John is in northern New York putting his family's cook pots and bedsteads in a wagon to come here and set up house. We're engaged to be married! I belong to him! A man *takes* a wife!"

"Wait," Abe says. His eyes narrow. He doesn't want to say it, but he has to know.

"Have you written to John?"

"Well...."

"We decided that you'd tell him we was going to get married and he had to let you go."

"I know...."

"You know... but?"

"I couldn't do it!"

"You couldn't? You said you would!"

"You weren't here! I was alone with...."

"With what? What on earth is stopping you?"

She pauses as if she doesn't know how to answer. Her tone softens. "Maybe it's not on earth, Abe."

His heart goes out to her uncertainty. He hesitates, dropping all blame, just wanting to persuade her. "*We're* on earth, Ann. Things happen, yes, but we make things happen too. We can't choose everything, but when we get a choice, we have to make it. John's been gone for three years and I don't think he's coming back, but we can't just wait and see. You can keep him from coming back. If you want to. You want to, don't you? Write him like you said and we'll be free!"

"I'll never...."

"A giant stride...."

"I gave my word ,,."

"John gave his word then disappeared."

"But...."

"But what?"

"There's something you don't know."

Ann closes her eyes and breathes deep then looks at him and says slowly: "Why do you think we're in this house in Sand Ridge?"

"Because... we...."

She stops him with a slow sad shake of her head: "Because it's John McNeil's house."

What? Abe is too puzzled to speak and Ann goes on.

"My father says he *got tired* of the tavern and mill and *wanted* to go back to farming, but he *failed* at the tavern and mill and *had* to go back to farming... what little he farms. Daddy lost the tavern, and the mill. For all of his being a kind, respected, and learned man, the founder of the town for the love of God, he got to where he couldn't pay his bills, but he wouldn't let on. John paid them for him. This is John's farm. He's letting us live here. John owns us. If I don't marry John, my family is ruined! Mother and Father and me and Bobby and Nannie and the little ones! John owns us! Owns us all! Where is this in your Plan? Do you buy us, Abe? Do you buy us with your debt?"

199

"Yes!" he cries, with no idea how he'll do it, and starts striding. "I'll raise cash. Sam will take my note, and Stuart, and Row, and Hardin Bale. Notes I'll pay when I'm a lawyer. Or I'll quit the law nonsense and make money surveying. I'll find lots and buy and sell them like John did…. I'll take care of your family. I'll find Offut if I have to. I'll raise cash to buy the kingdom! Sam was right. John's a son of a bitch and we'll put him in his place!"

Ann stares at him while unconsciously squeezing the wedding gown, *her* wedding gown, in both hands. He makes it sound easy. Can he do what he said? She remembers seeing him speak at Row's farm. The vision of what *can* be. Not what *must f*be.

It can't be, she thinks, then sees his Henry Clay jacket on the chair. *It can!*

"Write him, Ann. Write him and tell him. We get to choose. You do. You. I'll do my part and you do yours."

Ann drops the gown and stands so abruptly her chair clatters on the floor.

"Paper, counselor!" she cries, and picks up the gown and throws it on her mother's bed and pushes their coffee things aside and pulls the pins from her coiled hair and flings it unbound, red tresses flooding down her back and over the breast of her night-blue dress. "Let there be paper and pen from Daddy's roll-top desk. Yes, the middle drawer, O unknown prince. For it is John and not thou who art banished, and the edict shall go forth anon!"

Ann spreads the paper Abe brings and sits to write, then looks up at him from behind her sheltering hair with a peaceful gaze and an amused afterthought: "What does *anon* mean, Abe?"

"Forthwith!" he cries and throws his hands wide in histrionic annunciation, and they laugh the open-hearted laugh of the reunited in love, and she turns to the paper before her and writes… what she *chooses.*

30

Abe needs money to create the future. He stays in the village now that he's back from Vandalia, grateful he can be in the center of things when he needs to earn more. He goes back to the twice-weekly post office hours he resumes from young Daniel Burner, schedules all the surveying jobs he can get, and does some clerking at Sam Hill's store. He rooms as he did last summer at Dr. Allen's barn loft across from the Tavern, but being that he's a legislator now the Doctor insists that he take a little rough table and chair out to his living space and lets him hang his formal suit in a wardrobe closet in the house until he needs it next fall. How long will it be, Abe wonders, until it's Ann and not the Doctor who knows better than he does what furniture he needs?

Money! He never cared much about it until love had a price. The old love stories didn't warn him about this need, but he wrestles with it now, and the wrestling is worse because he can't know the size of the giant he has to throw: how much he'll need to take care of the

Rutledge family. He can't ask McNeil or Mr. Rutledge about this until he and Ann can make their intentions public, and that has to wait until John knows Ann has changed her plans.

He wonders at himself. He who so loves to calculate, has he taken on cost without measure? Cost that heaps on top of his personal debt, which got worse while he was away at the legislature and his partner Berry died, merging totally into his spirits, holy and otherwise, and leaving Lincoln to pay his share of the thousands in notes he and Lincoln signed. Lincoln didn't think much about his debt when he was jawboning bills every day in Vandalia, but back in New Salem it's at him and at him all the worse when he feels caught alone with it in the fog's vault-like walls.

April seems March all over. More rain, then less. Less rain, then more. Rain. And May. Rain. It's so foggy much of the time that you can't tell where you are by looking around. Sound dampens. *Life* dampens when you're alone and whatever's near you seems all there is.

Luckily, Abe and Ann have a way to meet. If they're careful.

On Thursdays Ann comes to town in Abe's post office hours. Knowing they mustn't call attention to themselves and risk the reputation of the famously engaged young lady of the place, they make small talk standing by the pigeon-hole desk where he sorts mail in the dark back end of the store. His eyes feast on her form and he aches to hold her as she bends to count out pennies on his desktop to mail her mother's letter to South Carolina, but there are shoppers in the store.

Sometimes he insinuates.

"I'm glad if I can make you happy," he says looking boldly at her as he gives her change. "I wish there was more I could do for you today." In the first month and more after Ann has written John they can't expect to hear back from him at such a distance, and this sets them free from worry about his reaction. For a while. One time with no one nearby in the store Ann stands behind Abe at his pigeon-hole desk and grips his hand with hers to show him how to write a more flowing script. She presses into his back and he loses his breath and stops writing and turns to her. Seeing in his eyes how innocent and lost he's suddenly become she steps back and says, "Maybe that's as far as we can go… with our lesson… today." And they both glance over at old Mrs. Johnson a row away fingering pound sacks of sugar with her canvas bag on her arm and hope she's as deaf as everyone says, or at least too old to take an interest in what they're doing.

Or does everyone know? Surely Ann's mother must, waiting outside in the wagon so long, and with Ann urging her to write new letters when she hasn't heard back from the ones she's sent. Ann has taken to writing more letters back to South Carolina too. And she asks Abe if he'll post her letter to their old grammar-mate Arminda across the river in Athens… a marvelous way, she tells him, to practice her language.

"Why, did you know," she says, "Arminda and I are studying the forms of adjectives? 'Wise… wiser… wisest'?"

"Yes," he says feeling the rise of a risk inside, "and loving…."

"More loving," she says.

"Most loving." They stare at each other, amazed at their daring.

She doesn't say, "But if there are only two of us there can only be a 'more' and no 'most.'"

He doesn't say, "If 'more loving' is all I can be then that's what I will do."

"Goodbye, Mr. Lincoln," she says and turns to go.

"More goodbye," he calls after her.

She smiles back at him but doesn't stop and turn and say, "No, that's not right at all," because she knows what he means and she likes it and takes it away and says it to herself for days as if it's the most wonderful thing she's ever heard: *More goodbye!*

31

Now Ann needs to really talk to Abe and he has some bad luck that gives her the chance. The time comes as it had to that one of Abe's creditors needs cash, so the Sheriff seizes the only assets he owns, his surveying tools. When Jimmy Short generously buys the tools at auction to return to his friend, the embarrassed Abe hikes to Jimmy's house in Sand Ridge to fetch them so he can get back to work. Knowing Ann will appreciate it, Jimmy tips her off that Abe is coming, and she comes out early to wait for him.

Seeing her line of moisture-loving Forget-Me-Nots shouting tiny hellos in the gray air as she comes down from the porch, Ann shoves away the thought of her tomato and basil plants out back coming up with thin stalks and leaves mottled brown from roots drowning in the soil. Everyone's soggy before morning chores are done these days and by noon there's no ambition. But it's early and as cool as the day is going to get while Ann waits at the crossroads in front of her house. Or in front of where her house would be if the fog hadn't eaten it whole.

When Abe emerges from the mists on his way home from Jimmy's with his tools, she rushes at him to say that she can't get out of the June Camp Meeting coming up and she wants him to come and her mother reckons he can sit with them 'cause he's a family friend and will he come, please.

Abe stops with his clanking gear. He doesn't know what to say, stewing in a turmoil of gratitude and shame at Jimmy's returning his tools. Now he can work again, yes, but thanks to turning another friend to a creditor. For a few months he was the Honorable Abraham Lincoln and now he's a poor boy who sleeps in barns and owes money to all his friends and is about to owe a lot more. Which reminds him of what he really wants to talk with Ann about: whether she's heard from John. He drops his satchel and rods to the ground with a frustrated sigh.

"Mother said, 'Annie, you know you haven't looked good lately. Something's wrong and maybe the Lord can make a difference.' I wanted to tell her that the Lord got me looking the way I look and I don't want to look any moreso."

She watches his glum face which still hasn't started looking happy to see her, even after her joke about god she was sure he'd like.

"'It's what everybody expects,' Mama told me. She doesn't know that's a reason to not want to do it."

She sees his gaze grow more forlorn until he looks away and shakes his head with regret. He feels how she needs him, and he wishes he weren't holding off and leaving her low.

How bad can it be to go to the thing? he thinks. He might have too *good* a time. As a child at the Pigeon Creek Baptist Church he enjoyed the preachers so much that back home he'd jump on a big rock and imitate their sermons while the other kids laughed until his daddy came and hit him on general principle.

Then why not go? he thinks. *The preachers will be as funny as ever. And where else can I be with Ann but family get-togethers and crowds? I'll sit beside her. Our legs will touch. When no one's looking I can squeeze her hand.*

But is it... what?... hypocrisy?... when I won't believe a holy word that fraud of a preacher says? But I don't have to sing the songs, much less get saved. I sit with the family and say pleasant things. And remember what Ann said? When spirits get lifted, skirts get lifted.

Lincoln thinks about Peter Cartwright, the politician-preacher he's seen hold forth in public, demanding that everyone kneel and be saved. If you don't agree with him and his god you're under Satan's command. Abe turns back to Ann with the pained but determined look of a man deciding against himself. He thinks: *I'll be damned if I'm getting down on my knees before Peter Cartwright.*

He says: "I'm sorry, Ann. I can't do it." He wants to move on to ask about John but he can't add that to the woe he knows he's already inflicting on her.

Ann sags. His face in the damp gray air has a look that says there's no use. She turns away and mutters goodbye in a tiny voice and drags her fallen shoulders back to the house while Abe goes off sad and self-justifying. *We and not some itinerant evangelizer in a robe two thousand years ago are responsible for our lives, and I can't pretend otherwise.*

Will Ann's spirit get lifted when he's not around? *I'd better ask Jimmy to keep an eye on her.*

Lincoln picks his way down the muddy road again, alone in the fog with his burden of metal surveying tools.

Why is Ann so hurt that I won't bend for her? Doesn't she know that besides my debts my principles are all I really have?

On the road back to New Salem he changes arms again and again, iron rods in one hand, bag of chains in the other. Tired and thirsty, he stops and drinks from a spring at the edge of a field pooled with standing water.

Nothing's moving, he thinks, *but I have to,* and he picks up his heavy rods and chains and starts walking again. *It's almost June and no McNeil. Maybe he's not moving. Maybe Ann's letter stopped him.*

Or maybe he's coming right now.

32

The wet heat wears on. The water table is up and the waste stays up and neighbors warn each other that springs are going bad so people boil their water for drinking and make hot houses even hotter. Or they boil water outside where the damp fires make ominous smoke in the blanket-like air. Cows dizzy from the heat get fevers from bad grass and pass the fevers to people in milk.

Where's the wind when I need it? Ann thinks. *When everybody does?*

June's Camp Meeting comes and goes with nothing to tell. Nothing that comes up at least when Abe and Ann get to share light talk and furtive looks on her visits to the post office, or at the Saturday markets where she brings cabbages and pound cake to sell and they share the best they can with glances and code what they can't do and say in the open.

At last in late July Ann has the house to herself while her family goes off for the last Camp Meeting of the summer where Peter Cartwright again favors the godly with his sin-hating conversion service. Abe is curious how she kept from going this time. Whatever her strategy, their freedom from the preacher's brimstone is evidence to Lincoln that you can be saved in this world without getting on your knees to a martyr from 2,000 years ago.

"Hello?" As Abe steps into the house, he sees the moss has gotten there ahead of him and is climbing over the threshold into the Rutledge living room.

"Is that you Abraham Lincoln?" Ann calls from the kitchen. "You just come in here and explain yourself!"

"That's a big order, your honor." They embrace uncertainly because they've been distant for a while and didn't part that well the last time they met, but when they step apart they're glad for any way of being together, and he sees she has scissors in her hand. He looks and sure enough Parthena's wedding gown shimmers on the table, and the sight takes him back to the wedding.

A week ago. Sam and Parthena facing Reverend Berry in the little log church with their backs to their family and friends, Parthena in the gown Ann fitted for her. They turned to each other, gave rings. *You may kiss the bride.* And then it happened. When Parthena raised her veil. The gauzy white veil hanging over her face and almost down to her waist came up over her face and back on the top of her head and the top of her dress was revealed. *She* was revealed. The crowd gasped at the display. Some said it was shameless because it was French, some blamed it on New York City, the empire waist-line gathered high below her breasts to project them in their deep wide scallop.

But Abe didn't see Parthena in that bold city dress.

He saw Ann, her breasts soft white temples of her heart, and his heart stopped shocked and he turned where she sat across the room. Their eyes met, she looked down and he looked down and breathed in deeply because he had to and he wanted to look at her again but he didn't dare. When the wedding ended he followed her out of the church at a distance, saw her standing with a group around Parthena,

208

went to shake Sam's sweaty hand and made off before… what? What others might see if he got close to her?

A week later he can be lighthearted. Or try. "Ann, I think you're the one with explaining to do. Will there always be a wedding gown spread on the table?"

She smiles, remembering. She doesn't say, "I know you'll see me in that gown forever and I haven't even worn it yet." The last time he was here she was building it out for Parthena. Now that Parthena's married, she's taking it back in. *Taking it*, she thinks. So she can be *taken*. She shouldn't say more but she can't stop herself. "I guess it'll be spread on one table or the other until it's time to spread it on a bed." She blushes.

He blushes. He doesn't say, "When will that be? Have you heard from John?"

"It's been so hot," he says.

"Yes," she says, "Parthena and Sam are the lucky ones."

"Because they're married?"

"Because being honeymooners they can be naked while we have to wear clothes."

He marvels at how daring she can be, but he hates his own frightened reserve and he's glad when she leads him out of it.

He says, "We owe a lot to Christianity."

"How can a scandalous non-believer say such a thing?"

"First because it tells us that when we meet the conditions we get to lie together…"

"Lie together and…."

"And second we couldn't be here with you teasing me like this if your family didn't have Camp Meeting to go to."

"Amen. Sit down, Brother Lincoln." Ann gestures to the table where Abe takes a chair while she puts down her scissors and gathers the silver-spangled white gown and moves it to the bed across the room.

"And how did you keep from going with them?" Abe says. "And what happened when you went last month? And… and… everything!"

"That's a big order, counsel. Especially from one who has not yet explained himself as initially required by the court. Might I assist the process with a gingerbread procedure?"

"Gingerbread!" he exclaims. "Nobody likes it more…"

"…or gets it less," she finishes for him. "I know your line. And so does Mother. She knows, Abe. I didn't tell her but she knew you were coming. I swear it. But she won't say anything, and I won't ask. She made gingerbread for Camp Meeting but made sure there was plenty to leave with me. More than she knows I'd ever eat."

"Have you told her?"

"Never. She just *knows.*"

"Well, thank heavens it drove her to gingerbread!"

"I'll bring some, but you get started talking. What have you been doing?"

"Tending the mails, studying law, surveying, killing mosquitoes lest they grow so great on my very blood that they bear me off whole to feed all who live in their giant swampy nest. And now going to Springfield to clerk with Stuart a few days at a time. There you have me, your honor. And you?"

Ann brings gingerbread cake on pewter plates and sits and they start to eat and their talk slows as surely as if she wants it to. She looks prim to him this evening, with her hair pulled back tightly and her long dress buttoned high at the neck. As if she has something to be formal about. Or just careful. She isn't newsy but thoughtful, picking at the moist brown square before her. "Mother knew that Christmas day. And when we studied grammar. And when I went to see you speak. And every time I looked up quickly when someone said your name."

"And maybe when you made your excuse for not going to Meeting?"

"Maybe."

"What *was* your excuse?"

"Oh, Abe...."

"Was it a terrible lie?" he asks sympathetically. "Because lying can be justified. I have the rulebook on that, *Lying for Lawyers*...."

He gets the smile he wanted, but not for long. "No," she fights back against his being lighthearted, "and don't you try to excuse me! It was a truth! A terrible truth. I got out by telling her one conversion is enough." She drops her fork on her plate and throws herself back in her chair and looks away. "I got converted at the last Meeting!"

Invited by his gape of disbelief she spills it. "I didn't want you to know. I knew you'd hate it. I don't know why but I went down to the benches in the front where the sinners find god and sobbed on my knees for most of a day and thought like the Pastor said about how low I was and he stood over me and prayed and prayed and at last I stood up and raised my hands and cried *Halleluia!* and accepted Jesus and everybody sang and when it was done I told Jimmy Short that if he told you I'd kill him and we made our way home on the crowded road like sheep back to pasture and I remembered what you said about not letting me see you get shorn and I'd been shorn...."

Still baffled, Abe takes refuge in asking: "Was it true? Was it a lie?"

Ann's voice is small. "I don't know what it was, Abe."

He sees a way out. "Then should we have more gingerbread?"

Ann laughs with tears on her cheeks. She looks at him with a kind of recognition. "I guess I survived it."

"The conversion or the first gingerbread?"

"Stop it!" Ann says, and gets up grinning for cake.

But the important question. He has to ask. His stomach tightens. *Now,* he thinks, *while she's over there and everything is light.*

"You're helping me," she says coming back as if on a cue he doesn't hear but she does, "through the thorns."

"Ah," he says, relieved to be freed from his act of courage. For the moment. "Professor Kirkham. And will his wisdom save us?"

"Yes!" Ann quotes Kirkham's song of praise for grammar as she raises the two plates of cake before him. "It will elevate us to our proper rank in the scale of intellectual standing…."

"Existence," he corrects her. "Intellectual existence."

"… which" she carries on, lifting both hands higher and wider as if gingerbread were unfolding the soul of the world on high between them, 'lifts the soul from earth, and enables it to hold converse with…,' she stops to bring the cake down on the table before him so he can bless it with the final line and he throws his arms wide and proclaims it:

"A thousand… worlds!"

"Amen!" Ann says and bows her head and presses her hands together as if in prayer where she sits across from him smiling.

Abe doesn't know what to make of an "Amen!" from Ann after she's said she's been converted but he trusts her and lets it go.

"We'll do it, Ann," he promises with his gaze going right at her the way it can while it also goes to the sky. "We'll change our worlds. We'll live on a leafy street in Springfield. I'm going there tomorrow to study with Stuart for a month, and in a few years we'll move there and I'll hang my shingle and build you a two-story house like Sam's building Parthena, and you'll have linens and china and teach children in a schoolhouse with real slate blackboards."

"Nothing will stop us?"

He tightens as he thinks of his debt, her family to care for. *But that*, he thinks, *is in the distance. Now I've got to do something else,* he thinks. *I've got to.*

"John," he starts, with an inquisitorial coldness he doesn't like. But he's doing it. "You wrote John in March. Haven't you heard by now?"

Ann rises abruptly and knocks her fork to the floor.

"Maybe I've had too much gingerbread," she jokes as she picks up her fork and takes it to soak with the dirty dishes as if that were the most important thing in the world. Then she turns on him pretending to be playful as she adjusts a loose pin in her hair.

"I thought I heard you ask how I could not have heard from John when you know very well that it has rained continuously for the four months since I writ... wrote... my letter in March. There's not a stream you can still ford without a horse or a rope in Sangamon County. Bridges are out all the way to Cincinnati, five-foot stage-coach wheels are clamped three feet deep in mud, and the steam-boats that carry mail are crashing into rocks in angry river currents. It's going to take you all day to pick your way through the fifteen miles of marshy ruts to Stuart's place when you run out on me to-morrow to study law again in glorious Springfield. The whole United States of America west of New York is practically under water. Maybe that's how I could not have heard from one long-gone traveler a thousand miles away in the East across the vast ruins of Noah's flood!"

He's impressed with her barrage but sure he's in the right. "For four months?"

Ann looks away. "Some of us," she says, defiant, "must maintain a positive view." She goes to the wedding gown on her mother's bed and spreads it carefully and turns to her sewing basket on the bedside table. With her seam-ripper in hand, she goes back to Abe and sees he's as hurt as she is.

"Hold me," she begs.

He rises from his chair and their arms go around each other and he feels her body surrender into him. Their embrace is so comforting and exciting he never wants to let go. She seems small but he knows she's not. She gives him a squeeze then gently pulls away and bends smiling to the gown on the bed to distract herself quickly, finds its seam, proclaims, "Let the gown be prepared for the daughter of the rightful duke!" slices the seam, cuts her finger and shrieks. She spins quickly from the bed to keep blood from the gown but she's late and red drops stain the white as she presses her finger where she's pierced it.

In the chaos of the moment, Lincoln thinks: *Natural language? But....*

Ann looks almost gay.

213

"Mother taught me the Indian trick," she says, and licks her wounded finger. She lifts it to him with blood on its tip. "You put it in your mouth and the bleeding stops."

How does she keep doing things like this? Time slows as her blood-tipped finger come closer to his face. *So... bodily.* He thinks of her "washed in the blood of the lamb," hates Cartwright, hates her kneeling to Cartwright, hates himself for letting her go even a minute into that tyrant's power. Will he remember this when he beats the stern preacher for Congress ten years from now by the highest vote margin Illinois ever saw? No matter, now he takes Ann's finger into his mouth for revenge, takes her into his mouth to taste her salt and sweet in a way he triumphantly feels Cartwright would condemn, and he's drunk and doesn't want to let go, wants all her fingers. Does she see it? She slips another finger between his lips and presses his tongue and his thrill rises and their gazes hold onto each other.

"Captive!" she cries and seizes his tongue between her fingers and his eyes fly wide with the surprise and she frees him and slides her fingers from inside him and they laugh and laugh because there's nothing else they can do. Unless....

"We must clothe my nakedness," Ann says and holds up her cut finger, and Abe marvels at the things she says and breathes deep and cuts a bandage from clean cloth at her direction and they wrap it and tie it on and she's changed the subject as she wanted, but as she folds the gown up to put away she sings unconsciously, almost as low as a thought:

Hard is the fortune of all womankind....

Blood, he thinks. *Flood.* He can't let go of the question on his mind. "Ann, where's that big map of your daddy's?"

Ann's tone says she doesn't like it because she suspects why he wants it. "It's on the shelf right there, right next to the Bible. But you know half the country's changed since they made that map."

"Yes, but they didn't change the rivers."

214

"The rivers?"

"The rivers where the mail goes on steamers when it's not in a stagecoach. And will you point me where his ruler is?"

He moves the dishes and spreads the map on the table. "And a pencil and paper? I'm going to calculate the time the mail would take. John has to have gotten and answered your letter by now."

"You surveyors," she complains while getting what he needs, "think you can measure the world. And speaking of surveying will you be seeing your dear and generous Mrs. Abell?"

"I might," he says and deliberately keeps his head down, busy angling the ruler she's brought him on the map and reading it closely the way she read seams a few minutes ago. "I hadn't thought of it."

"You stayed with her when you first starting surveying. She gave you... Byron."

"Yes." *And may only she know what else.*

"She believes in your future."

"She does. Yes."

"She's felt... what you have to give...."

He stops his note-jotting over the map. *Could she know?* "Ann, no one has ever inspired me like you do."

"She sewed skins on your pants!"

"Yes, she did." He goes back to measuring.

"I can sew!"

"You're the best seamstress there is, Ann. Everyone knows it."

Ann throws herself down in a chair while he stands bending to the map and wishing he could go to a refuge somewhere in it.

"Then why," she complains, "did I cut my finger? If I'm the best at something, why am I a prisoner? Doing what I must for Daddy. What I must for John McNeil. And now you measure my fate on a map like an abandoned lot!"

He stops. "You know you're the only woman I ever cared for."

"I know you went into the woods with Nancy Burner!"

"But we didn't...." He lets that drop and makes some notes.

"Remember when she eloped with Jason Duncan?"

215

"Everybody knew," he says and pauses to make a note then goes on, "she and Jason were…." More notes.

"But people said it was yours!"

He tries to be done with this by leaning closer to his map with his ruler and saying softly, "People get so foolish."

"When?" she demands, standing to look into his face and insist on attention.

"When?" he repeats.

"What makes people turn foolish? Why did I accept Jesus when I don't believe?"

"You'd have to tell me, Ann," he says with a glance before looking back at the map. "But as a humble surveyor I can tell you some facts." He looks at his notes while she slumps into a chair as if she doesn't care.

"You wrote your letter to John on the day I came back from the legislature, March 12, which was a Thursday. And the next day I took it to my post office," here he points where the tiny New Salem dot would be on the map if there were one, "where it waited until the next day, Saturday, for Harvey to take it by horseback to Athens…." His pointing finger traces the route, neglecting with silent pride to mention the section of road he surveyed from Athens to Sangamo Town. "… from which it went on to Sangamo and Springfield. Time: one day at the most from New Salem to Springfield, even if the bridge is out and the rider has to ford the river."

"What do you suppose 'repent' means?"

"Repent?"

"That's what Pastor Cartwright said I had to do."

Abe's face stays intent on his mapping project while at the same time slipping easily into the spelling and defining procedure Mentor Graham taught him.

"Repent. R-e-p-e-n-t. Define? In the language of evangelical preachers converting farmers by the thousands at tent meetings across the western plains to give up sin and be converted to a newer

216

and truer Jesus. Use in a sentence? The preacher told Lincoln that if he'd...."

"I know that, Abe, but what does it really mean? Why is it '-pent' like to keep something in? Pent-up? Keep your sins in? 'Re-pent'? It can't mean to put the sins back in."

"I don't know that I believe in sins, Ann." He reads his ruler and makes a note. "About two inches," he goes on, "by stage coach from Springfield to Cincinnati... and the scale of miles.... Sheep get pent. Whether they do wrong or not. So maybe.. what?... 350 miles to Cincinnati, or even say 500 if the road has to wind through a lot of hills, and the stage makes – what? — five miles an hour? – so maybe a hundred hours there — say four or five days and some. Wait. The sheep? Not in New Salem."

"Not in ?" Ann misses his connection.

"The sheep," he stops to look at her. "They don't get pent here, they wander free."

Ann looks pleased that someone isn't imprisoned. "They're the lucky ones!"

"It doesn't seem like much of a life," he says then goes back to the map. "At Cincinnati the mail goes on a steamer up the Ohio...."

"At least they're free of sin," she argues.

"... to Pittsburgh. But they can be shorn."

She knows so well. "So when Pastor Cartwright said to repent I got confused."

"It looks like Pittsburgh's another 350 miles or so... but eight miles an hour on a steamboat. That's what the *Talisman* Captain told me. So that's... 34 hours. And a few hours for stops. I was five when I first saw a steamboat in Indiana. Wait. Why were you confused?"

"At camp meeting? I wanted to let something out, not put it back in."

"What?"

"John. I wanted John to be gone."

"He is gone, Ann! He's so far away he can't even get mail. He probably doesn't even exist!"

"But he does exist, Abraham Lincoln, and I'm engaged to be married to him! What you and I want can never be! John won't let me go. He's stubborn. He won't let anyone best him. He's inside me and is holding me with a demon grip!"

She blinks her eyes and looks away. "He's coming."

"He's gone."

"His hands take my waist."

"No."

She's urgent. "He presses toward me." Is she imagining, foreseeing or remembering?

"Ann...."

"His eyes fasten...." Abe sees her alarm and reaches for her hand.

"He doesn't exist."

"...his lips...." She twists to escape.

"He's a cold and deceiving man who never cared but to own you."

She clutches her heart. "He owns me."

"He's gone. He doesn't care. He doesn't answer your letters. He...."

"He does!" she shouts. "He sends fevered messages I tear open with trembling fingers. Hundreds of letters come in through the windows. They fall from the trees when I walk in the oaks. They fly in the wind when I walk in the storm. He must have me, they say, he'll never let me go!"

"Ann...."

She weakens and her voice gets small. "If he wrote that's what he would say. That's what...."

"Ann, come here by me and sit." He leads her gently by her hand and he guides her to the chair beside him.

"Gingerbread," he says and takes both of her hands in his as she sits and looks at her softly. "Gingerbread will save us. Let's forget all the rest for a while."

Ann's face relaxes into her weariness and she gets up and goes slowly to the kitchen as they go on talking.

"Mother *knows*," Ann says. "She knows I'm a sinner. That's why she wanted me to go to Meeting."

"What did you ever do wrong?"

She pauses. Then speaks slowly. "Well... here I am... *flirting*. Is that what this is? With you... while I'm... promised...."

"You wrote John. That was honorable. You told him. And where is his answer?"

Ann presses her heart in dread and says in a low voice, "I'm afraid it's here in my breast."

"And I'm afraid," Abe says, impatient to beak up the gloom, "that it's lost in the mail." He stands and pulls the map close before him as Ann cuts fresh slices of gingerbread on the other side of the table.

"Then from Pittsburgh," he says, and puts his ruler down there. "I don't know for sure how the mail goes from Pittsburgh, but probably up to Cleveland or Erie on Lake Erie, like...so... and then east on the lake to Buffalo and the Erie Canal and at last your letter's in northern New York where John's family is."

"John's family...."

"I'd say two days from Pittsburgh up to Lake Erie. Even in the worst of weathers. A day or two across the lake to Buffalo? Then a day... call it two to be generous... two more days on the canal boat with horses towing?" He writes his numbers.

"He's bringing them here to live." Ann's voice has no life now but Abe's too excited by the climax of his calculation to notice.

"Not since he's gotten your letter, he's not. That's... say... six days from Pittsburgh. Then probably horseback from the canal to his town. What's the name of his town?"

"New Ohio."

"New Ohio?" he repeats studying the map. "Did he say what it's near?"

"Not that I recall," Ann says as if nothing matters now. "It's on the Black River, he told me. Does the map have Black River?"

"Black River... Black River.... Yes, here it is!"

"It's here too," Ann says, touching her heart. "Black River."

219

"Well, it doesn't look more than a day from the canal to any place on Black River as far as it goes. Let me add up the days…."

Ann mutters, "Black River in my heart."

"So, it's one day to Springfield and five to Cincinnati and two to Pittsburgh and six more from Pittsburgh up to the lake and across, and then maybe two finishing off to a place on Black River… sixteen days. Sixteen days in normal weather. Now let's double the whole thing. Double it all for the flooding and call it a month and a little more." His words quicken as he goes on. "A month to get there, and you gave me your letter for the mail in late March so John would have gotten it in late April, or call it the start of May. And if we figure another month for the return, then John could have gotten a letter back to you at least by early June. And even if it took until the middle of June, that would have been six weeks ago!"

"But…."

"But… yes." His words speed faster, his face quickening with a new idea. "Say John didn't want to answer your letter because his heart was heavy as any man's would be with your loss, and say it took him a month to make himself write you a reply and post it. You still would have gotten his answer weeks ago!"

There's a silent pause, and then Ann gets up and goes toward the kitchen and says, "I don't want John's answer."

He's confused. "Are you all right, Ann?"

She comes back with tin mugs of coffee and looks at him defiantly and puts them on the map. "No. I'm not all right. I'll never be all right."

"Well… I think it's unfair of him not to write. Promise me that if his letter comes in the next month while I'm in Springfield, you'll send word right away."

Ann drops her hard mood and says in a low voice, "I've failed you."

"Impossible!" he exclaims.

She looks at him with an appeal for forgiveness. "I was heartless to you after Row killed his wife."

220

"We got through those thorns," he says. She's stepped toward him and her face is close. "You tell me I can do anything. I saw your face behind the falling stars."

"You're on your way to something… grand…."

"I am, Ann, thanks to you. And you are too. We'll go to balls and you'll wear gowns…." *Gowns* gives him the right to look at her from the top of her head to her toes, and he does. "And they'll marvel what a beauty like you is doing with a homely cuss like me."

She leans back to appraise him, happy with his roving eyes. "They won't say that when they see you dance."

His excitement vanishes with the threat of dancing. "Dance? You know I can't dance."

Ann's eyes brighten. "Oh, no, Governor Lincoln, but you can dance and will! The bailiff will remove the prisoner's shackles." She takes his hand and steps him toward the center of the room. "Yes, you, Mr. Lincoln."

"Are you sure?"

"I believe you remember, Mr. Lincoln, the night of the wicked *Talisman* captain? The jaded-looking one who danced a strange dance on the deck with the woman who was *not his wife?*"

Ann looks flushed, but she has him by the hand and she's leading him into something the way she knows she can and he feels it coming and it scares him but it's all he wants.

"Well," Ann raves on, "this infamous 'waltz' was the talk of the township's women, who had heard its reputation, and thanks to the roguish captain seen by mystical torchlight it was suddenly manifested from Lord Byron's Europe direct to our sleepy frontier. And it wasn't so awful. It doesn't hurt a bit. I learned from Arminda the next week, and I can teach you. Arminda's father does it! If it's good enough for the postmaster of Athens, Illinois, it's good enough for the postmaster of New Salem!"

She pulls him gently to the center of the room. "You know that Colonel Rogers has more books than Daddy. And Arminda has been to the Methodist Female Academy in Jacksonville, and she would

221

never teach me anything truly evil. At least not unless I begged her. Now hold out your hands like this."

Abe resists giving up control, but there's no way out. *Delay.* "Do you really know how to waltz?"

She smoothes back and re-pins her hair. "Every daughter of a ruined duke knows how to waltz."

What can he do? He reaches out as Ann again mimes for him and she shows and tells him how to hold her with his large left hand high with her small right hand in it and the long calloused fingers of his right hand pressing her back and their fronts just barely touching.

"Does this seem scandalous?" she teases as if seeing inside him. "Don't answer. Yes, your right hand between my shoulder blades."

"Between your wings?"

"Yes. Like that. My wings? Am I a bird?"

"An angel." He steps back slightly to stop thinking about their touching.

She shakes her head. "If only you knew."

"A messenger angel." He leans close to smell the message of her hair.

"The President," she says, "does this in Washington."

"This close?"

"This close."

"They say the country is going to hell," he says.

"But you like it?"

"The Baptists say it's a sin." He banters to escape his growing excitement.

"Waltzing?" she says.

"Dancing."

"But do you like it?" she insists with a teasing smile, feeling his urge to pull her close, and his fear.

"That it's a sin?"

"The closeness!" She lunges to give him a squeeze for a make-believe penance then breaks off and starts moving things, and he sees what she's up to and is relieved to stop having to hold himself back and helps her widen the open center of the room.

"Our ballroom," she says as they set aside the rocker, a lamp and lamp table....

"Our private ballroom where no one can see my clumsy...."

"Our intimate island nation where only we...."

"The duke's daughter."

"And the prince disguised as a swineherd...."

"A swineherd!"

"*Disguised* as a swineherd. A woodsman. But in truth a noble."

"A wooden noble," he concedes.

Enough furniture moved, Ann goes to the center and gestures him to her. "Ah, but be not stiff my wooden noble, for the time has come to step lightly."

"M'lady knows not what she asks," he says and wonders what she does know and stands next to her as she directs so she can show him the step before he leads her.

"Lead you?" he exclaims. "There *is* a first time for everything!"

"You watch my feet."

"Your feet are so small."

"Next to your great flatboats they are. But yours will be a gentleman's feet when they step as you will learn if you hush and follow," Ann says, and standing beside him she takes him through it, starting with his left foot forward on one, his right foot forward and to the right on two, the left closing to the right on three. Going back starts with the right, then the left back and to the left on two, the right closing to it on three.

They repeat until he sees the pattern and sees where it gets him: "The back undoes where the forward went."

Playfully scorning his philosophizing, Ann faces him with her best contessa pose and extends her right hand upward to invite his left. As her left hand goes to his shoulder the long reach of his right finds her back and draws her close.

"I'll count and you move your feet as we practiced and I'll do the opposite facing you," she says, and they set forth with care on her slow counting:

"Fore… two… three. Back… two… three. Fore… two… three. Back…."

"Doing…," he says.

"…two, three."

"What none thought…."

"One…

"Could be done."

"…two, three. Hush… two, three. One… two, three. One… two, three. One… two, three. One… two, three…."

She looks up and smiles at the merriment on his lips, his eyes sparkling against his will.

She's in my arms, he thinks.

He counted the time for her letter, she counts it for their dance. But faster.

"See?… two, three. How we… two, three. Fly?… two, three."

"I…." Abe's grinning but at the edge of control. "I don't…."

"Like the wind!" she calls with her head back and quickens. "…, two, three. One, two, three. One, two, three."

"Too…," he says.

"One two three…."

"…fast!"

"Onetwothree. Onetwothree. Onetwothree. Onetwothree…."

"Ann!"

"Onetwothreeonetwothreeonetwothreeonetwothree…."

"Stop!" he shouts and pulls away but keeps her hands to slow her.

"Stop!" Ann loses her balance against his strength and she falls and he falls on top of her. Unhurt, he gets to his knees to see if she's hurt and sees tears on her cheeks where hair clings like red streaks of resentment. She pulls herself up to sit and looks at him angrily and looks away.

"Maybe I wanted to burn it out," she says.

"Burn what?"

"The answer."

"The answer? What do you mean?"

"Here." Her fingers press the cloth between her breasts.

"What do you mean?"

"The letter. Here. Hold me tight, Abe. Hold me."

She reaches out and he pulls her to him and they cling on their knees.

"What letter?"

"John's letter."

"John's letter? What do you mean?"

"It's here. You're pressing it. Hold me!"

"It's here? A letter that flies in the wind?"

"A real letter."

"His letter came?"

"I hid it in my breast."

"What does it say?"

"Poison. Death."

"But...."

"You were away when Daddy brought it from town."

"Why didn't you tell me?"

"I couldn't."

"You couldn't...."

"I couldn't. It fused with my heart, it put roots in my blood. I'm frightened, Abe!"

"What does it say?"

"Read it. Take it from me."

"Me? But...."

"You have to do it. My finger. You take it out."

"I can't."

"Open my dress." She touches her bodice. "Put your fingers here...."

"Ann...." Does she hope the danger of touching will stop him?

"Unbutton me.... Spread my dress!"

225

"But…. I don't…." Clumsily, shaking, kneeling with her, he starts her top button.

"Yes! It burns me!"

"But…." He has her dress unbuttoned to the white frill crossing the cleft of her breasts.

"You must. Down in my chemise."

"Your…." He says uncertainly and reaches timidly into her dress.

"Yes!" she cries as his fingers slide between her breasts, and she squeezes his shoulders as his fingers stretch to explore the softness there.

"I have it!"

"Did Nancy cling when you touched her?"

He brings a cylinder of paper out.

"When you opened her?"

"I'm going to…"

"Did she open you?" She reaches for the buttons of his shirt.

He sees only the letter. "I'm going to open…."

"Like this?" she says, unbuttoning his shirt.

"…the letter."

"Don't open it!" she cries. She tries to take it but he twists away.

"Ann…."

She lunges to her feet and rushes a few steps off and stands looking away with her arms folded while Abe gets up too as if to take the letter standing and he reads it to himself in the silence and then exclaims: "He refuses!"

She nods with her arms crossed and a tear rolling down her cheek, and says as if to herself: "He owns me."

"But what does this mean?" Abe says, and he reads from the letter:

> Beyond regard for financial matters in which I
> have no desire to see you and your family hurt,
> you will understand better than anyone else
> why your marriage with another man would be
> inappropriate after the things you and I have done
> together. Things which out of concern for you I
> would not want to come to public knowledge.

226

Ann unfolds her arms and spreads them upward in supplication as if she were the wife in "Matty Groves" when the lord pins her to the wall with his sword. She cries, "Where is the wind that will take me from this world?"

"Ann, what does it mean?"

"You won't want me," she mutters and turns to him but avoids his eyes. Then she looks up, animated. "John marked me! Inside. Before he left...," she stares into Abe's eyes as she floods out the hated history, "...he said he was going away and I had to show him I was his. Doing *that* would make us married. He was urgent and took me to his store, the one you moved into later. It was night. It was empty and he unlocked it and we went in and he *made* me. Made me *his* on the counter. I was so weak! Afraid! Would he hurt Daddy? Ruin my family? Better me. Me. And we were going to get married. I was an object! His object! Governed, pushed into by the demon... *taken*...."

Abe's shoulders are slack, his face gray. Ann steps to him and throws her arms around him but he doesn't move, only mutters trance-like, "... cursed..." and Ann steps back from him and quickens.

"Cast it out, Abe!" He hears a force in her voice that won't be denied and raises his gaze to hers. "We'll cast it out," she says, stepping toward him with her eyes fixed on his as she unbuttons her disheveled dress. "Together!" She pulls the top of her dress back from her shoulders and tears the pins from her hair to set it loose down her breast and his arms open wide and he knows that if there's promise in the world she brings it rushing to his embrace.

"Make me yours, not his!" she says and spreads his open shirt while he follows her eyes to his belt and reaches to unbuckle it. "Lay hands on me," she implores him as she slips his shirt off his shoulders and kisses his chest. Warmly she implores as she kneels on the bed and pulls down her chemise and draws his hands to her breasts: "Touch me and heal me..." and when their lips come together they're lost and Ann's breasts sway free as she turns to draw him down to the pillows and Abe pushes her skirt up to her waist and she reaches

227

between his legs to bring him to her. She moans as she takes in his longing. "Possess me!" she whispers into his mouth as if her words are his, and again and again he clings and she swings loose and as if in a dream she runs and he catches her, she flies and he soars to find her, and each time he's to her she turns and captures him in the moist center of the world. "Possess me…" she whispers into his mouth as if to put words there for him to say while she takes him, "Possess me and set me free!"

At last they return to themselves in the stillness and lie touching in the low lamplight, stunned at what they've done. Ann pushes herself up on her elbow to lean down to him. He sees the fires in her eyes between the falls of her auburn hair.

Softly she asks, "Now is my face in the stars?"

"Better," he says.

"How can that be?"

"I'm in the stars with you," he says. He thinks for a moment. "Or are they in us?"

"Nobody talks like you!" she cries and throws herself on him and he gives himself up and he's inside her again and slowly, slowly the wind takes them once again starward, and later when he dozes he dreams that she tells him she's not going to be a teacher but a constellation.

"You were right," she tells him in the dream. "The light is in us. Along with the darkness."

33

It rains so much until the end of July that when it stops a few hours, even if you wait before you go into the woods, you still feel the trees crying on you in the dark. Bird song is a surprise not a constant, as if the rain stole it all except a few notes of warning here and there under heavy branches. Nobody can explain how it's so wet and so hot at the same time. Then August brings such a change that nobody cares what used to be.

In August the clouds go, the ones overhead and the ones you got used to walking and talking and doing your work and eating your dinner in. The clouds go away and there's nothing but sun. People think: *Hooray!*

But it's a mean sun. Its big hard dry yellow blare withers the rain-mottled wheat and corn and burns people's skin bright red and keeps animals, including humans, lying all day in the oven-like shade that's as precious as food. More precious than food because who feels like eating.

Late in that foundry of an August its over-hot stillness explodes into a tornado tearing through New Salem slamming barns into splintered boards and toppling fences and trees and uprooting the last hopes of farmers that they might still have a crop after their corn and wheat and beans have mostly died slow deaths from the flooding of their roots beneath the ground. A torrential rain the twister brings-in overnight flattens the last of their mottled plants and the next morning the sunny quiet comes back like something you thought you wanted but you might never trust again. A mother duck of a kind Ann's never seen before scurries past her window followed by two quacking ducklings, and an hour later two wolves go by in the same direction with their tongues out, not even looking around. That afternoon Ann takes to bed with a fever.

A few days later Abe knocks a courtesy knock and walks into the Rutledge living room where Ann smiles at him from the first floor bed her parents have given her so they don't have to nurse her up in the loft.

"And is it the great lawyer Lincoln himself descending from his cloud?"

"It's jack-of-all-trades Lincoln stumbling off the bumpy stage from Springfield when I heard you need me. What's wrong, Ann?"

"Tell me how we got here, counsel," she says kindly.

He pulls up one of Robert Johnson's ladder back chairs from the table on the other side of the room and sits by her bed and takes her hand. "You mean how did we get here with you lying down receiving callers like the queen? Your hand is so warm! Should I call Doctor Allen?"

"He was here this morning."

"Good," he says, though it doesn't look good to him. "Lay back, Ann, and let me get you a drink. How long have you been sick?"

"It's just a fever. But how else could I receive you in my nightie?"

"The fever hasn't changed you. What does Doctor Allen say?" He's up and pouring a tin cup of water from a pitcher on the bedside table.

"He says not to worry. Did you hear about the tornado?"

"I saw it. All the way from Springfield... we heard the rumble, and the bunch of us ran out of Stuart's office and saw it coiling across the sky out this way. Did anybody get hurt? Here," he says and he can feel her heat as he lifts her head to help her drink.

"Crops and animals and years of repairs," she says and her head drops on her pillow like stone.

"Thank heavens I'm not a farmer," Abe says.

"Lawyer Lincoln...."

"Now, you might not get another drink if you tease me, Ann. You know I'm not a lawyer yet. I just had most of a month in Stuart's office, but tomorrow I'll be a surveyor again, poking through the brambles to divide a farm. In the inferno. Maybe you got your fever from the heat. Maybe we've all got fevers. In Springfield the judges let the lawyers in court in their shirtsleeves, and the women are abandoning petticoats. Or so the married men tell me. But I'm worried about you...."

"Don't do that, Abe. We mustn't disobey the doctor, and he said not to worry. And what I've got is scenic. Do you see the roses on my neck and shoulders?"

"I see them. But...."

"A girl gets herself up and he doesn't make a fuss."

"I noticed when you put flowers in your hair."

"I did, didn't I? And I thought no one really ever did that, only girls in songs. But that day I couldn't help it."

"I couldn't help it either, Ann. Any of it."

"Tiny blue flowers... and I danced instead of walking!"

"You ran!"

"I ran but I let you catch me."

"You *let* me?"

"And then we decided."

"Everything."

"Everything. In the mud and the rainbow and fording the swollen river when you carried me."

231

"I did?"

"I made that up."

"I like it. And I've been thinking about everything."

"Everything, Abe? How like you. But you know of course, that I *am* everything."

"Of course you are, Ann. And I thought about you all the time in Springfield."

"And?"

"We said we'd get married after John comes and we talk with him but I think we should get married right away."

"And if he tells the world about me?"

"That's *his* dishonor. And besides, Ann, it doesn't matter. Half the children in New Salem are conceived without marriage. Lovers couple at Camp Meeting while the Christians listen! The only women who can claim to be pure as snow are the ones so cold they don't matter."

He's resolute and she sees it and turns to the window.

"After what I did?" she says and looks at him so he knows she wants an answer. She sees him get wavy as her fever rises.

He smiles, embarrassed. "After what *we* did."

She's grateful but worried too. "But what I did *to you*. I deceived you. I spoke to you cruelly. Can you forgive me?"

He's earnest. "I thought about it in Springfield. I tried to escape everything but I couldn't. The mess we're in. It's like the stars falling. Every day. Somebody in Stuart's office would say something and it was like they were waking me up. But then I saw it."

"What?"

"Your face." He takes her hand again. It's so warm he wonders if he'll make it worse by holding it, but he can't let go.

"You saw my face?"

"Like that night the stars fell but your face was still there. With that one star that winked."

"A star that winked? Did it really?"

"I made that up."

"I like it." She wants to grin but she's weak. She's weak but not as weak as the times she hardly knows where she is. And sometimes her fever dips and she's cold and she's frightened how clear and sharp-edged the world gets. But it's worse when she gets wound up and her fever runs her mind around and around.

In her weakness she feels him lift and kiss her hand, and hears him say: "Every sorrow you give me shows me how much I love you."

Ann starts to smile, but her smile wanes and she takes her hand from his and turns to the window and says as if to herself, "Will your next sorrow be as good for you?"

He asks what she said but her strength's coming back and she's moving on. She turns to him. "You made me think of *Kirkham.*"

"Professor Kirkham," he says cheerfully, "who brought us together?"

"The very one, counsel. How I miss him! Can you put into evidence our famous lines from Lecture One? About lifting our souls?"

"I'll try, your honor, but it might be patchy. There's something about unfolding and maturing our powers… and… yes… elevating our… what? something about the scale of intellectual existence…."

"Yes!"

"And…" here Lincoln can't keep from rising slowly from his chair, "lifting the soul from earth…."

"…the very soul from earth!" Ann raises her arms and lifts her head from her pillow as Abe rises, and they elevate together with Kirkham's language while laughing inside.

Standing, Abe lifts his palms to the sky while his upward gaze gives thanks for the miracle: "… to hold converse with a thousand worlds!"

"Ah!" Ann's head falls back to her pillow in consummation. And exhaustion.

"How did my story," Lincoln asks as he sits back down, "remind you of that?"

"It wasn't that. No. Your adventure with the stars reminded me of mine with the wind."

"And Kirkham?"

"Remember what he wrote about 'natural language'?"

"Signs."

"Exactly! I heard what I heard out behind the barn. What I needed, crude and what does he say, *brute*? I held converse! But the winds disappeared." Ann stops and pats the sweat on her forehead and upper lip with her sheet. "Could the winds have been there all summer and I didn't notice? I don't know. But I know they came back hard and wrecked the town and here I am."

Abe knows better than the drift of this, he thinks, but what is it?

"Abe?" He's glad she interrupts his thinking. "I need you to do something for me."

"Of course, Ann."

"It's just for a minute and then I want you to go right back to Kirkham, or the stars…." She's losing focus and he won't hold still for her to see.

"I'll go back to getting married."

"Getting married, then," she says absent-mindedly. "Is there a bucket of water at the foot of the bed?"

"Yes."

"I need you to pick that up and pour it on my sheets."

He notices what he missed in his urgency to see her. Ann isn't just covered by the single light cloth you might expect in weather like this, but piled with a mound of wet sheets. Above them the tips of her hair, dark with moisture, cling to her neck. Her hair seems a deeper red now, almost brown, and the floor boards around her bed are dark with dampness.

"Doctor Allen," she says, "has us do this to bring down my fever."

Abe's up now and going for the bucket, relieved to be able to help. "How does it feel when that water comes on you?"

"It shocks me. Then my mind gets clear."

"That's good," he says as he lifts the heavy water.

"Sometimes I don't like it."

Leave it to Ann. "Why not?" he says. He rests his bucket on the footboard.

"Because I see… well…. But I don't like it either when I'm hot and undone… things… float…." He's struck by the way her thinking's coming apart and her face is flushing so pink he can hardly see the freckles he knows her by.

"Shall I?" he says.

"Yes. Please. Pour away."

"From your neck to the bottom of your bed?"

"Yes," Ann says, "that's fine. Splash it on."

"The whole bucket?"

"Now!" she cries. "Stop measuring and pour…!"

He dashes the water on her.

"Aaaaaaaaaaaaaa!" she cries. "God, that's cold! God, god, god!

"Are you all right, Ann?"

"I am, I am, I am, I really am. Yes, O god, that feels better. I'm sorry I was hard, Abe. I'm sorry." Tears shine in her eyes which stand out a darker blue now that her skin's so white with cold.

"Why are you crying?" he says, but he's comforted too as her freckles emerge again in her whitening skin.

"It's all right. That's not crying… it's just… some tears… it's over now. Now… tell me what you were talking about. Your closing argument, and then I'll rule."

"And where was I, your honor?"

Ann's wet eyes go wide with alarm. "No, Abe! Where was *I?* I failed you so badly!"

He sits again and takes her hand to soothe her. "Objection, your honor. Such sentiments are out of order when your health and happiness are paramount and I am determined that all will be well."

Ann calms as he pets her arm, and he goes on. "Your behavior has been as it had to be, and is guaranteed to have the finest of results according to an advanced and subtle theory I will explain."

She sighs. "The Plan? You dazzle me, Mr. Lincoln."

"My goal, entirely, your honor."

235

"Proceed." Her strength is coming back and she wants to be a partner in his venture. "And you will clarify the benefit of my failing at first to send to John for my release when I promised I would?"

"That, your honor, was a Test of my Love."

"Really?" She sees him blurring. "You're getting…. I'm getting…."

He's up now and pacing because he sees it. He doesn't know where he'll find the money… *Money!*

"I couldn't let it stop me…. what John did. He's the one dishonored and I'll tell him. Paying off your father's debts and taking care of your family is the least I owe your father for building the dam that stopped me at your tower."

"Water, Abe!" she calls out. "Water!"

He sees how red she is and she points him to a row of a dozen buckets of water her daddy and Jimmy Short have lined up beneath the window, and he grabs one and pours a deluge over sheets and bed and floor.

"God, god, god!" Ann shouts and starts shivering and something reminds her of Pastor Cartwright's conversion that was so intense but didn't last. "Oh! That's so good and so bad!"

"Does it really help?" He looks down, concerned.

"I can see you so clearly now, Mr. Lincoln. Ah!" she exclaims compassionately, "Mr. Lincoln!"

Abe doesn't like being suddenly Mr. Lincoln, but Ann is Ann. "What, Ann?"

"You are so wonderful, but you will be so tragically sad. But you need not be."

He sits down and takes her white hand and its coolness seems alarming. "What do you mean, Ann? Tell me."

"I'll tell you, Abe. But first you must tell me. You must tell me so that I, who am the judge, may judge. Counsel will please put into evidence the lovely and dreadful poem he so clings to on the subject of mortality.

"Really, Ann?"

"Absolutely."

"You want me to say the poem?'
"Exactly. Will you?"
"O why should the spirit…"?
"The very one."
"Of course, your honor. But are you sure I shouldn't go? You seem…."
"Continue, please."
"I rise to recite."
"Please."
Abe stands and puts both hands over his heart, then opens his arms and slowly spreads his palms wider as he declaims stanzas from the poem of life's transience he's nourished his gravity on for years.

> Oh, why should the spirit of mortal be proud?
> Like a swift-fleeting meteor, a fast-flying cloud,
> A flash of the lightning, a break of the wave,
> He passes from life to his rest in the grave.
> They loved – but the story we cannot unfold;
> They scorned – but the heart of the haughty is cold;
> They grieved – but no wail from their slumber will come
> They joyed – but the tongue of their gladness is dumb.
> 'Tis the wink of an eye, 'tis the draught of a breath,
> From the blossom of health to the paleness of death,
> From the gilded saloon to the bier and the shroud,—
> Oh! why should the spirit of mortal be proud?

Ann interrupts. "My heart is breaking, Abe." Her face becomes forlorn at how forlorn he'll be.
"What's wrong, Ann?'
"It's not me, Abe. It's you."
"What do you mean?"
"…the thorns."
He looks at the red marks brightening again on her neck and worries. "But you're a garland of roses, you said so."
"But roses have thorns."

237

"Thorns… interspersed," he quotes Kirkham, "like intricacies too difficult for the juvenile mind to unravel."

"Yes! That's how it is! Oh! More water, Abe. I'm on fire!"

Abe again splashes water over her sheets and she shivers and moans, and then smiles. "How can that be the worst thing and the best!"

"Intricacies too great for the juvenile mind…."

"Yes! Do you remember when we talked about death? We were joking like Shakespeare characters, and you said something like, "All men do think death wrong.""

"Yes?"

"Well, maybe it's not death but people who are wrong. Maybe death seems the worst thing that can happen but is the best."

"Do you mean it's good to die?" He sits and pulls his chair closer. He loves when she philosophizes.

"What if everyone who dies is trapped," she says, "and needs to go on? If we're stuck on the dam or in a web or our body's walls and we need to move on like water or wind. A motion and a spirit through all things in the living air! We see death's sorrow, but not its joy!"

He doesn't follow her. "What's joyful in death?"

"Freedom!" she exclaims in blue sparks from Forget-Me-Not eyes.

"To be free of the body?" he says, trying to follow.

"Ah, milord doth grip in hopeful air."

"Or grasp nothing."

"Or nothing he could lose."

"Ann, what are you talking about?"

Her voice is level. "I'm dying, Abe."

"No!"

"I heard Dr. Allen tell Daddy."

"No!" He grabs her hand to pull her up and steal her but stops and closes his eyes and tears start and his head falls toward hers and he caresses her face with his fingers. "No, no, no."

"Your hands are so cold!" she says, worried for him not herself, but he shakes his head slowly and she puts her free hand to her cheek and knows. "It's me. But am I fevered with death or life?"

He takes both of her hands in his and shakes his head. "I won't let you die! We'll get the doctor back. All the doctors!"

"Abe, remember when you said that your accepting my not writing John… that that was a Test of your love? Well, this is a Test. Now. A bigger Test."

"What do you mean?"

"If you keep crying like that, you'll be as wet as I am."

"I'm sorry, Ann."

"The court gives counsel leave to cry. But listen to me now. You say your love has overcome a lot?"

"Yes?"

"Now it will overcome death."

"Impossible!"

"Because none have done it? What was that line from *Kirkham* we had to repair?

My ancestors virtue is not mine? Well, good riddance! No more virtues of women slaves all their lives. No more lists of what I must do and not do just to be proper. Begone! You would have been proud, Abe. This morning. Dr. Allen started to shave my hair. I said No. He said, Annie, we have to expel your fever to save your life. I said I doubted he'd save a life that way, I'd seen it done with three others and nobody lived. He said I'll have them hold you down if we have to. I said I have a mother who loves me and won't let that happen. I looked at her and she looked at Daddy across the bed and Daddy turned and walked away. God bless them both. If there were a god. I did it because of you."

"I don't care how you look, Ann."

"I don't mean that! I wouldn't let you see me shorn! You taught me! I'll stay with my wet clumps and bolts and threads and kites of hair… kites to carry me… soaring…."

"Nobody talks like you."

239

"Nobody has you. You and *Kirkham*. Where is *Kirkham,* Abe? Will you get it?"

"On the bookshelf," she says as he gets up to find his way through his blur of tears. "With Mother's *Bible* and Daddy's map. There! Bring it. Read it, will you? What I've marked?"

Abe opens the book's chapped deerskin cover and finds his pressed blue flower marking a page and reads aloud Ann's penciled underlining:

> Don't be afraid to *think for yourself.* You know
> not the high destiny that awaits you. You know not
> the height to which you may soar…. Go on, then,
> boldly, and… unyielding….

"You see?" Ann says. "…boldly… unyielding…. If you love me you must go on boldly and love what dies as well as lives!"

He doesn't know what she means but he knows he'll do anything. "I do love you, Ann."

She smiles. "Do you remember when I said *I do* when I should have said *I will?*"

He sees back to the rainbow over the mud when they decided.

"Well," she says, "now is the time for us both to *do*. You said so when you came in."

"What?"

"We must get married right away."

"As soon as you're better…."

"There is no soon, Abe. Now!" Her face in natural language says: *Nothing will stop me.*

"Sheets off…" she commands. "…that the ceremony might begin!" She tugs, weak but determined, at her pile of sheets, and he helps her peel and heave off the mound of wet cloth until sharp flecks prick his fingers in the final cloth.

"What's this around you?"

"My gown."

240

He sees on the damp-dimmed cloth she's wrapped-in the spots of her blood that escaped like hidden truth when she cut herself in July. "You've got...."

"... the wedding gown, my groom."

"Parthena's...."

"Mine. Mine as *you* are. For I have *taken* you, have I not? And you me. And will you join me in church? The Holy Church of Impropriety?" She pats the bed next to her, and he knows what she means.

"Our ancestors' virtues are not ours," she says as he comes to her. "No rings, or matrons, or preacher, or flowers...." Abe is so won by her unlikely wedding plan that he feels the terror men feel at their weddings as he sits beside her and she closes her eyes and he folds his long legs in next to hers and slides close and lies with her warmth in her gauzy gown.

"Ann..." he says and he wants to tell her something but he doesn't know what and can only put his arms around her and press to her fevered body. Her hair floods his cheek, and her lips at his ear whisper like wind through sky roaring and tumbling with stars: "And she is everything as she spreads her wings!" And with her lips on his lips she whispers in his mouth as she whispered when he was inside her: "And they are one with the spirit that moves through all things... life and death together...." Her voice thins to air: "... moving... moving...."

Her eyes are closed, her breathing light.

He waits, holds her. *Is she sleeping?* He lingers, remembers, wishes, prays... yes, prays. Lulled by her low breath, he dozes.

The wind moans at the open window and wakes him. Ann's eyes are closed and he stands carefully so he doesn't disturb her and he looks down at her and sees her at peace and sees her plundered from him with her blood-dark hair spilling on her sparkling white gown from a fairy tale. He remembers the gravestone the night he walked to her...

Life is not forever
And neither is death

... but there's no consolation and he collapses on his knees and his head falls on her breast and he surrenders to the storm of his despair.

34

Lincoln sees people he knows in Concord Cemetery. It's twenty-six years later and he's visiting New Salem from his home in Springfield and here on his left as he comes in the graveyard is his old partner Berry's stone and Abe remembers Berry in his brown tweed jacket lifting his warped green bottle to his Holy Spirits. Right ahead, close to the center of the place, set off with an iced-over black iron rail, is the thick silver granite marker for Mr. Rutledge, a place of honor for the man who built the dam that started the town and made...well... *everything*... possible.

Abe turns at Ann's father's grave and crunches his big flat steps through the snow past the grave of her mother who always knew, and his hand goes reflexively to his jaw to feel the strangeness of the beard Ann never saw.

Will she know me? She always knew me. Will a rose and thorn twine up from her grave? No, he thinks, *that isn't our story. Our story is our story.* He looks out to the wider world as if for confirmation and sees

243

from the hillside graveyard a view over miles of flat white fields to one tiny cabin lifting a thin curl of woodsmoke from its chimney in the hazy cold. *Even if we're the only ones who know it.*

"Hello, your honor," he says looking down at Ann's slender gray headstone with shining white snow on its thin top edge. "Did you watch me coming up the hill? Not much moving on that prairie, is there? Not much moving in the territory. I came up through New Salem and you wouldn't know it. Sam and Parthena moved to Petersburg since the last I was here. And grim old Onstot and his cooper's shop with them. The Tavern's closed now, but Dr. Allen's still there beside it. Henry McHenry's gone to Bobtown, Jimmy Short's in Iowa, and Mentor moved west too… South Dakota, I think."

Thinking he should shut up but not knowing what to do but talk, Lincoln sways from foot to foot at the stone that's so unlike her that he stops seeing it and sees her instead. "'Course some of our old friends are here with you. Do they come out at night?" He smiles. "I saw Berry on my way in. And your daddy… and your mother over there who knew.

"And talk about knowing, I remember you said we don't know what death is. Now do you know?

"I don't know much," he goes on. "But I know this: I'm going to Washington. Four years. I'm going to be President, like you said. Or wait. Did you say that? You didn't? That was my other wife?"

"My other wife!" he goes on. "That's what you'd say, isn't it?"

And she says, "You know what I say, Abe. We can't let death shut me up. So, the prince disguised as a woodcutter came into his own?"

"Came into his own, your ladyship?"

"No naughty thoughts, Mr. Lincoln. That's more my line of work. Which reminds me, counsel, that the poem you put in evidence in our final hearing was in error."

"How so?"

"Remember that line: *They joyed – but the tongue of their gladness is dumb*"?

"Yes."

244

"Well, the tongue of my gladness is not dumb."

"That's true, your honor."

"And neither is the tongue of *your* gladness dumb, because I, as you know, have always *been* the tongue of your gladness, you being somewhat less gifted at that."

"I've never talked with anyone the way I talk with you."

"I rest my case."

"You should have been the lawyer, Ann."

"We do what we have to do."

"And choose when we can choose."

"Well then," she says with a womanly sweetness acknowledging everything they chose to do and don't need to say, "tell me why you're going to Washington."

"The whole thing got away from me."

"You're going to your rightful throne."

"To my uneasy lies the head that wears the crown."

"We knew you had to rise."

"I'm sorry you had to fall, Ann."

"I fell to rise, and you will too."

"You're always up there, Ann. I don't know what will happen in Washington, but when the stars fall I'll look up and you'll be there."

"With that one star that winks?"

"Exactly. You'll watch me in Washington like you looked down from your daddy's mill that day my boat got stuck on the dam. And I won't let you see me shorn."

"I know you won't. You've always made the best of things."

"I have?"

"Even when you have to dance."

"When I dance, someone else has to make the best of things."

"You leave that to me."

"You mean…."

"Exactly."

"Now?"

"You're my partner, aren't you?"

"I am."

"How often do I get you in my arms in the graveyard?" She spreads her arms wide.

"Come then if you dare," he says stepping to her because with her *he* dares and his face drops its habit of grief as his mouth and cheeks rise in a grin all the way to his glimmering eyes.

"And come bravely," he says, "because even the dead might dread my dancing… your right hand in my left up here, my right on your back between your wings. One-two-three? Yes… again: one-two-three…. Will you get… me in troub… trouble, Ann? Soon-to-be. Pres-i-dent. Dancing a… lone around… watch that grave!… talking to… one-two-three…. holding you… like the day… when you called… me to bed… and I laid… with my skin… one-two-three… on your skin…god, two-three… how we burned… burned with life… yes and death… I had, yes… I had…. Wait! Stop!"

His hands grip her waist as he looks at her celestial blue eyes and her rich auburn hair spilling down the front of her dress.

"Do you know what I had, Ann?" He lifts her and sees her above him where his tears of joy make stars around her shining face.

And she says it: "Everything!"

"I had everything, Ann!"

"*Have,* Abe! *Have* everything!"

†††